There was no denying Oliver's appeal

His hair was a deep, russet chestnut, warm and vibrant. As for his body... Well. Mackenzie would have cast him as a love interest on her TV show in a heartbeat if his audition reel had come across her desk. He had the kind of body women fantasized over—broad shoulders, deep chest, flat belly, tight, firm little backside....

Fantasizing just like she was doing now. Furtively watching him through the window as he romped with his dog in the backyard.

Sad, Mackenzie. Very, very sad.

Giving herself a stern talking to about spying on neighbors—especially on neighbors she wasn't sure she actually liked—she tried to turn away. But at that moment, he pushed his hair out of his eyes, and a smile lurked around his mouth. She froze, captivated by what that smile did to his very attractive features.

Suddenly, her other priorities slid away and getting to know him better seemed the most important thing to do.

Dear Reader,

When I initially conceived the idea for this book, I imagined my heroine being fresh from the breakup of her marriage, with a very bitter taste in her mouth. I imagined a reclusive, grumpy hero who was recovering from illness—perhaps something potentially life-threatening. I imagined these two people brought together by the fact that their two dogs couldn't stay away from one another.

As this idea noodled its way around in my mind, I started wondering what would happen if I reversed their backgrounds. What if she was the reclusive curmudgeon, and he the recently burned victim of divorce? Well, my brain lit up like a New Year's Eve fireworks display. I figured I was on to something.

I confess, there's a lot of dog love in this book, because I recently acquired a small, black Cavoodle—or Cavapoo as they are sometimes known—named Max. Max is funny, loyal, sweet, affectionate and playful, and I am putty in his small but perfectly formed paw. He has made my writing days less lonely, and coming home to him when we go out is pure joy. How can you not smile when a dog does the happy dance the second you walk through the door? As you can imagine, many of the antics in this book are culled from my experiences with Max—although, to my knowledge, he has yet to do what Mr. Smith did in this book.

I hope you enjoy reading about Oliver and Mackenzie and their dogs. I had a lot of fun writing their story, and I particularly wanted Oliver to find his happy ending after having the rug pulled out from beneath his life.

Happy reading, and please drop me a line via my website at www.sarahmayberry.com. I love hearing from readers.

Best,

Sarah Mayberry

The Other Side of Us

SARAH MAYBERRY

Recycling programs for this product may not exist in your area.

ISBN-13: 978-0-373-71824-5

THE OTHER SIDE OF US

This edition published by arrangement with Harlequin Books S.A.

For questions and comments about the quality of this book, please contact us at CustomerService@Harlequin.com.

www.Harlequin.com

Printed in U.S.A.

ABOUT THE AUTHOR

Sarah Mayberry lives by the bay in Melbourne in a house that is about to be pulled apart for renovations. She is happily married to another writer, shades of whom can be found in many of her heroes. She is currently besotted with her seven-month-old Cavoodle puppy, Max, and feeling guilty about her overgrown garden. When she isn't writing or feeling guilty or rolling around on the carpet with the dog, she likes reading, cooking, shoe shopping and going to the movies.

Books by Sarah Mayberry

HARLEQUIN SUPERROMANCE

1551—A NATURAL FATHER
1599—HOME FOR THE HOLIDAYS
1626—HER BEST FRIEND
1669—THE BEST LAID PLANS
1686—THE LAST GOODBYE
1724—ONE GOOD REASON
1742—ALL THEY NEED
1765—MORE THAN ONE NIGHT
1795—WITHIN REACH
1812—SUDDENLY YOU

HARLEQUIN BLAZE

380—BURNING UP
404—BELOW THE BELT
425—AMOROUS LIAISONS
464—SHE'S GOT IT BAD
517—HER SECRET FLING
566—HOT ISLAND NIGHTS

Other titles by this author available in ebook format.

Dearest Wanda, most generous and benevolent of editors, thank you for your unstinting patience with me with this book, and your endless faith in me. You are always on my side, you always challenge me and you always say the exact right things at the exact right time. Bless you.

A big thanks also to Chris, because he puts up with a lot of rambling and general craziness when I'm deep in the throes of a book. He always has my back, one of the many reasons I love him.

Finally, a big scratch, tummy rub and liver treat to Max, for being such a sweetheart and for making my days infinitely fuller and richer.

PROLOGUE

OLIVER GARRETT STARED at the rolling digits on the gas pump, willing the damn thing to finish filling his tank so he could get back on the road. He had a nine-o'clock appointment with an up-and-coming country-and-western band who could become regular clients—if this first recording session went well. Being late would be an awesome start to their relationship—the rule was, it was okay for the talent to be late, but not the sound engineer. That was simply the way the world worked.

It was exactly like his wife, Edie, to suggest they swap cars for the day and not notice her Mini was low on fuel. It wouldn't have even crossed her mind to check last night on her way home from work, let alone before she took off in his wagon this morning. Just as she never seemed to be aware when she used the last of the hot water or put an empty milk carton back in the fridge.

He frowned, annoyed by the whiny, resentful tone to his own thoughts. Admittedly, he wasn't exactly a dream to live with, either. He left his shoes to clutter up the bedroom floor and liked to drink juice straight from the container. Sometimes he even left whiskers around the sink after he'd finished shaving. Tolerating another person's little habits and preferences was part of marriage, and getting bent out of shape about the small stuff was a surefire way to make himself—and Edie—miserable.

The pump hit the thirty-buck mark and he called it

quits—half a tank was more than enough to get him where he needed to go. He leaned into the car to grab his wallet, but it was nowhere to be seen. He swore under his breath. Why did keys, passports and wallets always go missing when time was at a premium?

He crawled into the car, checking first the floor, then under the seats. He found his wallet wedged between the passenger seat and the door, along with a fistful of crumpled papers and an empty chocolate-bar wrapper. He pulled it all out, dumping the trash in the nearby bin before hustling inside to pay.

He tossed his wallet onto the passenger seat when he returned to the car, his gaze gravitating to the lone piece of trash he'd missed. He reached for it impatiently, the neat freak in him unable to leave a job half-done, even though he was running late. The curse of the detail-minded.

He was about to lob the crumpled piece of paper through the open car window and into the garbage when something caught his eye: a line of dark printing, visible from the wrong side of the paper.

The Annandale Motel.

Huh? He smoothed the paper flat on his thigh. Sure enough, it was a receipt for a queen room for one night, along with minibar expenses—a bottle of wine, a package of pretzels. Total $187.50.

Everything in him went very still.

The date was Wednesday of last week. The same day Edie was supposed to have given singing lessons to one of her many private clients, followed by a girls' night out with her friends.

There had to be an explanation. Maybe the receipt had fallen out of one of her friend's bags. Maybe—

Someone tooted the horn behind him. He was blocking the exit. Feeling oddly disconnected from his body, he shoved the car into gear and drove out of the service station, turning onto the nearest street and pulling over. He read the receipt again, his gut churning. Looking for proof that what he was thinking was impossible.

The last four digits of a credit-card number were printed below the total. He grabbed his phone and launched his banking app. He and Edie had separate accounts, but he knew her access code, the same as she knew his. His hands were shaking as he punched in her number then waited while the program processed his request.

Finally the screen filled with data. He scrolled through until he found last Wednesday's transactions. His hand tightened on the phone when he found a payment to the Annandale Motel for $187.50.

Not a mistake, then.

Edie was having an affair.

He felt… He didn't know how he felt. Angry. Shocked. Disgusted. Hurt. And that was just the tip of the iceberg.

He bowed his head, trying to think. Trying to get past the tight, hot sensation in his chest.

They'd been married six years. Their relationship wasn't perfect, but this was real life, not some fairy tale. Marriage was tough, and he'd signed up for the long haul because he loved Edie and because he wanted to grow old with her.

And she'd cheated on him. She'd gone to some sleazy motel and slept with some other man and then come home and lied to him.

He started the car and drove in the opposite direction of the studio. He knew exactly where Edie was—teaching vocal lessons to a bunch of overprivileged kids on the North Shore. Battling his way through rush-hour traffic, he focused on getting to her. He needed to talk to her. Needed answers. Beyond that… He had no idea.

His phone rang as he exited the freeway and headed

into Cremorne. Caller ID told him it was Rex, his business partner.

"Where are you?" Rex said the moment he took the call.

"I'm not going to make the session," Oliver said.

Someone cut in front of him and he leaned on the horn, a surge of fury rocketing through him. He wanted to put the pedal to the floor, wanted to blast past all this traffic so that he could be there, standing in front of Edie, looking into her face. So he could know for sure if this nightmare was real or some kind of messed-up misunderstanding.

"What do you mean you're not going to make it? You're the one who roped these guys in, Ollie."

"I think Edie's having an affair." The words were thick in his throat, so thick he didn't know how he got them out.

"What?"

"I found a receipt in the car. I'm going to talk to her."

Rex swore. "Mate, do you think that's a good idea?"

Oliver laughed. "There's nothing else I can do."

He had to know. Now.

"Okay. I'll cover for you. Somehow."

"I'll make it up to you."

"Don't worry about it. And...look after yourself, okay? Call me when you know more."

Oliver tossed the phone onto the passenger seat and concentrated on driving. Twenty minutes later he pulled into the parking lot at Cremorne School for Girls. He could see his wagon sitting halfway down the row. He parked the Mini and got out. His legs felt strange as he made his way into the school, as though they belonged to someone else.

It was easy enough to find the music wing, and once there he simply zigzagged along the corridor, looking through the window of each door, searching for Edie's familiar dark head.

He found her midway down the hall, dread thudding in his gut like a bass drum.

He watched her for a moment, aware of the adrenaline firing his pulse. She was demonstrating a breathing technique, one hand on her diaphragm, the other gesturing in the air. She wore slim, thigh-hugging jeans tucked into tan knee-high boots and a green asymmetrical top that hinted at her spectacular cleavage. She looked beautiful and vibrant.

His wife. The liar.

He opened the door. Edie turned toward him, a confused smile curving her mouth when she saw him.

“Ollie. What are you doing here?”

“Can I have a minute?”

Her smile dropped like a rock as she registered his tone. She glanced at the class.

“I won’t be a minute, girls. Go over the chorus again, and concentrate on your breathing.”

She joined him, her gray eyes wide with panic. She grabbed his jacket sleeve. “It’s not Mum, is it? God, please tell me it’s not Mum.”

Her mother, Naomi, had had a minor stroke several months ago and Edie had convinced herself it was the beginning of the end.

“She’s fine, as far as I know.” He pulled the motel receipt from his pocket and handed it to her.

Was it his imagination, or did she blanch as she read it?

It seemed to take forever for her gaze to return to his.

“I found it in your car today,” he said.

She opened her mouth and he knew from the look on her face and in her eyes that she was about to lie. Funny that he could see it now. When it was too late.

“I checked the account,” he added.

There was a small pause.

“Ollie. I’m so sorry.” Her eyes filled with tears.

"Who is he?"

"Does it matter?"

"Who. Is. He?"

She swallowed, a single tear snaking down her cheek. "I was with Nick."

Shock was a physical thing, rocking him back on his heels.

"Nick?"

Of all the men in her life—in *their* life—Nick was the last person Oliver would have suspected. Nick had been their band manager in the early days, and he and Edie had gone out for two tumultuous, tempestuous years. Nick had broken her heart and crushed her spirit and when things had finally ended, Oliver had been the one to help her pick up the pieces.

Nick was the past, a face they saw occasionally at other people's parties and barbecues. A mistake Edie had openly regretted more times than Oliver could count.

And yet she'd slept with him last Wednesday.

Edie wiped the tears from her face. There was something about the way she was watching him that made the tightness in his chest ratchet even tighter.

"How long?" The question came from his gut, inspired by pure, primitive instinct.

She closed her eyes, as though she couldn't bear to look at him as she—finally—spoke the truth. "Since he and Lucy broke up. On and off."

"Jesus." Oliver took a step backward, blinking rapidly, struggling to get his head around that news.

Lucy and Nick had broken up *five years ago,* barely six months after Oliver and Edie had returned from their honeymoon.

Five years. Edie had been sleeping with her ex, screwing around behind Oliver's back for *five years.*

He felt as though the world had shifted beneath his feet. Everything he thought he knew about her, about their marriage, about *himself* was suddenly as insubstantial as dust.

Five years.

That was when it hit him—nothing would ever be the same again.

CHAPTER ONE

IT WAS WET and dark and cold. At first she didn't know where she was, then she realized she was in the car, the wipers working overtime, the road a shiny black ribbon stretching in front of her. She gripped the steering wheel tightly, but it felt rubbery and insubstantial beneath her hands. Panic welled inside her. She knew what was coming next. What always came next.

Then she saw it, the dark mass of rocks blocking the middle of the curving mountain road. Her scream was swallowed by the explosive crash of glass breaking and metal crushing as the car hit, then there was nothing but pain and the realization that she was going to die out here on this godforsaken stretch of road....

Mackenzie Williams bolted upright, heart racing, sweat cold and clammy on her body. The bedclothes were a heavy tangle around her legs and for a few disoriented seconds she fought to free herself before reality reasserted itself.

She was alive. She was at the beach house in Flinders. And she ached. God, how she ached. Her hips, her shoulder, her back…

She scrubbed her face with both hands, then let out her breath on an exhausted sigh. It had been almost two months since she'd had a nightmare and she'd hoped they were a thing of the past. No such luck, apparently.

She threw off the covers then swung her legs to the floor. Her joints and muscles protested the action, as they always did first thing in the morning or when she'd been sitting in the same position for too long. She gritted her teeth and pushed herself to her feet anyway. If she waited till the pain stopped, she'd never get anything done.

It was still dark outside and the floor was cool beneath her feet. She shuffled forward a few steps until she found her slippers, then reached for her dressing gown.

She could hear the skitter of Mr. Smith's claws in the hall outside her bedroom and she smiled as she opened the door.

"Hello, Smitty. How you doin'?" she asked as he began his morning happy dance, walking back and forth in front of her with his tail wagging madly, his body wiggling from side to side.

"I'm going to take that as a 'very well, thank you very much.' Shall we go outside?"

Mackenzie made her way to the living room. The bitter morning chill was like a slap in the face when she opened the French doors, but it didn't stop Mr. Smith from slipping past her and out into the gray dawn light. Mackenzie followed him, stopping at the top of the deck steps, arms wrapped around her torso as she looked out over the jungle that was her yard.

The air was so frigid it hurt her nose. She inhaled great lungfuls of the stuff and let the last remnants of the nightmare fall away.

It was just a dream, after all. She wasn't dying. She was alive. She'd survived, against all odds. Better yet, she was on the track to a full recovery and resumption of her former life.

Which reminded her…

She left the door open for Mr. Smith before collecting her iPad from where it was charging on the kitchen counter. One click told her that Gordon hadn't responded to her email. Again.

This was getting ridiculous. Twelve months ago, her boss wouldn't have ignored an email from her. Then, she'd been a valuable commodity, the only producer in ten years who had managed to improve the ratings for the production company's longest-running serial drama, *Time and Again.* Now apparently she was a liability, an employee on long-term sick leave who didn't even merit the thirty seconds of his time it would take to respond to her email.

He doesn't think I'm coming back.

The thought made her blood run cold. She had worked hard to land the job of producer on a network drama. She'd kissed ass and gone beyond the call of duty and even trampled on a few people in her rush to climb the ladder. She'd sacrificed her time, her social life, her marriage…and then her car had hit a landslide at sixty kilometers an hour and flipped down the side of a mountain. She'd fractured her skull, broken her pelvis, her hip, her leg, several ribs as well as her arm, torn her liver and lost her spleen.

And it looked as though she was going to lose her job, too, even though she'd been driving to a location shoot when the accident happened. Gordon had promised that they'd keep her job open for her, filling the role with a short-term replacement. He'd given her a year to recover—a year that was almost up. And yet he wasn't returning her calls.

Lips pressed into a tight line, she opened a blank email and typed a quick message to Gordon's secretary, Linda. Linda owed her, and Mackenzie knew that if she asked, the other woman would make sure Gordon called her.

At least, she hoped she still had that much influence.

Mr. Smith pressed against her legs, his small body a welcome weight. She bent to run a hand over his salt-and-pepper fur.

"I'm not giving up, Smitty. Not in a million freaking years."

She wouldn't let Gordon write her off. She would walk back into her job, and she would claw her way into her old life. There was no other option on the table. She refused for there to be.

She had a hot shower, then dressed in her workout clothes. Together she and Mr. Smith made their way to the large room at the front of the house she'd converted to hold her Pilates reformer and other gym equipment when she left the rehab hospital three months ago. She sat on the recumbent bike and started pedaling. Smitty reacquainted himself with the rawhide bone he'd left there yesterday and settled in for the duration.

After ten minutes on the bike, she lowered herself to the yoga mat and began her stretches. As always, her body protested as she attempted to push it close to a normal range of movement. Her physiotherapist, Alan, had warned her that she might never get full range in her left shoulder and her right hip. She'd told him he was wrong and was determined to prove it.

The usual mantra echoed in her mind as she stretched her bowstring-tight hip flexors.

I want my life back. I want my job back. I want my apartment and my shoes and my clothes. I want to have cocktails with my friends and the challenge of juggling too much in too little time. I want to be me *again.*

Gritting her teeth, she held the stretch. Sweat broke out along her forehead and upper lip. She started to pant, but she held the stretch. Her hips were burning, her back starting to protest.

She held the stretch.

Only when pain started shooting up her spine did she ease off and collapse onto the mat, sweat running down her temple and into her hair.

Better than yesterday. Definitely better.

The thought was enough to rouse her to another round. Teeth bared in a grimace, she eased into another pose.

THE MORNING SUN was rising over the treetops as Oliver turned onto the unmarked gravel road that he hoped like hell was Seaswept Avenue. He was tired and sleep deprived after a long drive from Sydney and more than ready for this journey to be over.

Craning forward over the steering wheel, he checked house numbers as he drove slowly up the rutted road. Not that there were many houses to check. The lots were large, the houses either old and charming or new and sharp edged, and there was plenty of space in between. Aunt Marion's was number thirty-three, and he drove past half-a-dozen vacant lots thick with bush before spotting a tired-looking clapboard house sitting cheek by jowl with a much tidier, smarter whitewashed cottage. As far as he could tell, they were the only two houses at this end of the street.

He didn't have enough optimism left to hope the tidy cottage was number thirty-three, and the rusty numbers on the letterbox of the shabbier house confirmed his guess.

It seemed like the perfect ending to a road trip that had featured not one but two flat tires and a motel with fleas in the carpet.

Driving from Sydney to Melbourne had seemed like a great idea four days ago. Four days ago, he'd been so sick of the burning anger that seemed to have taken up permanent residence in his gut that he'd been willing to do almost anything to change the record in his mind.

How could she do this to me? How could I be so freakin' stupid? How could she do this to me?

He pulled into the driveway and let his head drop against the seat for a few seconds. God, he was tired. Strudel made a forlorn sound from the backseat and Oliver shook himself awake and exited the car to let her out. She immediately availed herself of the nearest patch of grass. Would that he could be so lucky, since he'd cleverly tossed the keys to his aunt's house into the bottom of his duffel bag. But he wasn't about to start his stay in what was surely a close-knit community by exposing himself to his new neighbor.

Stretching his arms over his head, Oliver grabbed his duffel from the rear. Strudel joined him on the weathered porch as he dug in among his clothes for the key. Miracle of miracles, his hand closed over it on the second dip. Moments later he was inside, walking around flicking on lights and opening windows to relieve the stuffy, musty smell. He passed quickly through the living room filled with heavy, old-fashioned furniture, and the two bedrooms with their stripped-bare beds, ending his tour in the kitchen.

Aunt Marion had died over a year ago now, but neither he nor his brother, Brent, had been in a position to do anything about their joint inheritance until now. Traveling south to put things in order had seemed like the perfect excuse to be out of Sydney so he could lick his wounds and get his head together.

If that was even possible.

Of course it's possible. Edie was your wife, not your whole life.

Logically, he knew it was true, but it didn't feel true at the moment. Six years of his life had been exposed as a lie. His whole marriage. He didn't know how to deal with the anger and grief and humiliation he felt.

Strudel whined, drawing his attention to where she was sniffing and scratching around the base of the oven. No doubt she'd found a nest of mice or something equally unpleasant.

"Good girl, Strudel. Good girl." Strudel came to his side and lifted her head for a scratch. He obliged, rubbing her behind the ears where she liked it. Some of the tension left him as he looked into her big, liquid eyes.

For the next five weeks, he had no one but himself and Strudel to please. Edie and Nick were a thousand miles away, his job was on hold. This time was all his and he could use it to rage and be bitter and brood—or he could start putting himself back together again.

He really hoped it would be the latter.

He walked to the back door and stepped onto a broad porch that overlooked a yard thick with grass and overgrown garden beds. A shed huddled in the left-hand corner. He considered it briefly, then decided he would inspect it later.

His gaze shifted to the cottage next door. It occurred to him that he should probably go introduce himself to his new neighbor, since they were more or less isolated at this end of the street. His aunt's place had been vacant so long he didn't want some old dear with three cats and a hearing aid freaking out because a strange man had moved in.

Then maybe he'd head into town to grab some food and other supplies.

It wasn't much of a plan, but it would get him through the next few hours.

MACKENZIE RETURNED THE reformer carriage to the starting position and let her hands drop to her sides. She was officially done for another day, every exercise on her chart completed and ticked off. Even the ones that made her want to curl into a ball and cry, they hurt so much.

She reached for her towel and blotted her sweat-dampened face and chest. The sharp taste of bile burned at the back of her mouth, a sure sign that she'd overexerted herself again.

Well. A little nausea was a price she was willing to pay if it meant she made a faster recovery.

She stood, running the towel over her cropped hair. Mr. Smith stood, too, tail wagging as he looked at her expectantly.

"Yes, little man, it's time for breakfast."

If she could stomach it.

She wrapped the towel around her shoulders like a cape and headed for the kitchen. A sharp noise stopped her in her tracks before she'd gotten halfway. It had been so long since anyone had come to the door that it took her a full second to recognize the sound as a knock. She glanced over her shoulder. A dark form filled the pebbled glass of the door. She frowned. Who on earth would be visiting her at ten o'clock on a Thursday morning?

Her first thought was that it was Patrick, but she dismissed it instantly. He was hardly going to drive an hour out of town to visit her—not when he hadn't bothered to pick up the phone in more than four months. No, she had a better chance of finding Elvis on the other side of that door than her ex-husband, and an even better chance of finding a complete stranger who probably wanted to sell her something.

The joy. Just what she wanted to deal with when she was shaky with fatigue and nausea.

She swung open the door, ready to give short shrift to the cold-calling salesman on her porch.

The man on her porch was definitely not a cold caller. Nothing about this man was cold, from the deep chestnut of his wavy, almost shoulder-length hair to his cognac-brown eyes to his full, sensual mouth. Then there was his body—nothing cold there, either. Broad shoulders, a chest Tarzan would be proud of, flat belly, lean hips. All wrapped up in faded jeans and a moss-green sweater that was the perfect foil for his coloring.

"Hey," he said in an easy baritone. "I'm Oliver Garrett. I

moved in next door." He gestured toward the house on the other side of the fence. "Wanted to give you a heads-up in case you saw me moving around and thought I was a burglar or something."

He smiled, so warm and vibrant and alive it was almost offensive. His gaze slid down her face, scanning her body in a polite but thoroughly male assessment. She tightened her grip on the towel, glad it was draped over her shoulders and arms. Managing a stranger's shock then polite sympathy once he got an eyeful of the impressive scars on her left arm was not part of her plan for her morning.

"Mackenzie Williams," she said briskly, offering him her hand.

They shook briefly, his much bigger hand dwarfing hers. She made a point of keeping her grip firm and looking him in the eye, a habit she'd acquired early in her career and one that had always alerted her about what kind of man she was dealing with.

Oliver Garrett held her eye and didn't seem surprised by the firmness of her grip. More importantly, he didn't try to grind her hand into dust with his superior strength. Both marks in his favor.

"I was hoping you could give me some guidance on where the best place is to grab supplies and whatnot," he said.

He hadn't shaved for a few days and his whiskers glinted in the sunlight, a mixture of dark brown, bronze and gold.

She tore her gaze away and concentrated on his question. "There aren't many shops to choose from in town. One of everything, pretty much, which takes out the guesswork."

Her legs were starting to tremble. She needed a protein drink and a shower and half an hour on her bed. She took a step backward to signal that she didn't intend to stand on the doorstep chitchatting with him, golden stubble or no golden stubble.

"Figured that would be the case. It's been years since I was here. But it doesn't look as though much has changed."

Nausea rolled through her, tightening her stomach and making her mouth water. She gripped the door frame. Any second now she was going to either throw up or wind up on her ass, and she wasn't about to do either in front of a complete stranger.

"Listen, I have to go." It came out more tersely than she'd intended, but there wasn't much she could do about that.

He looked a little shocked, but before he could say anything, a long, furry body rushed past her and onto the porch. For the first time she registered that he had a dog, too—a miniature schnauzer by the look of her. A miniature schnauzer that Mr. Smith was very pleased to meet, judging by all the tail-wagging and bottom-sniffing that was going on.

"Smitty. Inside," she said sharply.

"It's okay. He's just saying hello, aren't you, mate?" Oliver smiled indulgently and bent to scratch Mr. Smith between the shoulder blades.

Her stomach rolled again. She swallowed and leaned forward to grab her dog's collar. He was so involved with his new friend that she had to use considerable strength to yank him into the house, the effort only increasing the nausea burning at the back of her throat.

"I don't have time for this."

She wasn't sure who she was talking to—her new neighbor, her shaking body, her overeager dog. It didn't matter. The most important thing was that she was about to throw up.

One hand restraining Mr. Smith, she took a step backward and shut the door. In the split second before it cut her new neighbor from view, she saw his eyebrows shoot toward his hairline with surprise. One hand pressed to her mouth, she raced to the bathroom. She almost made it, the spasms hitting as she stepped over the threshold. Bracing her hands on her knees, her stomach released its contents all over the tiled floor.

For long moments afterward, she remained where she was, knees weak, a sour taste in her mouth. An emphatic reminder that her injured body had its limits. Finally she got down on her hands and knees and cleaned up.

At least she hadn't thrown up on Mr. Sunshine. There was that small mercy to be grateful for. No doubt he thought she was incredibly rude all but slamming the door in his face.

She shrugged. There wasn't much she could do about that, and it wasn't the end of the world. They were hardly going to become bosom buddies, after all. She'd moved to the beach house for one reason and one reason only—to recover. She didn't care who moved in next door or what he looked like or what he thought of her.

She only wanted her life back. And she would bloody well do her damnedest to get it.

OLIVER HAD TO THINK about it, but he was pretty sure that no one had ever slammed a door in his face before. Not even an angry ex-girlfriend. So much for easing the concerns of his elderly neighbor.

Not that there was anything elderly about Mackenzie Williams. If he had to guess, he'd say she was around the same age as him—thirty-nine—and judging by her firm, lean body, there was nothing remotely doddery about her. Nothing soft or warm or welcoming about her, either, from the cool, clear blue of her eyes and small, straight nose to her very short brown hair.

From the second she'd opened the door she'd wanted him

gone—he'd felt the force of her will like a hand shoving him away. More fool him for trying to do the right thing in the first place. He wouldn't make that mistake again, not where she was concerned.

He'd met a lot of women like Mackenzie over the years. Edie had gravitated to that type of woman—aspirational middle-class, with European luxury cars in their driveways, addresses in the "right" part of town, foreheads injected with Botox, fashionably skinny bodies and husbands who earned the big money in banking or law. The only wonder was that Mackenzie had taken time out from her no-doubt hectic social schedule to rusticate in the wilds of the Mornington Peninsula. Hardly the kind of place he'd expect to find an upwardly mobile, hard-edged woman like her.

He paused climbing the steps to his porch, aware that there was a considerable degree of vitriol in his thoughts. Perhaps a disproportionately large degree, given the length of his acquaintance with Mackenzie Williams. They had been talking for all of two minutes before she'd slammed the door, after all. Hardly enough time to drum up a high level of ire.

Before his life had turned out to be about as substantial as an empty cereal packet, he'd considered himself a pretty easygoing kind of guy. Not particularly prone to temper tantrums, reasonably long fuse, pretty quick with a laugh when something tickled his funny bone.

Lately, though… Lately he'd noticed a tendency to see only the darkness, the ugliness in people and the world. And his fuse had shortened considerably. Six months ago, Mackenzie's little stunt would have made him laugh and worry about her blood pressure. Today, it filled him with the urge to do something childish like put Led Zeppelin on the stereo and turn up the volume to bleeding-eardrum level so that it rattled her windows.

He released his breath on an exasperated exhalation. It didn't take a psychologists' convention to work out where the impulse stemmed from and who his anger was really directed at.

Edie.

Except she was a thousand miles away and he hadn't spoken to her for more than three months.

Because he didn't know what to do with all the anger Mackenzie had inadvertently triggered in him, he strode through the house and into the yard, aiming for the shed in the far corner. Nothing like a distraction to avoid dealing with his feelings.

Strudel kept pace with him, her whiskered face bright with doggy anticipation. At least one of them was getting something out of this.

He was struggling with the rusty latch on the shed when his phone rang. He glanced at the screen before deciding to take the call. It was Brent, his brother.

"You there yet or still on the road?" Brent asked.

"Got here a couple of hours ago."

"How's the place looking?"

"Old."

"Coat of paint will fix that. I've been doing some research. Looks like the big-gun real-estate agent in the area is Dixon and Lane."

Oliver gave the latch a thump with his fist. "It'll be a while before I can call the agents in, mate." The latch finally gave and he pulled the door open. "Bloody hell."

"What?"

"The garden shed is stuffed with furniture." His gaze ran over chairs, a sideboard, a dresser, a bed frame, all of it crammed cheek by jowl and covered with dust.

"Any good stuff?"

"I have no idea." It all looked old-fashioned and heavy to him, but what did he know?

"We should get an evaluator in. One of those guys who specializes in estates," Brent said.

"I guess."

"You sound tired."

"Lot of road between here and Sydney."

"That's kind of the point, though, right?"

Oliver shut the shed door and used his shoulder to hold it in place while he forced the rusty bolt home. "Yeah."

"I'll let you go. Speak again tomorrow, okay?" Brent said.

Oliver suppressed a sigh. Ever since he'd told his brother about Edie and Nick, Brent had been checking in with him daily. As though Oliver would "do something stupid" if he didn't have his hand held.

"You don't have to keep up the suicide watch, you know. I'm pissed off, but I'm hardly going to end it all," he said drily.

For a moment there was nothing but the sound of the wind in the trees and the distant thunder of surf.

"You're not on suicide watch," Brent said stiffly.

"Whatever you want to call it. I don't need my hand held."

"Excuse me for caring."

Brent sounded pissed now. Oliver ran his hand through his hair.

"I appreciate the sentiment, okay? But you don't need to babysit me."

"Sure. I'll speak to you later." Brent hung up.

Oliver congratulated himself on being a dick. Brent was a good guy. A little fussy sometimes, but maybe that came with the territory when you were the older brother. Rewarding his concern with smart-assery was a kid's way of dealing with an uncomfortable situation.

Jamming his hands into his coat pockets, Oliver promised himself he'd call Brent tomorrow. He surveyed the garden, looking for Strudel before he headed into the house. He frowned when he saw her doing the doggy meet-and-greet routine with the neighbor's dachshund.

"How did you get over here?" He glanced at the fence that separated the two properties. It was silver with age, but it looked solid enough. Obviously there must be a hole somewhere.

"Strudel. Come here, girl. Come here."

His normally obedient schnauzer didn't so much as glance in his general direction. She was too busy canoodling with her new best friend, sniffing and dancing around and generally being coy.

Oliver went after her, scanning the fence line as he walked. Sure enough, he found a half-rotted board and a hole that was sufficiently large for a determined dachshund to gain entrance.

"Party's over, buddy." He reached down to scoop up the dachshund. The dog wriggled desperately, but Oliver kept a tight grip, only releasing him when he'd arrived at the fence. He squatted, pointed the dog at the hole and stood guard until the sausage dog had wiggled into his own yard. There were a few loose bricks in the garden bed nearby and Oliver used them to build a blockade. He'd patch the hole properly later, but the makeshift barrier should keep Romeo out in the interim.

He returned to the house and did a thorough tour of each room, making notes on the work that needed to be done. He'd reached the kitchen when he realized Strudel had disappeared. He checked the living room, sure he'd find her making herself at home on the overstuffed couch. She wasn't there, however.

He glanced outside as he returned to the kitchen. He stopped in his tracks when he saw the dachshund planted at the bottom of the exterior steps.

Bloody hell. Houdini had done it again.

He found Strudel sitting at the door, gaze fixed longingly on the handle, almost as though she was willing it to turn. He had no idea how she knew that her furry friend had come calling, but clearly she did.

"You can do much better, girl," he said. "He's way too short for you."

He went outside, Strudel hard on his heels. He watched in bemusement as the two dogs greeted each other with what he could only describe as the canine equivalent of a twenty-one-gun salute. Didn't seem to matter that they'd seen each other less than an hour ago.

"Okay. Hate to break it up, but Houdini has to go home."

He picked up the dachshund and carried him to the hole in the fence. To his surprise, the barricade was still intact. He followed the fence farther into the garden, squirming hound under his arm

By the time he'd reached the rear of the property he'd found another three holes, which made the dachshund more of an opportunist than an escape artist. Oliver considered the problem for a few seconds, but he really couldn't see any alternative to biting the bullet and paying his not-very-neighborly neighbor another visit. She needed to be made aware of the issues with their shared boundary. As tempting as it was to simply attach a note to her dog's collar and send him through one of the many holes in the fence, Oliver figured the news would probably be better received in person.

He ushered the interloper inside and clipped Strudel's lead onto his collar. He had to practically drag the dachshund out the door, however, and he could hear Strudel whining beseechingly as he crossed to Mackenzie's driveway. He knocked on her door, then looked down. The dog was staring up at him with sad eyes, the picture of abject misery.

"Yeah, yeah, your life is hell. I get it."

He could hear footsteps inside the house. He braced himself for more rudeness. Mackenzie opened the door and stared at first him, then the dachshund.

"Why do you have my dog?" she asked, a frown furrowing her brow.

"Because he was in my yard. Twice. The fence between our properties is riddled with holes."

She crouched, one hand reaching for the door frame for balance.

"Mr. Smith, what have you been up to? Have you been out making new friends?" Her tone was warm, even a little indulgent.

She knelt, rubbing the dog beneath his chin. Oliver stared at her down-turned head, noticing something through her dark, clipped hair. A white, shiny line sliced across her scalp along the side of her skull, then curled toward the front just inside her hairline.

A scar.

A pretty wicked, serious one by the looks of it.

She glanced at him. "Thanks for bringing him back."

She wasn't wearing a scrap of makeup. Her skin was very fair and her long, dark eyelashes stood out in dramatic contrast to her piercing blue eyes.

She unclipped the leash, then straightened. Maybe he was looking for it after seeing the scar, but it seemed to him the move wasn't anywhere near as easy and casual as she'd like him to think. He reminded himself of the reason he was here—and it wasn't to ferret out her secrets.

"We need to do something about the fence," he said.

"There's never been a problem before. Mr. Smith isn't much of a roamer."

"I think he's more interested in Strudel than exploring the terrain."

"That's never been a problem before, either."

His back came up. Admittedly, he'd come here primed to be annoyed because she'd been so dismissive earlier, but there was a definite tone to her words. As though somehow he and Strudel were responsible for her dog's behavior.

"I guess times have changed. We should probably do a temporary fix and then get some quotes to have it repaired."

The phone rang inside her house and she glanced over her shoulder. The move drew his attention to her breasts—small but perky. He gave himself a mental shake. As if he cared what her breasts looked like. They were attached to the rest of her, which was toned within an inch of its life and way too scrawny for his tastes.

"I need to get that," she said as she refocused on him.

"Fine. But we need to deal with this fence or Mr. Smith is going to come visiting again."

"I'm sorry, but I really need to take this call. I'll get back to you." There was a distracted urgency beneath her words as she reached for the knob.

He opened his mouth to protest—as the door swung shut in his face for the second time that day.

"You cannot be serious," he told the shiny black wood.

But she was. She was also the rudest person he'd ever had the misfortune to meet. He was tempted to knock again and force her to deal with him, but he had an image of himself knocking till the cows came home and her ignoring him as she dealt with her vitally important, utterly life-transforming phone call.

He'd been de-balled quite enough by his wife's staggering infidelity, thank you very much. He had no intention of hanging around to play the part of supplicant.

He remembered an old saying as he returned to his aunt's house: no good turn goes unpunished.

Indeed.

CHAPTER TWO

MACKENZIE REACHED THE PHONE just as it stopped ringing. She checked caller ID and swore when she saw Gordon's number. She'd talked to Linda earlier and managed to convince her to prompt Gordon into calling. Linda had come through—and Mackenzie had been too busy dealing with Oliver What's-his-name to take the call.

Unbelievable.

She hit the button to return the call and prayed that Gordon hadn't already moved on to something else. She willed him to pick up as the phone rang at the other end. She was about to give in to despair when Gordon's voice came over the line.

"Mackenzie."

"Gordon. How are you?"

"Good enough. More importantly, how are you?"

"Getting there. Better every day."

He grunted. She pictured him sitting at his desk in Melbourne, feet up on the corner, big belly straining at the buttons on his shirt.

"How are the headaches?" he asked.

"Better. Much better." She didn't mention the fact that she still struggled to spend more than a couple of hours at a time on her feet before her back started acting up and that she struggled to stay awake after eight at night.

"That's good to hear." He sounded distracted and she knew she wouldn't hold his attention for long.

"Listen, Gordon, I've been wanting to talk to you because I know Philip's contract is coming up for renewal."

Philip had been brought in to fill her role while she recovered. An experienced producer, they'd been lucky to catch him between gigs.

"It is. Still got that steel-trap memory, I see."

What she had was a heavily used calendar function on her iPhone, but he didn't need to know that.

"So, have you spoken to him about renewing for a shorter term?" She wrapped her free arm around her torso, tension thrumming through her body as she waited for Gordon's response.

"We haven't had that conversation yet."

"Right. Well, I wanted to suggest you go for three months. I'll be more than ready to get back to it by then."

Gordon sighed. "Mackenzie…our hands are tied here. You have to understand that."

A chill ran down her spine. Was he saying what she thought he was saying? "What does that mean?"

"It means we can't afford to lose him. The show needs continuity. If he won't consider a short term, we'll have to look at something longer. It's a shitty situation, I know, but he's done a great job for us."

Mackenzie bit back the urge to remind Gordon that she'd done a great job, too, in the three years prior to the accident. She'd increased the ratings by nearly thirty percent, streamlined the story department and used her influence with her ex-husband, Patrick Langtry, to persuade him to join the cast—a move that had led to another ratings bump. Gordon knew all that, though. It simply didn't mean anything to him while she was sidelined.

There was a reason Hunter S. Thompson had described television as "a long plastic hallway where thieves and pimps run free and good men die like dogs." The industry was ruthless, ratings driven and peopled with huge egos. God only knew why she'd spent the bulk of her adult life loving the hell out of it, but she had and it was where she wanted to be.

Once she was on her feet again.

"I'll be back soon, Gordon. I've had some great ideas for the show, too. Something to really kick us into the new ratings period."

"You don't need to pitch yourself to me. I'm going to offer him a month-by-month contract. I'm not expecting him to be happy about it, and I know for a fact there are other production companies sniffing around. I'll do my best, but you need to understand that, at the end of the day, we have to do what's best for the show."

Even if that meant giving away her position while she was on sick leave for injuries acquired while on the job. If she hadn't been driving to that location shoot, she wouldn't have had the accident. It was that simple.

She opened her mouth to remind Gordon that he was legally obliged to keep her job open for her, then closed it again without saying a word. Nobody ever got ahead at Eureka Productions by resorting to lawyers at ten paces. No one who worked *behind* the camera, anyway.

"Don't worry, Mackenzie. You'll be looked after. You're still our little pocket rocket."

Mackenzie bared her teeth. How she hated that offensive, patronizing nickname.

"Will you keep me in the loop?" It was a testament to her strong will that she managed to keep her voice even and her tone pleasant. No way would she give Gordon the leverage of an emotional outburst. If he recognized a weakness, he wouldn't hesitate to use it against her. "Let me know how things go with Philip?"

"You'll be the first to know."

"Network negotiations must be coming up soon, too. Any indication they might go for the Christmas special again this year?"

"They like to play their cards close. Listen, Mackenzie, I'd love to chat but I've got a meeting in ten."

"Sure. Thanks for the call, Gordon."

"Look after yourself, sweetheart."

Mackenzie dropped the phone onto the coffee table and sank onto the arm of the sofa.

Shit.

If Philip played hardball and pushed to have her job permanently, there was a very real chance that she would be out in the cold.

The thought was accompanied by a flurry of panic and a stab of pain behind her right eyeball. She pressed her fingers to her temple, squeezing her eyes shut briefly before searching for painkillers. Normally she tried to get by without medication. At the worst of her recovery she'd been on so many tablets she'd had a special dispenser to keep them all straight. She'd been fuzzy headed and a step removed from the world most of the time, and she'd fought with her doctors to reduce her daily intake to the bare minimum. These days, she avoided anything that came in a foil sleeve, even a humble aspirin. But she could feel the headache building behind her eyes and knew from experience that it would snowball into something ferocious if she didn't nip it in the bud now.

Mr. Smith pattered after her as she made her way to the bathroom. Seeing him reminded her of her new neighbor and his concerns about the hole-riddled fence. She supposed she should be more worried, but Mr. Smith was ridiculously attached to her and he'd never run away before. She figured he was simply excited about having a little buddy next door. Once the novelty had worn off he'd settle down.

Still, she should probably look into having the fence repaired, as Oliver Golden-Stubble had suggested. Not that she wanted to pour her precious, limited energy into anything unrelated to her recovery, but if it had to be done, it had to be done.

She swallowed two painkillers. A noise started up outside as she chased them with a glass of water. Someone hammering—in what sounded like *her* backyard. She made her way to the picture window in the living room. The noise wasn't coming from her backyard, but the neighbor's. Oliver was out there, working away with hammer and handsaw. Repairing their shared fence, apparently. Obviously he hadn't been prepared to wait until they could hire a professional.

She watched him work, arms crossed over her chest. She'd never been attracted to redheaded men, but there was no denying this man's appeal. His hair was a deep chestnut, more of a reddish-brown than a true red. As for his body... She would have cast him as a love interest on *Time and Again* in a heartbeat if his audition had come across her desk. He had the kind of body women fantasized over—broad shoulders, deep chest, flat belly, tight, firm little backside...

He pushed his hair out of his eyes, then turned to say something to his dog. There was a smile lurking around his mouth. Both times she'd met him she'd had the sense that he was a man who laughed easily. One of those comfortable-in-his-own-skin men. She wondered idly if he was married. He seemed like a married man to her. Hard to put her finger on why, but she usually had good instincts about that sort of thing.

He glanced up, his gaze locking with hers across twenty meters of garden and fence. Feeling caught, she took an instinctive step backward, then realized retreating only made her look guilty and furtive. She forced herself to stand her ground and hold his gaze. After a beat, he broke the contact, refocusing on his work.

She escaped to the kitchen, feeling oddly rattled. She wondered how long he planned to hang around. She hoped it wouldn't be for long. She didn't have time for distractions.

The painkiller was starting to make the world go fuzzy at the edges, but it didn't ease the panic left over from Gordon's phone call. She returned to the living room and sat in the corner of the couch.

If she lost her job—

She clamped down on the thought. It wasn't going to happen. She wouldn't *let* it happen. That job was her life. No way was she letting it slip through her fingers.

OLIVER FIXED TWO of the holes in the fence before he'd exhausted the small stash of nails he'd had in his tool chest. He'd taken the precaution of packing it and a few power tools before he left Sydney, based on the assumption that Aunt Marion's place might need a few hinges fixed. He hadn't expected to be getting down and dirty on his first day.

There were still holes to patch, but he decided they could wait until tomorrow and packed his gear away for the night. He got takeout from the local Chinese restaurant and spent the evening staring into the fire he built, downing a six-pack of beer and feeling disconnected from the world in general. Since distancing himself from his old life had been the whole point of his trip, he figured he was off to a good start.

He woke to overcast skies and the realization that he should have turned on the water heater last night. An icy-cold shower left him shivering and pissy. He whistled for Strudel to get in the car then drove into town, wondering if he had a chance of getting the remaining holes in the fence repaired before it started to rain. Judging by the dark, moody-looking clouds overhead, probably not.

He spotted a small, soberly clad woman the moment he entered the hardware store. For a few seconds he thought it was his surly neighbor, then the woman turned and he saw she was much older than Mackenzie. Just as well. He wasn't in the mood to be polite this morning. Not that Mackenzie seemed overly concerned about social niceties.

He remembered the look they'd shared across the fence yesterday as he trawled the shelves for nails. He'd felt her watching him before he'd glanced up. Not that he'd known he was being observed per se; he'd simply known that something was not quite right. And there she was, watching him from her window, a slim figure, arms wrapped tightly around herself as she studied him.

She was one of those people who had perfected the art of giving nothing away—expressionless face, emotionless eyes. She'd held his gaze, cool, unreadable. Assessing.

He made a rude noise in the back of his throat. She'd probably been congratulating herself on getting her fence repaired for free. Certainly she hadn't seemed in a hurry to do anything about it when they'd spoken, and she hadn't rushed out to offer her assistance yesterday, either.

Belatedly he recalled her scar and the labored way she'd gotten to her feet. Maybe she wasn't in a position to offer her assistance, physically speaking. He immediately dismissed the notion as he remembered the lean strength of her body and the fact that she'd clearly finished a workout when he'd first knocked yesterday.

She probably simply considered manual work beneath her, in the same way that common courtesy seemed to be beyond her.

Aware that he'd let himself get bent out of shape over her once again, he concentrated on his search. By the time he'd completed a tour of the small store, he still hadn't located the nails and he gave in and approached the elderly man behind the counter.

"If you're looking for sandbags, we're all out, sorry," the salesclerk said before Oliver could open his mouth.

"I guess it's just as well I'm looking for nails, then," Oliver said, more than a little bemused by the man's opening gambit.

"What sort?"

"I'm repairing a fence."

"You'll want bullet heads, then."

Oliver followed the man to the far corner of the store and selected a carton of nails.

"Had a run on sandbags today, have you?" he asked as they returned to the counter, more to make conversation than out of real curiosity.

"People having conniptions over the weather report. Bloody drama queens, those people in at the weather bureau. Storm will probably pass out over the water and not even touch us. Same as usual." The clerk shook his head, clearly unimpressed with modern science.

"Is there a storm warning?" Oliver glanced out the window. Sure enough, the sky had grown even more forbidding since he'd left the house.

"So they say. Probably worth clearing out your gutters and downpipes, but I wouldn't go blowing up your water wings just yet." The old man laughed at his own joke.

"Thanks for the tip."

Oliver switched on the radio when he got to the car and scanned through the frequencies until he found a weather report. Sure enough, they were predicting heavy rain for the southern part of the Mornington Peninsula, with warnings of flash flooding and high winds.

Awesome. Was it just him, or was Flinders really rolling

out the welcome mat? A rude neighbor, a decrepit fence and now imminent flooding. And it was only day two.

Since the rain was holding off, he decided to finish the fence repairs. Strudel kept him company, sniffing around his feet and generally getting in the way. Twice he had to push her aside when he was nailing a board in place. He was about to put her in the house to save both her and his sanity when she trotted off into the garden.

"Smartest thing you've done all day," he muttered.

It wasn't until he'd finished repairing the second-last hole that it occurred to him to wonder where she'd gone. He tucked his hammer into his tool belt and went looking. He spotted her the moment he rounded the shed. More accurately, he spotted *them.* As in plural. As in, two dogs, one silhouette.

"Hey!" he yelled, outraged.

He'd let Strudel out of his sight for five minutes and Doggy Juan from next door had taken advantage. Unbelievable.

Neither Strudel nor Mr. Smith paid him any attention, the two of them being very occupied with being humped and humping, respectively. Oliver searched for the garden hose. It took him half a minute to find it, and by the time he'd dragged it across the lawn Mr. Smith had finished and was simply standing beside Strudel, panting and looking pretty bloody pleased with himself.

"Don't grin at me, mate. You're in big trouble."

"Mr. Smith? Smitty? Here, boy. Mama's got a bone for you."

Mackenzie's voice floated over from her yard. Oliver scooped up her miscreant dog and strode to the fence. Holding the dog under his arm, he gripped the top of the fence and stepped on the cross rail so he could see into her yard.

"He's here. Again."

Mackenzie stood on the deck, once again dressed in expensive-looking workout gear. She frowned when she saw Mr. Smith in his arms.

"I didn't realize—"

"No kidding."

He waited until she'd crossed to the fence before lowering the dog into her arms.

"You might want to keep him inside until the fence is secure. Since he doesn't seem good at taking no for an answer."

She smoothed a hand over her dog's head. "Sorry?"

"I just caught him humping Strudel."

"Oh." She had the grace to look embarrassed.

"Yeah." He was aware that he sounded like an outraged parent. Frankly, he felt like one. Strudel was barely eighteen months old. Still a puppy, really. She wasn't in the market for the kind of adults-only behavior Mr. Smith had dished out so enthusiastically.

"I'm sorry. I didn't realize he was out."

"You said that."

Her eyebrows rose as she picked up on his tone. "I know that technically he shouldn't have been on your side of the fence, but they're only following their natural instincts. There's no need to get all prissy about it."

Prissy? Where did she get off calling him prissy after she'd shut her door in his face not once but twice and then let her reprobate of a dog run loose to do as he pleased?

He fixed her with a hard look. "Keep your dog out of my yard, okay?"

She set the dachshund on the ground and brushed fur off her body-hugging top. "It takes two to tango, you know. I bet Mr. Smith didn't go where he wasn't wanted."

He opened his mouth to respond, then realized he was

one riposte away from a schoolyard squabble. He released his grip on the fence and dropped to the ground.

"Keep an eye on your dog," he said as he walked away.

The only response was silence, but he could practically hear her grinding her teeth. Good. She'd made him grind his teeth more than once in the past twenty-four hours. Turnabout was fair play.

Strudel once again shadowed his every move as he patched the last gap in the fence, taking every opportunity to lick his hand or rub up against his leg.

"Don't go sucking up. You barely know the guy. A little bit of restraint wouldn't have gone astray."

Strudel eyed him uncomprehendingly and he reached out to scratch her behind her ear. How could he resist that face?

Once he'd finished with the fence, he dragged the ladder out of the shed and inspected the gutters. Sure enough, they were full of leaves and silt and he worked his way around the house, scooping dead leaves and who-knew-what-else out from the gutters. It was a disgusting, messy, smelly job, and by the time he'd reached the front of the house he was well and truly over it. He glanced at Mackenzie's house as he cleared out the corner nearest her property, wondering if she'd heard the storm warning.

For a few seconds he toyed with the idea of passing on the information, then he remembered the superior way she'd looked down her nose at him while blaming Strudel for her dog's bad behavior. He was all out of favors where she was concerned.

Once he'd finished the gutters, he checked the downpipes, then cleared the drain that ran across the top of the driveway. Both his and Mackenzie's properties were on a slight slope, the street being higher than the house. If there was water runoff coming his way, he wanted to be sure it had somewhere to go, other than into his house.

He was putting the ladder away when the heavens opened, rain sheeting from the sky so intensely it stung when it hit his arms and face. Strudel at his heels, he bolted for the house. It wasn't until he was washing off the dirt beneath a hot shower that he registered that he hadn't thought about Edie or Nick once all day.

A new record.

Maybe walking away from everything and driving a thousand kilometers south hadn't been such a crazy idea after all.

MACKENZIE HAD PLANNED to take Mr. Smith for a walk along the beach that afternoon, but the weather had different ideas. Instead, she spent some time online checking out the various chat groups and fan sites for *Time and Again*. She liked to dip her toe in occasionally to take the temperature and see how viewers were responding to the show. The uneasy feeling that had sat in her gut since her conversation with Gordon yesterday intensified as she read excited posts from die-hard fans. According to them, the past few months had been some of the best in the show's history. Dramatic, exciting, romantic, funny...

It was hyperbole, written by fervent, biased fans. But it still made her feel edgy. She recorded the show religiously every night but hadn't caught up with her viewing for a few days. Since she was on a roll with the self-torturing thing, she watched three episodes in a row. Every time something caught her attention—a change in the lighting, some alterations to a set, the thrust of a storyline—she stopped and reviewed the footage. Two hours later, she'd bitten her thumbnail down to the quick and the edgy feeling had become full-fledged anxiety.

Gordon was right. Philip *was* doing a good job. Possibly even a great job. She'd been aware of it before, of course—

God, she'd even been foolish enough to be relieved that the show was in such good hands—but she hadn't consciously registered how good his work was.

She stared at the darkened TV screen, rain slashing at the windows, Mr. Smith snoring at her feet. If Philip held out for a longer contract, the production company would be crazy not to give it to him. *She'd* give it to him if she were in Gordon's position.

Please, please, please don't let that happen.

She wasn't even remotely hungry but she forced herself to make and eat dinner. In the good old days, she'd lived on Diet Coke, black coffee and take-out meals. These days, she made sure she gave her body what it needed to recover—organic vegetables, lean protein and all manner of virtuous things. She sat on the window seat in the living room and watched the trees thrash around in the rising wind while she ate her chicken stir-fry. The storm showed no signs of abating. Hardly unusual stuff for the Mornington Peninsula—she'd already endured several storms like this since she'd taken up residence in the beach house—but pretty spectacular to watch from the comfort of a warm, cozy house.

Her gaze was drawn to the golden light spilling from the house next door. It was strange to see it lit up after all these months of darkness. If her new neighbor hadn't turned out to be such an uptight ass, she'd have welcomed the signs of life. But after this morning's dressing-down, the only thing she'd welcome was his departure.

She made a rude sound in the back of her throat as she remembered the way he'd looked down at her from his position on the fence, telling her how to manage her dog and acting as though Mr. Smith was some kind of pirate king who had buccaneered his way into the neighboring yard and raped and pillaged its doggy occupants. Last time she'd looked, dogs were animals, with all the attendant urges and instincts of animals. Clearly Oliver was one of those uptight dog owners who policed their pet's every move. No doubt poor Strudel lived a regimented life full of rules and regulations.

Poor Strudel. Probably those few illicit seconds with Mr. Smith were the most fun she'd had in a long time.

Mackenzie scooped the last mouthful of rice from her bowl and swung her feet to the floor. She wasn't going to waste another second thinking about Mr. Uptight. Life was too short.

She was in bed by nine o'clock, listening to the rain drum against the tin roof. She drifted into sleep and woke to deep darkness and the sound of running water. For a few seconds she thought she'd left the tap on in the en suite bathroom, but it didn't sound like a tap running. The rain was still thrumming against the roof and pelting the windows and a horrible suspicion crept into her mind. She threw back the covers. The ominous feeling intensified when she discovered Mr. Smith was missing from the hallway outside her bedroom. Not a great sign. She turned on lights as she moved through the house, checking first the open-plan living area at the back before making her way to the front.

She found Mr. Smith at the door, ears up, posture alert in full defcon-five watchdog mode.

"What's going on, Smitty?"

He turned and gave her a darkly knowing look.

"That bad, huh?"

She opened the door—and froze.

Water rushed down her gravel driveway, a muddy brown torrent filled with leaves and gravel and other debris. Once it hit the paved area in front of her house, it had nowhere to go, and a lake was forming on her doorstep, the water already lapping at the bottom step.

Dear God, she was about to be flooded.

For a moment shock stole her capacity to think. She stared at the swirling, dark water, unable to comprehend what was happening. Then, suddenly, her brain snapped into action. There was a storm drain across the driveway. In theory, it should be channeling this deluge away from the house. Which meant it must be blocked. Maybe if she could unblock it, she could avert disaster.

Maybe.

She was barefoot, so she raced up the hallway, snatching her rubber boots from the laundry, along with her garden gloves and the yard broom.

She was soaked to the skin the moment she stepped beyond the shelter of the porch, sheeting rain turning her tank top and pajama bottoms into skintight apparel. Squinting against the downpour, she made her way to the drain. The problem was immediately apparent—gravel had washed down from the road and filled the grate covering the long channel, rendering it all but useless and creating a bridge for the water to reach the house. She pulled on the gloves and squatted, scooping the gravel away from the grate. She swore under her breath when she saw that as fast as she scooped, the rushing water replaced what she'd removed with yet more gravel.

She increased her pace, scooping the gravel away with cupped hands, pushing it between her legs like a dog digging a hole. After ten minutes it became painfully clear to her that she was rearranging deck chairs on the *Titanic.* Not only was the water faster than her, but also she could feel her energy flagging. She glanced over her shoulder and felt a sick jolt of adrenaline at the sight of the water lapping at the second step.

She abandoned the drain and returned to the porch, collecting the broom then wading into the fray. The water was already flowing around the house, rushing down either side, but not nearly fast enough to prevent the rising levels. But perhaps if she encouraged it on its way she could keep the water from invading her home.

Perhaps.

She began pushing the water toward the side of the house with the broom, gloved hands gripping the handle tightly. She worked doggedly, putting all her weight behind each push. Soon her arms were burning and she was panting

And still the water kept coming.

She paused to catch her breath, despair filling her heart as the rain intensified.

She was going to be flooded. There was no way she could stop it. The best she could do was retreat inside to roll up rugs and move as many valuables as she could off the floor.

She lifted a hand to swipe the water from her face—an utterly useless, pointless gesture, just as all of her efforts had been useless and pointless tonight—then lost her breath as a figure loomed out of the darkness.

Tall and broad, his chestnut hair was plastered to his scalp, his jeans molded to his thighs, his T-shirt to his chest.

Her neighbor, Oliver-the-ass.

He surveyed the situation, then zeroed in on the drain. She started moving forward, intending to tell him that it was no use, that he couldn't possibly beat the water. But he was already pulling the metal grate free, gravel and all, tossing it to one side to allow the water and gravel to surge into the channel beneath the grate.

He didn't wait to see if his radical surgery had had the desired effect. He turned to her, jerking his chin toward the house.

"You got another broom?" he yelled over the sound of the wind and rain.

She blinked the rain from her eyes. Tried to get her brain to connect with her mouth. "Yes."

He plucked the broom from her hands. "Go grab it."

He was gone before she could say anything more, striding to the side of the house. He swept with long, powerful strokes, pushing water down the side path.

For long seconds Mackenzie simply watched him, dumbfounded, overwhelmed, grateful and terrified all at once. He glanced at her, obviously wondering what she was doing, standing there like an idiot, and for the second time that night she snapped into action.

Her legs felt rubbery, her back was starting to ache, but she spun on her heel and went to find the second broom.

CHAPTER THREE

OLIVER GLANCED TOWARD the sky, willing the weather gods to take it easy with the rain. Apparently they weren't taking calls right now, because it continued to pound down, relentless and seemingly unending.

He returned to sweeping, pushing water along the side of Mackenzie's house, the weight of the water and his efforts creating a miniature river. He was aware of her working at the other corner of the house, a small, sodden figure in clinging pajamas. She'd looked terrified and exhausted when he'd arrived twenty minutes ago. As well she might be. He'd been momentarily staggered by the amount of water pouring down her driveway when he left his place.

The street was almost knee-deep, the storm drains clearly overwhelmed by the volume of runoff. The laws of gravity demanded that the water find the lowest point and it had—Mackenzie's driveway. And, to a lesser extent, his own. He'd already removed the grates on his own channel drains, but one glance at the water rushing toward Mackenzie's house had told him that her property was in far greater danger.

Lightning cracked overhead, a violent fork that turned the world silver. He spared the sky a glance before refocusing on his efforts, but a few seconds later he felt a tug on his arm.

"We have to go inside," Mackenzie yelled over the sound of the wind and rain.

"I'm all right," he assured her.

She didn't let go of his arm, tugging on it with surprising strength. "You can't be outside in an electrical storm. It's dangerous."

As if to punctuate her words, the sky split in two again, a fork of lightning spearing across the darkness. She flinched, her grip tightening.

"Inside!"

He glanced toward her porch, where water still lapped at the bottom step. If they stopped what they were doing, there was a very real chance she would be inundated.

"Don't worry about the house," she yelled.

He let her tow him toward the porch. She released him as they gained the shelter of the eaves and they stood side by side in the relative dry, watching the water rush down the driveway to join the miniature lake in front of them. Lightning lit the world again, a huge, jagged line that cut through the darkness, and he was suddenly glad that she'd insisted they seek cover.

"You're insured, right?" he asked, looking at her.

She had her arms wrapped around herself, and goose bumps peppered her skin. She nodded, her face very pale.

"You're freezing," he said.

"So are you."

"You should go inside."

"And miss the floor show?"

"If it means missing out on pneumonia, sure."

He could see her reluctance to abandon her post. He didn't know Mackenzie from a bar of soap, but his gut told him she wasn't the sort of woman who gave up on anything easily.

"You can't do anything until the electrical storm passes," he said.

Her mouth flattened into a stubborn line for a second or two, then she nodded. "Come on, then."

He paused on the doorstep to toe off his sodden sneakers then followed her inside, Mr. Smith hard on his heels. Mackenzie stepped into the first room on the left—a home gym with some kind of specialized equipment, from the look of it—and returned with an armful of towels.

"Thanks," he said when she offered him one.

Water pooled on the floor around him. He blotted his face and hair, then started in on his T-shirt and jeans. She did the same, briskly toweling her hair before moving on to her chest and arms.

There was an odd intimacy to the moment—the two of them alone in the narrow, dimly lit hall, tending to the needs of their bodies. It didn't help that now they were inside he was very aware of the fact that her pale gray tank top had become semitransparent with the rain and he could see the dark shadows of her areolaes through the thin fabric. To make things worse, her nipples were hard from the cold, too, an almost irresistible combination for any self-respecting heterosexual male.

He forced his gaze away and registered the vicious-looking pink-and-red scar that ran down her left shoulder and along her upper arm to her elbow. It was so unexpected he found himself staring. He remembered the scar on her scalp and put two and two together—clearly, something very serious had happened to her. Recently, too, if the pinkness of the tissue was anything to go by.

He became aware that Mackenzie had finished drying herself and lifted his gaze to look straight into her eyes.

Busted. Big-time. Heat singed his cheeks. He tried to find the words to explain why he'd been gawking like a five-year-old, but before he could open his mouth she turned away.

"There's brandy in the kitchen."

She disappeared up the hallway, Mr. Smith trotting after her. Oliver followed her to an open-plan kitchen/living room at the rear of the house. He saw that she'd draped her towel around her shoulders, effectively covering her injury. Between avoiding ogling her breasts and getting busted ogling her scar, he was feeling more than a little awkward, so he made a big deal out of checking out the room while racking his brain for something to say.

The kitchen was white and modern and pristine, the furniture in the living area a mixture of creams and whites and raw wood. Only the stack of magazines on the coffee table and the vase of half-dead flowers on the mantel saved it from being magazine-shoot perfect.

"This is nice. Much better than Aunt Marion's place," he said.

She opened a cupboard and pulled out two tumblers. "Scotch or brandy?"

He didn't drink either, but if ever an occasion called for the lubricating effects of alcohol, this was it.

"Scotch, thanks."

She poured a generous amount into each glass then handed one to him.

"Thanks for your help. I appreciate it," she said, lifting her glass to him in an informal toast. "Above and beyond the call of duty, especially since we hardly know each other."

And didn't exactly get off on the right foot.

She didn't say it, and neither did he, but he knew without a doubt that they were both thinking it.

"Once I saw the street I figured you might be in trouble." He took a swallow and Scotch burned its way down his throat to his belly.

"Oh, right. I guess it's flooded up there, too, huh?"

"You practically need a canoe."

"I've never seen flooding like this before. And I've had this place nearly ten years."

"My guess is the drains on the street are blocked. Mind you, when that much water comes down this quickly, most drainage systems freak out."

She nodded, then looked into her drink. He wondered if she was as uncomfortable as he was, and if she was finding this conversation as stilted and yawn inducing.

A bead of water ran down her temple and onto the curve of her cheek. She lifted one side of the towel to rub at her hair. When she lowered it again her hair was sticking up in spiky tufts like a little kid's and her scar was once again on display.

Oliver kept his gaze fixed on her face, determined not to make the same mistake twice.

"So, um, I guess the storm woke you, too, huh?"

"I guess. I heard water running and Mr. Smith was missing from outside my bedroom. I figured something must be up." She lifted her drink to her mouth and he saw that she was trembling, the fine movement making the amber fluid shiver in the glass.

"Maybe you should sit down."

"I'm fine."

"No, you're not."

She was pale and she was soaked and she was shaking. Patently not fine, despite her bravado.

"This is normal. I just need a few minutes, that's all."

"Why don't you humor me and take them sitting down? Because if you keel over we're both in big trouble, since what I know about first aid could fit on a postage stamp."

"How about *you* humor *me* and trust that I know my own strength?" Mackenzie snapped.

He took an instinctive step backward, retreating from the anger in her suddenly fierce blue eyes. This was why he'd hesitated before following her into the house—for whatever reason, this woman and he were not destined to get on.

"Why don't I go check on the situation outside?" He set down his glass and headed for the door, his mind on only one thing—escape.

"Oliver, wait," Mackenzie said. "Please?"

There was a softness, a sincerity to her words that made him pause on the threshold.

"That was…out of line. Hugely out of line. I'm really sorry, okay?" she said as he faced her.

He nodded, very aware of his wet, cold clothes, keen to simply be gone now.

She sighed and ran a hand through her hair. "I was in a car accident a year ago. A pretty bad one. I was in hospital for months, then rehab… I guess what I'm trying to say is that people telling me how I feel or what I can do or not do—or even if I'm okay or not—is a really hot button for me. When you've been a patient for months, regaining control of your body and your life is a precious, precious thing. That's not an excuse, by the way, just an explanation. You came to my rescue when you didn't have to, and I am so, so grateful for that. Can we rewind and erase the last sixty seconds?"

She scanned his face, clearly waiting for his response.

He didn't doubt her sincerity, but he still wanted to be gone. He wasn't up for negotiating with prickly, difficult personalities right now. He had enough crap in his own life to deal with.

"Sure. But I should probably still check on the storm."

The words were barely out of his mouth before lightning flickered once again, closely followed by the clap of thunder.

She collected his glass and offered it to him. "At least finish this before you go. Never let it be said that I drove a man screaming into the night without letting him finish his drink first."

"Actually, I'm not the biggest fan of Scotch." He figured he might as well be honest, since he had nothing to lose.

She looked dismayed. "You should have said. Why didn't you say?" Then she shook her head. "Don't answer that—I know why. Because you're a nice guy, and I'm a harpy."

"You're not a harpy."

"Yeah, I am. A harpy with a horny dog and zero social skills." She sank onto the arm of the sofa. "Believe it or not, before the accident I was actually not too bad to be around. I may have even been likable."

She looked sad, sitting there in her soggy pajamas with her ruffled hair, her expression equal parts bemusement and regret.

"You're not a harpy. Just a bit scary."

She blinked, then huffed out a laugh. As he'd hoped she would.

"Scary, huh?" she asked.

"In that intense, I've-had-too-many-coffees-today kind of way." He said it lightly and she smiled.

"You know what's funny about that? I haven't had a coffee for months. Makes me feel sick now. Which is weird because I used to live on the stuff."

For a moment they were silent, the first easy, undemanding moment they'd shared.

She stood. "Right, where were we? You were escaping, I believe."

"I was going to check outside."

"Like I said, escaping. And who could blame you?"

She started up the hallway and Oliver followed her. The storm seemed doubly furious after the quiet inside, but when they walked to the edge of the porch and peered out, it was clear that the volume of water pouring down the driveway was far less than it had been, and the water around the house had subsided an inch or two.

Oliver tilted his head and assessed the cloud-choked sky. “You know, I think you might be in luck. The rain is definitely easing.”

“God, I hope you’re right.”

Mr. Smith descended to the lowest dry step and crouched to sniff at the encroaching water.

“Back from there, Smitty,” Mackenzie said.

Predictably, the dog ignored her, leaning even closer to the water. Oliver and Mackenzie started down the steps at the same time—just as the dog lost his balance and toppled in. To her credit, Mackenzie didn’t hesitate to jump in barefoot after him, even though there was no risk of the dog drowning—Mr. Smith might be on the ground-hugging side, but the flood was barely a foot high now. She scooped up the wet dog then climbed the stairs trailing muddy water.

“I see an RSPCA medal in your future,” Oliver couldn’t resist saying.

“Whereas I see lots of muddy towels and a wrestle with Mr. Smith in the bathtub.”

He decided he was ready to take his chances. A hot shower and a warm bed were very high on his must-have list right now.

“Send up a flare if you need more help,” he said, tugging on his shoes.

She met his eyes over Mr. Smith’s head. “I owe you,” she said simply.

“No, you don’t.”

“I do.”

“I held a broom for five seconds.”

“You came over in the middle of the night to help out a stranger.”

"Not much else to do when you're awake at two in the morning."

She smiled faintly and shook her head. "You're not going to talk me out of my gratitude, so you might as well go home and get warm and worry about what I might do to thank you."

Since she seemed determined to feel under an obligation to him, he simply lifted his hand in farewell and descended the stairs. He waded up the driveway and into the street, stopping to marvel at the lake it had become. Once the water subsided there would be a serious mess to clean up.

His feet slipping inside his shoes, he made his way home. Thankfully, there were still embers glowing in the fire grate and he stopped to throw on some more kindling. He stripped in the chilly bathroom, leaving his clothes in the tub before stepping beneath the shower. He closed his eyes as heat enveloped him. Next door, Mackenzie was probably doing the exact same thing, standing beneath the shower, water cascading over her small, perky breasts....

Oliver opened his eyes and frowned at the tiled wall.

Was he really such a cheap date that a few minutes with a woman in a wet tank top was enough to crank his engine, despite the fact he wasn't sure if he even *liked* said woman?

He thought about Mackenzie's breasts again, about how round and firm they'd looked the handful of times he'd allowed himself to peek at them, and admitted to himself that it might be low and base and animalistic, but yes, he was that cheap.

He was a man. He hadn't had sex in over seven months, and he'd just been in the same room with almost-naked breasts. Some things a guy didn't have much control over.

It didn't mean anything. It certainly didn't mean he was going to be rushing to spend more time with Mackenzie again. Granted, she had apologized for her prickliness and shown a rather charming willingness to mock herself, but whichever way he cut it, she was hard yards. He wasn't up for hard yards, even if he thought there was a chance in hell that he'd get to see for himself how perky and round her breasts were. He was fresh out of a marriage, heading toward an ugly divorce.

More than enough for any man to deal with.

MACKENZIE PULLED ON fresh pajamas after her shower and went to check that things hadn't taken a sudden turn for the worse out front.

It wasn't pretty outside, but it was definitely better, and she retreated to her bedroom and pulled the covers all the way up to her ears. The bed had been kept warm by her electric blanket and she wiggled her toes against the toasty sheets and contemplated how she would make things right with Oliver.

Because she needed to. Big-time.

Not only for the way she'd snapped at him tonight, either. From the moment she'd met him she'd been rude. Shutting the door in his face not once but twice, then getting defensive with him over Mr. Smith when she should have been thanking him for repairing the fence. She had excuses for some of it—her nausea, Gordon's much-anticipated and hard-fought-for phone call—but the bottom line was that she'd behaved poorly.

She winced, remembering the way Oliver had described her as scary, in an "intense, I've-had-too-many-coffees-today kind of way." He'd been joking, trying to ease the tension, but she was a big believer in the many-a-true-word-said-in-jest maxim and she didn't doubt for a second that that was how he saw her: scary and intense. And, of course, overly sensitive and snappish.

Hardly a flattering portrait. In fact, it made her squirm.

The defensive part of her said to hell with what he thought of her. He wasn't her friend, after all, or a colleague. Once she picked up the threads of her former life and moved back to Melbourne, he wouldn't even be her neighbor.

But everything in her balked at leaving the situation the way it was. As she'd told him tonight, he was a nice guy. He'd come over to introduce himself, he'd repaired the fence without hassling her or asking for a contribution to pay for materials, he'd come riding to her rescue and downed half a glass of Scotch simply to be polite. He was funny, too, with an easy charm and a deceptively quiet, dry wit.

I like him. And I want him to like me.

The thought made her eyes pop open. She'd been so caught up in herself and her recovery that she hadn't given any consideration to the outside world and other people for a long time. She'd deliberately sequestered herself here on the very tip of the Mornington Peninsula, shutting herself away from her friends so she could concentrate on her rehabilitation. She'd been isolated from life by her accident, and she'd made the decision to continue that isolation, and now she was…what? Lonely? Antisocial? A cranky, prickly hermit crab, holed up in her shell?

There wasn't much she liked about this new perspective on herself and her current life.

Then do something about it.

She could invite Oliver over for dinner, for example, to say thank-you to him. And, maybe, as a byproduct, improve his impression of her. Not that she thought it was likely they would become fast friends after such a rocky start, but at least she could show him that she wasn't a complete cow.

She could try, anyway.

MACKENZIE WOKE TO bright sunlight streaming through the gap in the curtains. Muzzy headed, she peered at the clock and saw it was nearly midday. She never slept in, but clearly her body had needed the rest. When she tried to roll over she realized how much—she ached as if she'd run a marathon, as though thugs had broken in during the night and given her a thorough going-over with baseball bats. She was used to a low level of constant pain, a sort of background hum of discomfort, but this was a whole other ball game. Her breath hissed from between her teeth as she swung her legs over the side of the bed. Moving like a much older woman, she shuffled her way to the bathroom.

She looked at her gray, washed-out face in the mirror and knew that she wouldn't be cooking dinner for anyone in the near future. Last night had tapped whatever reserves she'd built in recent months, and unless she was hugely mistaken, her next few days would involve lots of lying around in bed and on the couch, being bored out of her skull.

She let her head drop forward, frustration and disappointment at her own weakness momentarily getting the better of her. She'd thought she was stronger than this. Further along in her recovery. Apparently she was still a slave to her injuries and her broken body.

For long seconds she felt immeasurably heavy, defeated by the sheer breadth of the challenge that still lay ahead of her. She had no choice but to fight on, but right now it would be nice to be able to call a time-out and curl up in the corner with her thumb in her mouth for a while.

Life didn't offer time-outs, though. She needed to keep plowing on with her rehab program, and she needed to keep getting better. Otherwise, losing her job wouldn't only be a possibility; it would be a certainty.

She spent the day in bed and woke feeling marginally better the following day. She swapped the bed for the couch, and the evening found her ensconced on the window seat, Mr. Smith warming her toes as she ate a bowl of soup. The sun had set long ago and the world outside was dark except for the glow of Oliver's window next door.

She could see him moving behind the thin net curtain. By the way he kept moving in and out of sight, she deduced he was in the kitchen. She watched him idly, her thoughts slow and lazy. She wondered what he was having for dinner, and how he was feeling after their shared ordeal, and if he ever glanced out his window and wondered what she was doing.

Why on earth would he do that?

It was a good question, since she'd already established that she'd given him precious little reason to be interested in anything she might do or say. Plus, he was a married man—she was almost sure of it—so he had no business wondering about her. At all.

She set down her bowl and picked up the book she'd been reading, getting lost in a world of murder and mystery and romance. When she tuned into the real world again she heard music emanating from next door. Acoustic guitar, low and mellow. She wondered idly who it was. She wasn't a huge fan of instrumentals, but this song was like a warm breeze on a summer's day, easy and undemanding and thoroughly pleasant. One song melded into another, then another. Then the music stopped and the only sound was Mr. Smith snoring from the other end of the window seat and the creak of the wind in the trees outside.

When she saw Oliver again, she would have to ask him who the artist was. In the meantime, it was time for bed again.

Tomorrow I will start back with my exercises, she promised herself. She would also leave the house, and she would go grocery shopping and, depending on how she felt, she'd invite Oliver over for dinner. Maybe not for tomorrow night, but perhaps the next, which was a Tuesday if her calculations were correct.

If he wanted to come, of course.

Potentially a big if.

CHAPTER FOUR

OLIVER DUMPED THE LAST wheelbarrow load of gravel at the top of the driveway and paused to wipe his forehead with the bottom of his sweatshirt. Most of the gravel had washed down the slope and collected in front of his house thanks to the storm, and he'd spent the past three days alternating between cleaning up outside and trying to set the inside of his aunt's house to rights.

He wasn't sure which was the least fun task—sweeping up dirt and shoveling gravel, or cleaning out cupboards filled with the flotsam and jetsam of a lifetime. So far, he'd made half-a-dozen trips to the local charity shop, offloading books and china and knickknacks. He figured there would be many more trips in his future, too, since he'd cleared out only one of the bedrooms and part of the living room.

He grabbed the rake and started spreading the gravel across the driveway. He caught movement out of the corner of his eye and he glanced over in time to see someone shifting through the front window of Mackenzie's house.

He hadn't had any contact with her since the storm. Hadn't even heard her calling to Mr. Smith or seen her out in the yard. The lights had been going out very early on her side of the fence, too.

Not that he'd been looking. He'd simply happened to glance out the window a couple of times and noticed she seemed to be keeping very early hours.

None of his business, any of it. Even if there had been a

small, completely testosterone-driven part of his brain that had been looking forward to seeing her again.

Amazing the power of a see-through tank top.

He resumed raking, but the sound of a door closing made him lift his head. Sure enough, Mackenzie was descending the steps, Mr. Smith on a leash.

"Hello," she said.

He lifted a hand in greeting. She approached, Mr. Smith pulling at the leash with the eagerness of a dog that had been indoors for several days.

She surveyed his driveway and grimaced. "I guess the flood messed with your place, too, huh?"

"Not too badly. Just putting this gravel back where it belongs."

There was something about the way she held herself—a sort of wariness—that made her seem almost fragile this morning. As though a puff of wind or a rough gesture could knock her over.

"I've been meaning to come see you," she said. "I wanted to thank you again for the other night."

He shrugged. "Really, I didn't do anything."

"You saved me from bailing out my house. And I'd really like to cook you dinner to say thank-you. Tomorrow night, if you're available…?"

Oliver did his best not to let his surprise show on his face, but he wasn't sure he pulled it off. A dinner invitation was the last thing he'd expected from the difficult neighbor. Any social invitation, really. She'd made it pretty clear she wasn't into chitchat and small talk.

She was waiting for his answer, her gaze fixed on his face. In full daylight, the color of her irises was nothing short of arresting, reminiscent of the deep, deep blue of tropical water or the clarity of the summer sky.

His first instinct was to offer a polite excuse and keep

his distance. They didn't have the best track record, after all. But there was something about the way she was waiting for his response that appealed to his better nature.

"Dinner sounds great," he said after a slightly too long silence.

She smiled, the action showcasing straight white teeth and the rather charming crow's-feet at the corners of her eyes. "Is seven okay for you?"

"Sure. What can I bring?"

"Your appetite. I'll take care of the rest."

Her dog was sniffing the cuffs of his jeans, clearly looking for eau de Strudel. Oliver bent to scratch him behind the ears.

"Sorry, mate, but she's inside, staying out of all this mud."

Mr. Smith gave him a beseeching look.

"I think that's a plea for clemency. Maybe you could bring Strudel over when you come to dinner."

Oliver looked into Mr. Smith's pleading eyes and tried to remember that it had taken this furry Lothario less than twenty-four hours to impose himself upon Strudel in the most intimate way possible. Mr. Smith was the picture of innocence and worthy doggy loyalty.

"That could probably be arranged," Oliver said.

"Great. Then we'll both look forward to seeing you tomorrow night. Come on, Smitty."

Mackenzie gave a little tug on the lead and Mr. Smith fell in beside her as she headed up the road. Oliver stared after her, noting her undemanding pace, the slight stiffness to her gait and the fact that her black pants fit very snuggly over the curves of her small backside.

As he'd already observed, she was too scrawny for his tastes, but what there was of her was nicely proportioned. Small but very nicely formed.

He realized he was staring and shook his head, turning to his work. Tomorrow night was sure to be awkward. They didn't know each other, so conversation would be polite and superficial and no doubt stilted, as it had been the other night.

It was too late to take back his acceptance, so he would have to simply suck it up and take his medicine. Mackenzie would have a chance to get her gratitude off her chest and any sense of obligation that existed between them would be a thing of the past.

Then they could go back to being strangers and each get on with their lives.

MACKENZIE SPENT THE evening planning the menu for tomorrow night's meal, flicking through cookbooks and trying to work out what she could pull together given the limited supplies likely to be available at the local supermarket. She settled for a pasta dish—tortellini with salami, goat cheese and Kalamata olives, fresh bread and a baby spinach, Parmesan and pear salad. She made a shopping list sitting up in bed, more than a little amused by her own organizational zeal. She was planning this simple dinner with military precision—a strong indication her mind needed more to think about. The sooner she got back to work, the better.

She went into town first thing to do her shopping, then spent the afternoon pottering around the house. She started prepping for dinner at five o'clock so she could take her time and enjoy the process.

She was looking forward to tonight. There was no point denying it, even to herself. Having another warm body to talk to would be a welcomc novelty.

"No offense, Smitty, but sometimes a lick and a scratch don't quite cut it in the witty repartee department."

Mr. Smith lifted his head from his paws and gave her an uncomprehending look.

"Exactly."

She had everything prepped by six o'clock, the table set by a quarter past. At loose ends, she wandered into her bedroom and caught sight of herself in the full-length mirror. Her hair was limp and lifeless, her face pale. Her black leggings had seen better days, as had the long sleeved wool tunic she'd pulled on. Combined with her sensible walking shoes, she looked...*frumpy.* There was no other word for it.

As if he's going to notice what you're wearing. He's going to have one eye on the exit all evening.

She wasn't stupid. She'd noted Oliver's hesitation when she invited him. Given her not-so-enchanting behavior to date, it didn't surprise her that he might be cautious about breaking bread with her. The last thing he'd be concerned with would be if she looked frumpy or halfway presentable.

So what? It concerns me.

She opened the closet on a surge of determination. She was allowed to look nice if she wanted to. So what if Oliver was unlikely to register the cut of her pants or the drape of her sweater? She would know, and it would be a welcome change from workout pants and warm sweaters.

She pulled on a turtleneck made from cashmere and silk, matching it with her steel-gray wide-legged linen pants. They made her feel elegant, like the heroine from a thirties noir movie, and she felt infinitely better as she slipped on a pair of simple ballet flats and went into the bathroom to do something with her face.

Some blush worked wonders, as did a few swipes of mascara. Her hair, however, refused to cooperate. Amazing to think that it had once been her crowning glory, almost long enough to sit on, a sleek, smooth waterfall of hair that—in her own mind, at least—had made up for the fact that she wasn't exactly stacked in the breast department. She'd never been the frilly, feminine type, but the swish of her hair against her back had made her feel saucy and womanly and sexy without fail.

Those were the days.

The E.R. nurses had shaved it all off when they prepped her for emergency surgery after the accident. For long days and weeks afterward, it had been the least of her concerns, but there was no denying that it had been a shock to see herself in the mirror for the first time. The scars on her scalp had been visible through the regrowth by the time they let her look in a mirror, ugly and far too visible. She'd waited till she was alone in her room before letting a few silly, vain tears slide into her pillow. A small moment of mourning for her lost mane.

It had been tempting to grow it all out, but it was much easier to maintain this way. She didn't have to worry about tying her hair back when she was doing her exercises and it didn't require special conditioning treatments or take half an hour to dry.

She did what she could with some styling product, trying to coax some texture into it. Finally she rolled her eyes at her own reflection and turned away from the mirror.

Enough, already. She was having dinner with the guy next door, not attending a bloody state reception for the queen.

She was heading for the entry hall to turn on the outside light when the phone rang. She grabbed it from its station on the occasional table as she passed by.

"Mackenzie speaking."

"Mac. It's me."

She came to a dead halt as she heard her ex-husband's voice. It took her a moment to summon the casual tone her pride demanded.

"Patrick. How are you?" she asked coolly.

It had been more than five months since she'd last spoken to him. The ink was long-since dry on their divorce and technically he owed her nothing, not even a phone call or two. But the friends-with-benefits arrangement they'd slipped into in the months before her accident had led her to believe that there was still a degree of affection between them.

Yet another misconception to add to the many misconceptions in their shared history.

"I'm good. How about you?" he asked in the mellow, lovely voice that made women across the nation swoon.

Her ex, the matinee idol.

"I'm well, thanks."

"That's really great to hear. Really great. Gordon's been keeping me up-to-date with your progress."

"Has he? That's nice of him."

Her words hung in the small silence that followed. She could hear the click of a lighter on the other end of the line and guessed he'd started smoking again.

"Okay, fair call," he said. "I've been an asshole. I should have called and I didn't. I should have sent flowers and I didn't. I should have done a bunch of things, but it doesn't mean I haven't been thinking about you. It doesn't mean I don't care, Mac."

Mackenzie stared at the toes of her shoes. There were so many things she could say to him. She could take him to task for being lazy and neglectful. She could tell him that he'd hurt her, that while she hadn't expected undying devotion, she'd assumed he at least liked her enough to want to check for himself that she was doing okay. After all, that had been the raison d'être of the highly inappropriate affair they'd been indulging in before her accident—that, despite everything, they still liked and enjoyed each other.

There was no point, though. Their marriage was over, and whatever friendship remained was not worth stressing herself over. She only had so much energy to invest at the moment, and Patrick was a bad bet. Too much work for too little return.

"Don't worry. I'm not going to read you the riot act. You're officially off the hook."

"Don't be like that, Mac."

She pictured his face, the sheepish, naughty-boy hangdog expression he'd be wearing. Patrick was accustomed to skating by on the power of his charisma. Fortunately, she'd become immune to his powers during the first year of their short marriage.

"I've got someone coming for dinner any second now. Did you want something or was this just a social call?"

"It's about work."

So not a topic she wanted to discuss with Patrick. Anything he had to say was probably the result of gossip and innuendo. She would do better keeping her contact to the show—and her job—limited to conversations with Gordon. So did she really want to hear whatever it was Patrick had to say? "What about work?" Apparently she did.

"You're not going to like this, but as soon as I heard I knew you'd want to know. Gordon came out to the studio today to talk to Phil. It's not official yet, but the word is that Phil's signed on for another two years."

Mackenzie closed her eyes.

She'd lost her job. All those years she'd put in, slaving away like a good little worker ant. All the unpaid overtime, the days she'd worked when she'd been dead on her feet with a cold or the flu, the many, many times she'd gone beyond the call of duty to get the job done…

All for nothing.

Her loyalty, her passion, her dedication, none of it had

mattered when push had come to shove. She'd been replaced.

"Mac? Are you still there?"

"Yes."

Barely.

"I didn't want to be the bearer of bad tidings, but I figured you'd rather hear it from me than through the grapevine. For what it's worth, everyone thinks it's a shitty move."

Everyone being the other members of the cast, she assumed. Which also meant the whole world knew and there was absolutely no way for her to salvage an ounce of pride out of this situation.

"You'll get something else. The moment you're back on the market you'll be snapped up. Everyone knows how good you are," Patrick said.

It was nice of him to try to bolster her, but they both knew she'd struggle to find a position at the same level. The opportunity to produce a successful show didn't come up every day in the Australian television industry—and even if something did come up, her accident and extended convalescence were well-known in this tight-knit world. No one would want to take her on until she'd proved she wasn't a liability or a spent force. She'd have to start the climb all over again....

Despair gripped her. She could live with the fact that she might never regain full range of movement in her arm and shoulder. She could live with the occasional killer headache and the fact that she would never walk with a swing in her hips again. But that job had meant so much to her. She'd been so proud of it. She'd *earned* it, damn it.

It wasn't fair. It simply wasn't. She'd done all the right things. She'd *always* done all the right things—worked hard, sacrificed, kissed ass, taken shit, swallowed her pride. And a slick mountain road had taken it all away from her.

"Mac, say something. You're starting to freak me out."

"I'm okay."

It was such a lie she could barely get the words out her mouth.

"If you need me, I can be there in an hour. Hour and a half, max. Just say the word."

She pressed her hand to her forehead. Her fingers were icy cold.

"You don't need to do that."

"I want to do it. If I'd be welcome, that is. You don't deserve this, Mac. No one knows better than me how much you put into your career."

He'd blamed her work for the breakup of their marriage. Said that she cared more about her career and proving herself than she did about him. It wasn't true, but the long hours hadn't helped an already fraught situation, that was for sure.

"I half expected it, anyway." She had no idea where the words came from, or her almost-casual tone. "Gordon warned me. So it's not really that big a surprise."

Except it was, because she'd never really imagined that Gordon would choose Philip over her. Amazing to think that after all these years working in such a cynical industry she could still be so naive.

"You should sue them. You're still on sick leave, aren't you? They can't just give your job away."

"They can. They only have to offer me something similar. One of the game shows. Maybe the Christmas Carol special."

"You're better than a game show," Patrick said, his tone full of disgust.

"Listen, I need to go. My guest is here," Mackenzie lied. "I appreciate the heads-up, Patrick."

"Call me if you need to talk, okay? Anytime. Evidence to the contrary, I'm here for you, babe."

"Thanks and noted. See you, Pat."

She ended the call. She put the phone back on its cradle, then she turned on the outside light and went to the kitchen.

The ingredients for the pasta were lined up along the counter, neatly sliced and diced and ready to go. Two of her pretty Japanese glazed bowls sat to one side, waiting to be filled. In the living room beyond, the table was set with cloth napkins and shiny cutlery.

The last thing she wanted to do right now was entertain a virtual stranger. The thought of smiling and making small talk with Oliver when the rug had been pulled from beneath her life made her want to drop her head back and wail like a child. Yet she couldn't cancel on him. This dinner was a thank-you, an acknowledgment that he'd put himself out for her. No way could she pull the pin on their evening. It simply wasn't an option.

Instead, she turned to the fridge and grabbed the bottle of local white wine she'd bought to accompany their meal. She twisted the cap off and poured herself a big serving. She sipped as she gazed grimly off into space. Waiting for Oliver to arrive.

Waiting for this evening to be over so she could crawl into bed, pull the quilt over her head and hide from the world for a while.

Because even feisty, scary, too-many-coffees-intense women were allowed to have moments of weakness. Weren't they?

OLIVER SMOOTHED A HAND over his damp hair. His other hand gripped the neck of a bottle of wine and Strudel's lead as he stood on Mackenzie's doorstep, waiting for her to respond to his knock.

Dumb, but he was nervous. About what, he had no idea.

Annoyed with himself, he turned to study the paved area in front of her house. Unlike him, she hadn't done a thing about the damage from the storm so mud and gravel and debris were still strewn across the expanse.

The snick of the lock had him spinning around as the door opened. Mackenzie smiled at him, pulling the door wide.

"Right on time. The perfect guest."

Mr. Smith rushed out, launching himself at Strudel. A complicated exchange of sniffs, licks and tail wags took place, both dogs quivering with excitement.

"Well. That's them settled for the evening," Mackenzie said.

She looked different. It took him a beat to work out what it was—makeup and real clothes instead of workout gear. Small changes, but enough to make him realize something he hadn't admitted to himself before tonight. She was an attractive woman. Verging on beautiful, with her delicate features and striking blue eyes.

He offered her the bottle. "Not sure if you're a red or white person or an equal-opportunity wine swiller like myself, but this looked good."

She examined the label. "It is. One of my favorite local vineyards, actually."

She gestured for him to enter, making him clue in to the fact he was still hovering on the doorstep like a nervous schoolboy. He shrugged, feeling stupid and self-conscious, and stepped into her small entryway. Strudel strained at her leash, eager to cavort more fulsomely with her new beau.

"Hope you like pasta. And I bought a lemon tart for dessert," Mackenzie said.

"Sounds great." It did, too. Lunch had been hours ago, a cheese and Vegemite sandwich he'd shoved into his face one-handed while sorting through one of the many boxes of books in the back bedroom. "Is it okay if I let Strudel off the leash?" Before she choked to death trying to get at Mr. Smith.

"Of course."

He unclipped the lead and Strudel and Mr. Smith rampaged down the hall, disappearing in no seconds flat.

"No worries, guys, we're cool. We can look after our selves," Mackenzie called after them.

He smiled at her wry tone. "Hard not to feel like chopped liver sometimes, eh?"

"I think Smitty would be more interested in chopped liver, to be honest."

She led the way to the kitchen, her perfume leaving a scented wake.

"I never got around to asking, is this a permanent move for you or have you bought next door as a holiday place?" she asked as she opened the fridge and extracted a bottle of wine.

Let the small talk begin.

"Neither, actually. Marion was my aunt, and she left the place to me and my brother. We're both Sydney based so we decided it was best to sell."

"Oh. I'm sorry for your loss. I know it was a while ago, but she was a great old bird. I used to enjoy chatting with her over the fence whenever I was down here. I was really sad when I heard she'd died."

"Thanks. To be honest, I didn't know her that well. She lived so far away, we didn't see her much. Mostly it was Christmas cards and the occasional phone call."

"Right."

He thought over what she'd said. "Does that mean you don't live here permanently, then? I thought you were a local."

"I'm a city girl. But I've been masquerading as a local for the past few months so I can concentrate on my rehab." She handed him a glass of wine. "So you're the sucker who gets to prepare the house for sale, huh?"

"Guilty as charged."

"That's a big job. Your aunt had me over for tea a couple of times and that place is stuffed with furniture."

"And books and clothes and knickknacks. Then there's the shed out the back."

"You're a good brother," she said.

"Not really. It suited me to get away for a few weeks, that's all."

She raised her glass. "To being temporary neighbors, then."

He touched the rim of his glass to hers. "Cheers."

"Grab a seat while I make this happen." She waved him toward the stools parked beneath the overhang on one side of the counter.

He sat and watched as she moved around the kitchen, setting water to boil and washing a bunch of parsley. There was a restrained energy to her actions, as though she was constantly holding herself in check. Or perhaps it was her injuries that were doing that. He wondered what she'd been like before the accident.

Unstoppable, he suspected.

His gaze dropped and he couldn't help noting her small, round backside again. He wondered what it would feel like in his hands.

He forced himself to look away. He wasn't the kind of guy who went around checking out women and wondering what they looked like naked. He didn't make a habit of it, anyway. Yet somehow his thoughts always seemed to head in that direction when he was with Mackenzie. Even though she wasn't his type.

"So, what do you do when you're not clearing out old furniture?" Mackenzie asked.

"I'm a sound engineer. My business partner, Rex, and I have a small recording studio."

Her gaze was bright and assessing. "What sort of things do you work on? Music, commercial stuff?"

"A bit of everything, but mostly session work for albums."

"Interesting. How did you get into that?"

He shifted on the stool, not liking the direction of the conversation but he had no easy way of changing it. "I was a musician—long time ago. It seemed like the logical next move once the band broke up."

"You were in a band? What was it called?"

"Salvation Jake."

She set down the knife, her eyes wide with surprise. "Get out of town. Really?"

"Yeah."

"I loved you guys. I practically wore holes in your first CD."

Which, coincidentally, was also their one and only successful album.

He could feel his shoulders getting tight. It always made him uncomfortable talking about the band. It was so long ago, like a distant dream. The gold records, the packed gigs. He was well aware that he ticked more than enough boxes to qualify for the washed-up ex-rocker cliché. Eking out a career in an associated field, tick. Days of glory long behind him, tick. Anonymous, tick.

"Your lead singer, Edie Somers… She had such a sexy voice. So much gravel. And such an amazing stage presence."

"Yeah. She was something."

The last thing he wanted to do was talk about Edie. He took a big swallow of wine and focused on Mackenzie.

"How about you? How do you pay the bills?"

Her gaze dropped to the cutting board and she concentrated on brushing the parsley she'd just chopped into a small bowl.

"I work in TV. Producing, that kind of thing."

"I don't think I've ever met a producer before."

"We're not a very exciting bunch. More or less glorified field marshals."

"What shows have you worked on?"

She shrugged, her head still down turned. "Game shows, dramas. Most recently *Time and Again.* Really, it's pretty dull. I'm more interested in knowing what it's like to be a rock god."

"I was the bass guitarist. I don't think I even qualified as a demigod."

"No underwear flying your way, then? No groupies hanging out at the stage door?" Her words were light, but her grip was white-knuckle tight around the bowl of her wineglass, as though she was holding on for dear life. He studied her face, seeing past her smile to the misery in her eyes.

Something was wrong. He had no idea what, but he could *feel* it, and he had the sudden, odd urge to simply lay his hand on hers. Anything to ease the terrible turmoil he sensed in her.

Those were disturbing thoughts. He didn't go around touching strange women to reassure them. He wasn't about to start now, either. Particularly not with this woman, who had already proved that she could be prickly and difficult at the best of times.

"You're not going to go all shy on me, are you, Oliver?

I was hoping for some salacious tales of decadence and excess. At the very least I was hoping for some scuttlebutt."

She gave him what he could only describe as a cheeky look and he realized that whatever was going on, she had no intention of telling him. She was being a good hostess, keeping things light and easy breezy. The least he could do was follow suit.

As for touching her... No. That would not be a good idea.

So he talked about the band. He answered her questions and made her laugh with stories about how gauche and spoiled and dumb they'd been as they enjoyed their brief moment in the sun. She volunteered her own embarrassing stories, and before he knew it he was looking at the bottom of an empty pasta bowl, they'd finished one bottle of wine and she was opening the bottle he'd brought over.

"I'd better not," he said when she attempted to top up his glass. "The saddest thing about pushing forty is not being able to handle hangovers."

"Oh, God, I never could, even when my liver was young and pink and squeaky-clean. But it's not going to stop me from having more. Not tonight, anyway."

There was a determined, bright note to her voice but all he could see was the deep sadness in her eyes. For the second time that night he was gripped with the urge to ask her what was wrong. Then he reminded himself—again—that it was none of his business. She'd said it herself—they were temporary neighbors. Besides, his own life was mostly in the toilet. He was hardly in a position to offer anyone comfort or advice.

He looked away from her sadness and focused instead on the dogs. They'd settled in the corner on what was clearly Mr. Smith's favorite lounging spot, a big floor cushion made from coffee-colored corduroy. Strudel had claimed the prime real estate in the center of the cushion and Mr.

Smith had curled his long body around hers. His head nestled on his outstretched paws, and he watched her every move with a single-minded devotion.

"I think we might have a romance on our hands," he said.

She followed his gaze. "Smitty's definitely enthralled. And she doesn't seem to mind it too much."

"I'd say she was eating it up with a spoon."

"Speaking of which, time for dessert."

She cleared the plates. He watched her walk to the sink, his gaze drawn yet again to her small, pert bottom.

"You want ice cream or cream or both?" Mackenzie asked.

"At the risk of imminent cardiac arrest, both, please."

She was smiling when she returned with two plates bearing lemon tart, ice cream and cream. "Man after my own heart condition."

The lemon tart was just that—tart and sharp and sweet and sour and so good that an involuntary moan of pleasure escaped him.

"That good, huh?" she asked.

"Lemon is one of my favorite flavors, and it's been a while."

"I always make it a rule never to go too long between good desserts. Life is too short."

"That's a pretty good rule."

"It is, isn't it?"

Her expression seemed self-satisfied, although not in a bad way, and once again he was struck by how attractive she was. It wasn't just her eyes, although they were spectacular. It was the shape of her small nose and the plumpness of her lower lip and the laugh lines around her mouth.

Her smile faltered a little and he realized he was staring like...well, a little like poor, dumbstruck Smitty, if he were honest.

Mackenzie put an inordinate amount of attention into scooping up the last of her ice cream and he tried to pretend he couldn't feel heat climbing into his cheeks.

He was really, really out of practice with this man-woman stuff. Not that this was a proper date with any expectations attached to it or anything like that, but still. Apparently he needed to brush up on his social skills before he ventured out too far in public.

"That was really delicious," he said. "The whole meal was great. Definitely better than the canned spaghetti I had last night."

"That's a rather low standard you have there."

"What can I say? I'm a man of simple tastes."

He wasn't sure how, but somehow his words came out sounding loaded. As though he was talking about tastes other than the ones that originated in his mouth.

"So, will your wife be enjoying this lovely, restful break in delightfully wintery Flinders with you?" Mackenzie asked.

For a second he was thrown. How did she know he was married? Then he realized she'd probably assumed he was. Not the craziest assumption given his age, and one that would have been accurate four months ago. He opened his mouth to tell her he was in the process of getting a divorce—then the memory of the last time he'd told someone about him and Edie popped into his head. He hadn't stopped at sketching in the bare details, hadn't been *able* to stop, and all the sordid, messy ugliness had come pouring out. Trying to extricate himself—and the poor person who had been on the receiving end of his spewing—from that embarrassing situation had been almost as bad as baring his soul.

So no way was he gutting himself in front of Mackenzie like that. He'd already made her uncomfortable with his dopey staring and rusty social skills. Discretion was definitely the better part of valor in this circumstance.

"No, she won't."

"That's a shame," Mackenzie said.

He made a noncommittal sound as she poured herself more wine. The dogs stirred, shifting positions on the cushion. Mackenzie smiled indulgently.

"How old is Strudel?" she asked.

"Eighteen months. How about Mr. Smith?"

"Nearly three now. Poor little guy. He was so confused when I had my accident. He had to live with my friend Kelly for nearly eight months. I was worried he'd forget me after all that time, but he still did the happy dance when he saw me."

He knew what she was referring to—the complicated little dance Strudel did whenever he came home, complete with crazily wagging tail, bright eyes and lolling tongue.

"Gotta love the happy dance."

"Yeah, you do."

Her gaze rested on her dog, her expression suddenly pensive. "You know what I love about having a dog? They don't have moods." Her gaze met his, very intense and maybe even a little fierce. "He's always happy to see me. He always wants to be tickled on his belly. He's loyal and steadfast to a fault. Utterly and completely reliable. I know he'll never let me down. Ever. He's always got my back, no matter what."

A single tear trickled down her cheek as she finished speaking. She shook her head slightly and wiped her cheek. "Sorry. I don't know where that came from."

"You're okay. No worries."

She nodded and smiled but when she blinked two more tears slipped down her cheek.

"Sorry..." The look she gave him was anguished and self-conscious at the same time.

"Hey, what are a few tears between temporary neighbors?" he said.

Her chin wobbled, then her face crumpled and suddenly she was crying in earnest. He froze, unsure what to do, what to say.

"I didn't mean—" She stood abruptly. "Give me a minute."

Ducking her head, she strode from the room.

CHAPTER FIVE

OLIVER STARED at her empty seat, feeling sideswiped and stupid and more than a little inadequate.

He should have said something. He should have at least told her that he didn't give a shit if she cried. God knew, he'd shed his fair share of tears in recent months, deep in the dark of the night when no one would know that he'd compromised his all-important masculinity by letting his emotions get the better of him.

He started for the hallway. There he looked left, then right. Right seemed more promising, so he made his way toward the half-open door at the end. He could hear her sobbing as he approached and he paused to knock.

"Mackenzie..."

She didn't respond. He hesitated a moment, then pushed open the door and entered what was clearly her bedroom. She sat on the side of the bed, head down, arms wrapped tightly around the pillow pressed to her chest. Her shoulders shuddered with the force of her misery.

His first instinct was to put his arms around her. She looked so bloody sad and alone and he'd always been a sucker for crying women. He settled for sitting beside her and resting a hand in the middle of her back.

"What's wrong?"

She shook her head, still not looking up. He smoothed his hand in a small circle and waited. After a beat she lifted her head and took a shaky breath.

"They gave up on me. They were keeping my job open, but they've given it away. So it's all gone now. Everything I've worked for..."

Fresh tears welled. He pulled a handful of tissues from the box on the bedside table. He pressed them into her hand and she made a hiccuping sound that he guessed was thank-you.

"If they were willing to hold your job open that long, you must be good at what you do. There'll be other jobs, right?" he said.

She blew her nose. Her face was pink and shiny with tears, her eyelashes spiky with moisture.

"I want *my* job. The job I earned. *I want my life back.*" There was a plaintive, almost despairing note to her voice, like the wail of a scared child, and he understood that this wasn't only about the job. This was about everything—her injuries, the loss of the life and world she'd once taken for granted, her long recovery.

"It'll get better, Mackenzie."

"Will it? Will the headaches stop? Will my shoulder work properly? Will I ever be able to sit cross-legged again? Will I ever be able to take on a full nine-to-five working day without collapsing in a heap for a week?" The questions fired out of her, bristling with anger and frustration.

"I don't know."

She hunched forward, gripping the pillow tightly. "I need to know. I want to know *now* that it's all going to be okay. I'm sick of taking it on faith. I'm sick of proving everyone wrong. I need some kind of guarantee that it's going to be all right because I can't just keep trying and trying and trying when I can't see the end."

She started to cry again. This time he didn't resist the instinct. He folded his arms around her, pulling her close to his chest. She remained locked in on herself, arms banded around the pillow. He tucked her head beneath his chin and waited her out.

After what felt like a long time her body softened and her head rested more heavily on his shoulder.

"I'm so tired," she said, and he knew she was talking about more than physical tiredness.

"You'll be okay, Mackenzie."

Her breathing evened out. After a few more minutes she stirred in his arms, pushing away from his chest. She glanced at his face briefly before grabbing more tissues. The glimpse was enough for him to see she was embarrassed now that the crisis had passed. Self-conscious because she'd let her guard down in front of a man she'd shared a meal and a bottle of wine and not much else with.

"Don't," he said.

Her gaze found his.

"Don't give yourself a hard time for letting it get to you. You're only human. No one can be strong all the time. No one."

"You have to be strong in recovery. No one else will do it for you." Her voice sounded husky and thick.

"So, what? You're not allowed to feel shit? You're not allowed to have a bad day?"

"I don't know. Sometimes it doesn't feel like I can. Sometimes it feels as though if I stop, that'll be it. I'll be locked in that one place—never getting better, never moving forward, never getting back everything I had. That's why I wanted so badly to return to work. That was my benchmark. If I could fool them all into believing I was exactly the same, then it would all be okay. I wouldn't be different. My life wouldn't have changed. I'd just pick up the threads I dropped a year ago. But they gave up on me. They bloody gave up on me."

She blinked rapidly, clearly determined not to shed any

more tears. He thought about the scars he'd seen on her head and arm and the stiffness in her gait and it hit him that perhaps the hardest part of surviving the kind of trauma Mackenzie had been through was accepting that life would never be the same, no matter how hard you pushed yourself or willed it otherwise.

"Would it be the end of the world if everything didn't go back to being the way it used to be?" he asked quietly.

Maybe it hadn't occurred to her to ask herself that question.

"What are you suggesting I do? Slip into early retirement on a disability pension and take up crocheting and lawn bowling?"

"Not at all. I'm only wondering if there isn't another way of defining normal. That's all."

She stared at him. He could see her mind working, feel her sifting through her response to his challenge. Although it seemed low of him to leave her now, he knew Mackenzie well enough to understand she wouldn't want him hanging around while she grappled with redefining who she was.

"I'm going to get out of your hair." He stood. "Spare you any more of my amateur psychology. Such as it is."

She rose, too, quickly collecting the crumpled tissues from the bed and stuffing them into her trouser pocket. For the first time he glanced around, taking in the decor. The wall behind the bed was a muted green, the other three walls taupe. A hazy Asian-themed print hung above the headboard. Her duvet was green, the pillows snowy-white. Some clothes were draped over an antique chair in the corner. His gaze slipped away, but not before he'd noted the delicate black lace of a bra dangling over the chair back, the cups still curved to the shape of Mackenzie's breasts.

Feeling like a voyeur, he headed for the living room. Strudel was out cold, Mr. Smith draped across her neck. He clicked his fingers to wake her and clipped on her lead. She gave him a dark look but lumbered to her feet obediently.

Mackenzie was standing in the doorway watching him when he turned to go, her expression rueful and chagrined and awkward. "Tonight was supposed to make up for all the times I've been rude to you in the past few days."

"You don't have to make anything up to me."

"Right. Two doors in the face, belligerence over the fence, ridiculous preciousness and now this." She shook her head. "You must think I'm an absolute fruitcake."

He eyed her steadily. "What makes you think I'm in a position to judge anybody?"

She gave him a quizzical look.

"Everyone's got their own shit to shovel, Mackenzie. Believe me."

He started forward and she stepped aside so he could pass. She followed him to the entryway.

"Thanks for dinner," he said.

"It was my pleasure. Sorry about the entertainment."

"As I said, there's nothing to be sorry about."

He turned to go, but she caught his forearm. He glanced down as she transferred her grip to his hand. Her fingers were warm as they wrapped around his.

"More importantly, thank you for your kindness." She rose on tiptoe and pressed a kiss to his cheek. "You're a good passer of tissues."

She gave his fingers a small squeeze before releasing him and taking a step backward.

"Good night," he said, because he wasn't sure what else to say.

He walked away, Strudel padding at his side. The spot where Mackenzie had kissed him felt warm. As though she'd branded him with her lips.

She didn't shut the door and turn off the light until he'd

started down his own driveway. The house was cold and dark and utterly unwelcoming when he let himself in. He crouched in front of the fireplace and built a stack of kindling and paper twists. He lit a match and watched flames lick up the wood, trying to pretend that something hadn't happened when Mackenzie's hand closed around his and her lips brushed his skin.

But it had. Something had stirred in him, the same thing that made his gaze zero in on her breasts and backside every chance he got. The same thing that had turned him into a dazed yokel when she smiled at him tonight.

Desire.

So much for her not being his type.

He threw a log on the fire and used the poker to prod it into position, part of his brain already busy justifying his urges to himself. She was an attractive woman and it had been an unexpectedly intense evening. He was only human.... Just because he'd felt the pull of desire didn't mean he would necessarily act on it. He'd met dozens of women during his marriage whom he'd found attractive and never laid a finger on any of them, because he took his vows seriously. As far as he was concerned, marriage—

He sat back on his heels, a little stunned at himself.

Marriage? Really?

The fire popped, sending sparks floating up the chimney and snapping him out of his shock. He'd thought he'd drawn a line under his marriage the day Edie had confirmed the affair. But apparently a part of him still lived like a married man, still felt guilty about being attracted to another woman.

Which was nuts, because he was a free agent now.

Free to make his own decisions.

Free to desire other women.

Free to act on that desire, should he so choose.

An image filled his mind—Mackenzie's bra, a promise spun from delicate black lace and fine silk.

If he wanted to, there was nothing in the world stopping him from finding out how Mackenzie looked in that bra. Well, from trying to find out, anyway. He was single. Available.

And, apparently, more than a little horny.

For a moment, he allowed himself to wonder. Then he shut down those thoughts.

The truth was he didn't know tons about Mackenzie. He knew she was feisty and prickly and intelligent and challenging. She had a good sense of humor and a sharp, sometimes acidic tongue. She was also sexy as hell, it turned out.

She certainly wasn't the kind of woman a man took on lightly. Especially not a man who had next to no game where women were concerned—it had been a long, long time since he'd even thought about trying to get a woman who wasn't his wife into bed, and he wouldn't even know where to start where Mackenzie was concerned. He had no idea if she was remotely interested in him as a man. For all he knew, she was as likely to slap his face as kiss it if he made a move.

And no, that kiss on the cheek did not count as a *sign.* He wasn't that rusty or deluded.

He grabbed a couple cushions off the couch and settled in more comfortably in front of the fire.

This being-single thing was complicated. Fortunately, there was plenty of night left to ponder the subject.

I AM AN IDIOT. *I am an idiot. I am an idiot.*

The refrain echoed through Mackenzie's brain on an endless loop as she cleaned the kitchen. Who in their right mind invited a man to dinner and then had an almighty meltdown in front of him? Who did that?

You, you idiot.

She blamed the wine. She'd consumed four glasses in quick succession trying to numb the shock of Patrick's news. Instead of washing the pain away, however, the alcohol had eaten away at her defenses leaving her weak and emotional and unable to control herself when the tide of loss had risen up inside her—as it had on and off all evening.

She'd managed to laugh and talk and put on a good show the first few times the loss had threatened, even though inside she'd been wailing and pulling her hair and rending her shirt. Then she'd had one glass too many and suddenly there had been nothing between her and the pain and fear and she hadn't been able to stop the tears from coming.

She winced as she hung the damp tea towel over the oven handle. Oliver must think she was a bona fide head case. She hadn't had a single normal interaction with him since he arrived. If she were him, she would barricade the doors and windows and avoid any and all future contact with the crazy lady next door.

She trudged into the bathroom and squeezed toothpaste onto her toothbrush. The woman in the mirror had puffy, bloodshot eyes and a rueful expression on her face.

Well she might.

She brushed and flossed, then headed for bed. She stopped in her tracks in the doorway, pulled up by the sight of the twin indentations on her quilt. One for her, one for him.

God. What a ridiculous evening. The poor man.

Mr. Smith sniffed at her heels and she bent to give him a good-night pat before shutting him out in the hall. Then she changed into her pajamas, crawled into bed and tried to pretend that she hadn't lost it spectacularly in front of the lovely, warm, kind man from next door.

Flashes of her own self-indulgent monologue came to her as she squeezed her eyes shut.

I need to know. I want to know now *that it's all going to be okay. I'm sick of taking it on faith.*

He must think she was the worst sort of self-pitying sook—in addition to being emotionally unstable, of course.

His parting words came to her then.

What makes you think I'm in a position to judge anybody? Everyone's got their own shit to shovel, Mackenzie.

At the time she'd thought he was simply being kind—continuing to be kind, really—but now she thought...maybe not. There had been a look in his eyes as he'd spoken, a sort of hard, lonely bleakness....

Something else he'd said slipped into her mind. *It suited me to get away for a few weeks.*

It occurred to her that maybe she wasn't the only one struggling with a less-than-stellar life right now. The thought that she might not be alone in her messed-up state, that maybe she hadn't made as big a fool of herself as she'd imagined, loosened the tense knot in her belly. Maybe, as Oliver had suggested, she was allowed to have a bad day occasionally.

Maybe—revolutionary thought—she could even afford to cut herself some slack.

It wasn't exactly a philosophy she was familiar with. Everything she'd achieved in life she'd gained through hard work and determination. She'd attacked her recovery with the same zeal—every exercise a challenge, every milestone achieved a victory and a spur.

She had no idea how to turn off that part of herself. No concept of what it might be like to hold herself to a lesser standard. But maybe she needed to try, because, as she'd said to Oliver, she was so, so tired.

Tired of the constant fear she would never be able to reclaim her old life that sat behind her breastbone.

Tired of pretending to the world that everything was just dandy, that having her body torn apart had been a mere hiccup, a temporary hitch in her stride.

Tired of pretending to herself that she was still the same woman she'd been twelve months ago.

Would it be the end of the world if everything didn't go back to being the way it used to be?

She'd never really asked herself that question. She'd been so busy trying to make it as though the accident had never happened. But maybe she should be thinking less about resurrecting the past and more about what the future might hold. Maybe it was time to stop trying to alter an irreversible reality and instead work out how to live with it.

A few days ago, the notion of moving toward acceptance and away from defiance would have felt akin to heresy. Tonight...tonight it felt timely.

MACKENZIE WOKE TO the sound of birdsong outside her window. As always, she started planning her day the moment her brain came online, allocating time to all the things she needed to do, making lists in her head. Breakfast, then she needed to ramp up her rehab exercises so she could return to her regular workload. She had three days of downtime to make up for, after all.

She also needed to do something about getting a job. She wouldn't be fit for full-time work for a few months yet, but she needed to put her ear to the ground so she could find out who was where and what was happening and what opportunities might be on the horizon. She could renew her subscription to *Inside Film Magazine,* the industry bible, call a few contacts, put out some feelers....

She flung back the covers and swung her legs to the

floor. Instead of standing and plunging into the day, however, she simply sat there.

Not eight hours ago, she'd posed a number of questions to herself—or, more accurately, Oliver had—and she'd decided they were worth considering. Yet here she was, ready to embark on yet another day of pitting her will against her injuries, trying to alter reality by sheer dint of willpower and determination alone.

But what if this *was* her new normal? What if all the king's horses and all the king's men couldn't put her back together the way she'd once been? What would the world look like if she ceased trying to shove a square peg into a round hole?

Or, on a simpler, more practical level, what did she *really* want to do today, rather than subject herself to a grueling rehab session that would leave her feeling weak and potentially nauseous?

It was a novel question and it occupied her for all of five seconds. Then she stood to let Smitty in before returning to bed and pulling the covers high, because she knew the answer: she was going to stay warm and snug with her dog and read one of the books stacked on her bedside table. Then, when her stomach dictated, she would make herself something delicious for breakfast—pancakes, perhaps, or waffles. Then, and only then, she would figure out what else she felt like doing.

Smitty didn't need to be invited onto the bed—it was his favorite place in the world, and he was up in a flash. Mackenzie ran a hand along his back and smiled as he turned to lick her wrist. She picked up a book and wriggled herself into a comfortable position. Her conscience nagged at her for the first twenty pages, telling her to get moving and sweating and striving. She ignored it and continued reading until finally the nagging stopped and she was simply *being*.

How very…interesting.

After a while, a warm feeling of well-being stole over her and she found herself remembering the kindness and gentleness of Oliver's touch as he soothed his hand in circles on her back last night.

This respite she'd allowed herself felt a lot like that hand on her back. Reassuring and right and—perhaps most importantly—*kind.* She was suddenly filled with an overwhelming surge of gratitude toward her neighbor for his calm good sense and patience.

The jury was still out, but it was possible that last night hadn't been a disaster of epic proportions, as she'd first imagined. Maybe it had, in fact, been exactly what she needed.

OLIVER WAS BUTTONING his coat when a knock sounded at the door. Strudel raced down the hall, feet skidding on the polished floor, determined to be the first to greet their visitor.

"And yet I'm the one with the opposable thumbs and the ability to actually open the door," Oliver told her as he joined her in the foyer.

Strudel gave him an impatient look and pawed at the wood. He opened it to find Mackenzie on his doorstep, covered plate in hand. As usual, she was dressed in monochrome from head to toe, the only color the neon flashes on her running shoes.

"Long time no see." She gave an awkward, self-conscious wave with her free hand.

"Mackenzie. How are you?"

She looked surprisingly good for someone who had lost it in a big way not so long ago. Her eyes were bright, her shoulders square. Not a whiff of despair anywhere.

"I'm good, thanks. Which is mostly because of you. I wanted to thank you again for talking me down last night.

And to offer you this to make up for the world's most depressing dinner party." She thrust the plate toward him.

"Is that the rest of the lemon tart?"

"It is."

"In that case..." He took the plate. "I'd like it noted for the record that normally I'd refuse to take anything for simply being a reasonably decent human being, but this tart is too good to say no to."

Her smile was more genuine the second time around. "I was kind of banking on that. And you were far more than reasonably decent last night."

Strudel surged forward to sniff her shoes, quickly rising up to put her paws on Mackenzie's thighs.

"Down, Strudel. Four paws on the floor, please," he said.

"It's okay. She can probably smell Mr. Smith." She scratched Strudel's chest and beneath her chin. When the dog dropped down again, Mackenzie took a step backward. "Anyway. I wanted to say thanks. You said all the right things last night and I really appreciate that you didn't start looking for the exit the moment I started crying."

She shrugged, so self-conscious it was difficult to watch. He understood why—she'd been intensely vulnerable last night, stripped bare—but he hated the idea that she thought he was judging her for having such a human, understandable reaction to disappointing news.

"Four months ago I discovered my wife was having an affair with her former boyfriend." The words were out before he could think about it. "In fact, it turned out she'd never stopped seeing him for the six years of our marriage."

Mackenzie's eyebrows rose toward her hairline. Even though he could feel his face heating, he held her eye and kept talking.

"Like I said last night, everyone's got their own shit to deal with."

"God. I'm really sorry, Oliver."

He shook his head. He hadn't told her because he wanted her pity. "It is what it is. I'm dealing with it. Just like you're dealing with your stuff. And some days are good, and some days suck the big one."

"Yeah, they do."

"I figure there isn't a rule book for getting through crap. You get through it however you can."

She cocked her head. "Including driving a thousand miles south to clear out a dead woman's house?"

"Yeah. Including that, along with some inappropriate use of alcohol, punching of inanimate objects, self-pitying moping and late-night jam sessions on the guitar."

Truth be told, a part of him had envied her the crying jag last night. At least she'd found an outlet for her pain and frustration. And she hadn't had to do it alone the way he'd done those times he'd broken down.

"Hang on a minute—was that you playing the guitar the other night? The acoustic stuff?"

He winced. "You could hear that? My apologies."

"Are you kidding? It was great."

There was no doubting her sincerity. He shrugged. Apparently it was his turn to be self-conscious.

"I was messing around. Self-indulgent doodling."

"I meant to ask you who it was so I could buy the album."

He barked out a laugh.

"What's so funny?" she asked.

"It's been a long time since I've been on the other side of the mixing desk."

"Maybe you should reconsider that."

"Yeah, I don't think so." His days of being a professional musician were long gone.

She studied his face for a moment, her eyes warm and

searching. Finally she smiled. "Thanks, Oliver." There was a world of meaning and nuance in her voice.

His gaze dropped to her mouth and he found himself fighting the very inappropriate urge to lean forward and kiss her. She was complicated and a bit messed up, but so was he and he'd dreamed about her last night. About how she'd feel in his arms, and that kiss she'd pressed to his cheek and the round curves of her ass and breasts.

He really wanted to know what she tasted like. What that full bottom lip of hers would feel like pressed against his, and if the connection he'd felt when she'd touched him last night had been a fluke or something more important.

As though she sensed his intent, Mackenzie took another step backward. "Give me a yell over the fence when you've finished with the plate, okay?" She turned to go.

For the second time that morning Oliver found himself opening his mouth without first weighing his words. "Strudel and I were about to go for a walk along the beach. Would you and Mr. Smith want to come?"

She paused, and he couldn't read the expression in her eyes.

"Actually, that sounds good. Can you give me a few minutes?"

"Sure."

"Then I'll be back in five."

He stared after her as she walked along the driveway, wondering at himself.

What was he doing, exactly? Making a play for the neighbor? Exercising his rusty charm?

It was one thing to acknowledge he was a single man and another thing entirely to act on it. If that was what he was doing.

He thought about it for a minute, then went inside to find Strudel's lead.

The truth was he had no idea what was going on in his own mind at the best of times. And this was definitely not the best of times.

CHAPTER SIX

MACKENZIE SHED HER VEST and shoved her arms into her warmest wool coat, then reached for the fluffy scarf her niece had knitted her for Christmas. Made from multicolored wool, it was lumpy and misshapen and far too long, but it was also incredibly warm and it never failed to touch her that the niece she almost never saw had labored for hours to produce it. Wrapping it around her neck several times, Mackenzie headed for the door.

Her faithful hound did the happy dance when he saw her collect his lead and harness from the hook in the kitchen. She waited until his excitement had subsided before securing him. Then they went to join Oliver and Strudel.

As she'd half expected, he was waiting for her in the street, Strudel sitting patiently with a long-suffering expression on her face. The schnauzer perked up the moment she saw Mr. Smith, however, and Mackenzie and Oliver waited patiently while they fawned over each other before turning in the direction of the beach.

"Just as well you're with me. I wasn't really sure how to find the beach," Oliver said.

"Somehow I feel pretty confident you would have worked it out," Mackenzie said as they left the road and started down the path that led through a narrow band of bush to the sand. The sound of the surf was clearly audible, readily indicating which way the beach lay.

"You'd be surprised. I have a gift for getting lost. No sense of direction whatsoever."

"He said proudly."

He laughed. "I wouldn't say I'm proud. More resigned."

"Have you considered GPS?"

"That would be cheating."

They reached the part of the path where it narrowed to single file and Mackenzie fell back, an action that afforded her a perfect view of Oliver's backside as he strode ahead. He was wearing faded jeans today, the worn denim hugging his firm, round butt.

It occurred to her that it would have been far better for her peace of mind if he'd been one of those men with a tiny, disappearing backside or womanly hips.

No such luck, however.

"Does that mean you never stop to ask for directions, either?" she asked, forcing her gaze away from temptation.

"Correct. Directions are also cheating."

She could hear the laughter in his voice.

"Remind me not to take a road trip with you."

They emerged from the protection of the bush onto a windswept expanse of sand. The water was a dull pewter color, the waves white tipped as they hammered against the shore. An icy wind found its way beneath Mackenzie's coat and she immediately buttoned it all the way to the neck and thrust her hands deep into her pockets.

"Dear God, it's like Antarctica down here," Oliver said, copying her actions.

She watched as he flipped up the collar on his coat, feeling guilty for not having warned him that the beach could be harsh in winter.

"That's probably because the wind comes straight from Antarctica."

"No kidding."

They let the dogs loose and watched as they bolted along the sand, taking turns chasing one another.

"Kids, eh?" Oliver said, tucking Strudel's lead into his jacket pocket.

They started walking, following the trail the dogs had left in the wet sand.

"So, you ever been married?" Oliver asked.

The subject was such a non sequitur it threw her for a moment. Although, perhaps his curiosity made sense in light of their recent mutual confessions. "Yep. Three years." She pulled a face. "Not exactly a stellar achievement, but we both realized early on that we'd made a mistake."

"How long ago?"

"Nearly four years." It seemed hard to believe that much time had passed. Of course, part of her disbelief could be because she'd been silly enough to fall into an affair with Patrick more recently—but Oliver didn't need to know that.

"Edie and I should never have gotten married. I have no idea why she said yes when I asked her, since she pretty much picked up with Nick the moment we got back from the honeymoon."

Mackenzie winced mentally. He hadn't referred to his wife by name before, but she understood now that he'd married the lead singer of the band, Edie Somers. It was too unusual a name for him to be referring to some other Edie. And last night Mackenzie had blathered on about how special and talented the other woman was.

Open mouth, insert foot.

"Are they still together?" she asked.

"I have no idea and I don't want to know. If I could walk away from it all and never hear about them again, I would." There was a world of anger beneath his words.

She opened her mouth to apologize for prying but he stopped in his tracks and blew his breath out in a rush.

The look he gave her was rueful. "Sorry. That wasn't meant for you."

"I'd be pissed, too, if I were you. Six years is a long time to lie to someone you share a bed with."

"Yeah." He dug his hands deeper in his pockets, hunching his shoulders around his ears.

"If you don't want to talk about it, we don't have to."

"There's not much to say. I got married thinking I would stay that way until one of us was carted off in a wooden box. Instead, I get to make lists of my assets for the lawyers." He shrugged. "It sucks."

She studied him out of the corner of her eye. The wind was playing havoc with his hair, ruffling it and pushing it this way and that. He stared out at the ocean, his expression distant and stony—and yet he was still the most vivid, alive thing on the beach, with his rich chestnut hair and long stride. For reasons she didn't care to examine, she wanted to erase that air of disappointment.

"Tell me about your music. When did you start playing?" she asked.

The glance he shot her told her he was fully aware that she was steering the conversation to more neutral ground, but he followed her lead. They walked and he told her how he'd learned the guitar in primary school to impress a girl and discovered that not only was it an awesome pickup tool, it was also something that came easily to him.

"Don't tell me you're one of those revolting people who can hear any song and then play it a few seconds later?" she asked.

"I'm afraid to answer that question honestly for fear of not making it back from this walk alive."

"I took violin lessons for five years with a girl like you. She made me feel as though I had ten thumbs and a lobotomy."

"I'd like to point out—again—that I am utterly inept when it comes to map reading and general direction finding. If that makes you feel any better."

"It does, marginally. Thank you for reminding me."

"Can I ask why you persevered for five years if you hated it so much?"

"Overachieving child of overachieving parents. None of us knew when to quit."

"Funny. I would never have pegged you as an overachiever." His expression was so deadpan, his tone so dry she might almost have believed he was serious—except for the teasing light in his eyes.

"You should know that overachievers are known for not having a great sense of humor about their overachieving," she said, matching his expression and tone.

"Noted. Next time I will make sure to bring along a laugh track so you know when I've been funny."

She couldn't stop herself from smiling then. Her instincts had been right about this man—he was nice. A real, decent, sincere man.

He was also rather disturbingly sexy in a rugged, down-to-earth way that she didn't run into a lot in the highly groomed, fake-tanned world of television.

Edie Somers must have had rocks in her head to have had this man in her life and her bed and thrown it all away.

They'd reached the halfway mark and she checked to make sure the dogs were still in sight. They were, running in and out of the surf, chasing waves and each other.

"I know it's almost un-Australian to say this, but I prefer the beach in winter," she said. "No crowds, no screaming kids, no rubbish in the sand."

"You're right. This arctic wonderland is infinitely better."

More dryness. She was beginning to recognize it as his stock in trade.

His collar had flopped down and he stood it up again, a meager defense against the wind.

"If you're cold, we can turn back," she suggested.

"I'm fine. Besides, I want to see what's on the other side of those rocks."

"I'll give you three guesses."

"More rocks?"

"Bingo."

"Still. I think I need to see that for myself."

He glanced at her and she saw he was enjoying himself. Which was nice, because she was enjoying herself, too.

They talked some more about his music, then about her work. He peppered her with questions about the game show she'd worked on before *Time and Again,* feigning outrage when he learned that some of the segments were recorded several times for technical reasons. It wasn't until they'd reached the rocks at the end of the beach and he offered her a hand to clamber to the top of them that she realized how cold he was, his fingers icy against hers.

"This is ridiculous. I should have warned you it's brutal out here. You need to go home and warm up," she said, digging her heels in.

"I want to see the other rocks."

She assessed him. "Is this one of those man things, refusing to let the elements get the better of you, yada yada?"

"Maybe."

"Pathetic. Come on, we're going back."

She whistled to get Mr. Smith's attention, letting him know with a gesture that she was heading home. He loped to her side, Strudel hard on his heels, both of them wet and speckled with sand, tongues lolling happily.

"I'm really fine," Oliver said.

His shoulders were hunched even higher, his arms rigid

against his body as he buried his hands deep in his coat pockets.

"I feel cold just looking at you. Here, have this." She started to unwind her scarf.

"Get out of here. I'm not taking your scarf." Oliver waved her away.

"It's ugly but warm. And you need it more than I do," she said.

"I'm not taking your scarf, Mackenzie. End of discussion."

She frowned at him, the scarf hanging from her hands in big loops. "Is this another man thing?"

"This is most definitely a man thing."

"Okay, fine. If your pride won't let you accept the whole thing, take half."

Before he could respond, she looped the end of the scarf around his neck a couple times. There was still plenty left dangling so she looped the other end around her own neck. Oliver looked at her, then at the lumpy, multicolored band joining them.

"My God, it *is* ugly, isn't it?"

"My niece made it."

"Hence the fact you're actually wearing this in public."

They fell into step as they retraced their steps.

"This niece…she's, what, six?" He examined the scarf critically.

"Nearly twenty."

He looked startled. "Really?"

She laughed. "She's eight. And she tells me she's taken up beading now. Something to look forward to this Christmas."

"So I take it you have a brother or sister?" he asked.

"A brother. Older. They live in Perth. He's involved in mining."

They talked about their respective families as they walked. She heard about his brother, Brent, and Brent's two children, while she told him about Gareth and her niece and nephew. The shared scarf meant they were close to each other, and every now and then her shoulder or hip bumped his. It was strange and nice in equal measures. Strange because it had been a long time since she'd enjoyed this kind of casual intimacy with a man or, in fact, with anyone. And nice for the same reasons.

Oliver had to unwind a loop to allow them to walk in single file along the bush path. He kept her laughing all the way, comparing them to a couple of Buddhist teachers he read about a few years ago who made it a practice to never be more than fifteen feet from each other at all times. She suggested they were more like a line of elephants walking trunk in tail and Oliver produced one of the best elephant calls she'd ever heard from a non-elephant.

"You're freakishly good at that," she said.

"I have many pointless gifts."

Gravel crunched underfoot as they left the sandy path and started toward their houses, Oliver matching his stride to hers.

"Sorry for the slow pace," she said, glancing at his much longer legs. "The spirit is willing, the body not so much these days."

He was silent a moment.

"Does it hurt?"

She wasn't surprised by the question. She'd lost the natural swing of her hips with her injuries and was well aware that her walk appeared stiff and ungainly.

"Walking on its own doesn't hurt. My hip is compromised, though, so things don't move around as easily as they used to. Which isn't to say that learning to walk again was a lot of fun. Still, it was better than the alternative."

There had been a few days following the accident when the swelling on her spine had been so severe there had been a question mark over her ever being able to walk again.

"Can I ask what happened?"

Another not-surprising question, but one she still wasn't comfortable talking about. Recalling the scene, however briefly and succinctly, tended to resurrect the entire experience. Still, they had been swapping horror stories.... "We had an early morning call-out for a location shoot. I was driving to the location to meet the crew. The weather was terrible, it was still dark, the road was wet... I came around the corner and there'd been a landslide. I hit the brakes, but it was way too late."

"Jesus."

For a second she was lost in the memory, the world a dark, scary place, death screaming toward her at sixty kilometers an hour. Then she blinked and the sky was once again blue overhead, the wind chill on her cheeks, Oliver at her side.

"I was lucky someone came along a few minutes later and called for help. Probably wouldn't have made it otherwise," she said matter-of-factly.

They'd arrived at the houses and he turned to face her.

"Scary stuff."

"Yeah. I guess the downside of a long recovery is having an excess of time to think about it—repeatedly. I like to think I've mostly desensitized myself—" a slight exaggeration, perhaps "—but who knows. I definitely make a point of noticing and appreciating the small stuff these days."

"I bet." He unwound the scarf and handed his end to her. "Thanks for sharing your bounty."

"I'll pass your compliments on to my niece."

"Tell her it's the warmest half scarf I've ever had the pleasure of sharing."

"Will do."

Neither of them said anything for a beat. Mackenzie glanced toward her house. It was cold out here and she wanted to be inside, but she didn't want to stop talking to Oliver. He was easy company, fun and fast on his feet. She wondered what he'd say if she invited him in for coffee.

"I suppose I should finish sorting through the back bedroom," he said.

"Sure." She shortened Smitty's leash to signal that the canine love fest was about to end. "I'll see you around, okay? Thanks for the walk."

"Yeah, you, too."

She started up her driveway, very aware of the fact that Oliver still remained in the street, watching her. She concentrated fiercely on her stride, trying to make it as smooth and effortless-looking as possible. She didn't want him pitying her.

It occurred to her that a year ago she would have been more concerned about the size of her ass than the way she walked. Amazing how the world could tilt on its axis and things that had once seemed so vital could be rendered so insignificant.

She allowed herself a quick glance over her shoulder when she reached the porch. Oliver was still there, crouched beside Strudel as he attempted to brush sand from her damp coat. He was talking to her and shaking his head and Mackenzie wished she could hear what he was saying. Something funny, no doubt.

She was staring—again—and forced herself to go inside. Mr. Smith headed up the hallway at a leisurely trot, clearly tuckered out after his romp. She didn't immediately follow him. Instead, she stood in the foyer, hand pressed to her belly, trying to understand what was happening to her.

Somehow, she'd gone from acknowledging Oliver's attractiveness to being attracted to him. A thin line under ordinary circumstances, perhaps, but at the moment it seemed a huge leap. For months she had been nothing but a body, a collection of bones and muscles and organs that the doctors had stitched and stapled and screwed back together and that she had nurtured back to strength. She hadn't thought about sex or desire or men or anything even close to it. She'd been sexless, essentially, and she hadn't even noticed.

Then Oliver had arrived less than a week ago and she'd caught herself feeling nervous and primping and dressing to please him, even when she'd suspected he was happily married. Now he was unhappily on the verge of divorce and her awareness of him as a man had expanded exponentially.

Which meant…what, exactly? That she was horny? That she was lonely? That he was an attractive man and that her libido hadn't been crushed in the accident after all?

Without really thinking about it, she lifted his end of the scarf to her nose and inhaled. She smelled wool and ocean and something with hints of sandalwood and musk. Oliver's aftershave.

She remembered the way his shoulder had bumped against hers as they walked, how good it had felt to find the rhythm of another person's stride and match her own to it. How good it had felt to be connected, intimate.

He's a mess. And so are you.

Hard to disagree with the logician in her head. Bunching the scarf in one hand, she made her way to her bedroom and returned it to the cupboard. The odds were strong she wouldn't see him for a while now, anyway. Which would be a good thing.

Apparently.

OLIVER SAT AT his aunt's kitchen table, warming his hands around a mug of coffee. If he was a smoother guy, more practiced in the art of seduction, he would have somehow inveigled Mackenzie into inviting him to her place and right now he'd be sitting at *her* table, warming his hands on *her* mug and doing his best to make her laugh some more.

But he wasn't practiced, and he hadn't pressed his advantage. Instead, he'd retreated. Not exactly *Art of War* tactics.

He sipped his coffee and thought about how she'd had to stand on tiptoes to loop the scarf around his neck. His soon-to-be ex-wife was almost as tall as him, and he'd always believed that he preferred women of stature. But there was something about the sleek compactness of Mackenzie's body.... She may have been broken by the accident, but she'd clearly worked hard to regain what she'd lost and she was lean and toned and perfectly proportioned. He kept catching himself wondering how it would feel to throw her over his shoulder and take her off to have his way with her.

Good, he suspected.

It was absolute knuckle-dragging caveman stuff, of course. Embarrassing to admit even in the privacy of his own fantasies. And yet there it was.

Mackenzie brought out the caveman in him.

Which is why you're drinking coffee with only a wet dog for company. Right?

He grunted and pushed back his chair, taking his empty mug to the sink. Sometimes, the voice in his head was way too much of a smart-ass.

He spent the afternoon clearing out the bedroom, stopping only in the early evening. He bought himself a pizza for dinner and ate it at home in front of the fire, booting up his laptop to check his email and make sure everything was going well at the studio. They'd hired a freelance sound engineer to cover his absence, but there were a couple of queries from Rex that were easily resolved. Apparently, his world hadn't fallen apart because he'd absented himself from Sydney for a few days. Go figure.

Perhaps inevitably, his thoughts turned to Mackenzie again as he took the empty pizza box to the kitchen.

She was an interesting woman. An admirable woman. A lot of people would have been defeated by the blow she'd been dealt, but she'd come out fighting. He glanced toward the window. He could see the French doors into her living room from here. He wondered what she was doing. Then he wondered what she'd do if he showed up with a bottle of wine.

He could take Strudel and say she'd been pining for Mr. Smith. Not the most sophisticated approach ever, but it would probably work.

He returned to the living room and reached for his guitar.

Mackenzie made him laugh, and she made him think, and she got him out of his own head. She also made him want things he probably shouldn't be wanting so soon after his breakup with Edie. He was in no state to start a relationship with someone. Even on a very casual basis.

He picked at the guitar, fiddling with a harmony that had been sitting in the back of his head for a few days now. Just for fun, he dropped it down a key, and suddenly a couple of other ideas he'd had fell into place. He played until the notes ran out, then went over it again, listening and feeling his way through the music.

Before he could think it to death, he grabbed his phone, opened the dictation app and recorded everything he'd come up with. He felt a disproportional degree of satisfaction as he played it back. It was probably nothing, just a funny little harmony that no one would ever hear except himself. But still…

He continued to tinker with the song, making adjustments, coming up with a bridge. He played it through one last time, humming along in parts.

It needed lyrics, of course. He had no idea what they would be. Yet. But they would come, eventually. With the melody providing a backdrop to his days, the verses would slowly form—especially when he wasn't thinking about the song. That had always been the way songwriting worked for him. When he and Edie had written together, the process had moved faster because she'd always pushed him, forcing the lyrics even when he'd wanted time to let the music settle into his bones. She'd been the one to keep abreast of what was on the charts, casting their songs into a popular mold to produce something commercial and catchy. He could hardly complain about the method—it had earned the band two platinum singles and a bestselling album and a slew of awards after all—but he'd never enjoyed it and he'd never believed in it.

He sat with the realization for a moment, examining it from all sides and understanding that it was a fundamental truth, something that had come straight from his gut. Edie had always been about success first and the music second. That had never been the way he worked, however, and he'd always felt shoehorned into a role that didn't suit. Didn't matter how many times they'd come up with good songs—and there was nothing wrong with the band's repertoire—Oliver had never felt a sense of ownership and connection with that music.

He strummed a few chords of his new composition, enjoying the way the sound bounced off the hard surfaces in the room. Enjoying the thought that this was *his* song, and he was going to let the lyrics come to him in their own time. Because he could. Because there was no one but him to please now.

It was a liberating thought. The first he'd had since finding the receipt all those months ago.

Writing music was better without Edie.

Hard on the heels of that thought came another: What else might be better without Edie?

His hands stilled on the strings. So much of his current anger and hurt stemmed from the fact that he'd convinced himself he'd been perfectly happy and content in their six-year marriage. But what if, in the same way that he'd always told himself he liked writing songs with Edie, he'd also convinced himself he was happy, too?

He stared into the abyss of the question for a full sixty seconds before standing and putting his guitar in its case. It was late and he was tired. And—possibly—he wasn't ready to answer such a revealing question just yet.

TWO DAYS LATER, Mackenzie was standing in the dairy aisle of the local supermarket when she looked up to see Oliver enter the store. Ever since their walk she'd been alternating between attempting to come up with a bulletproof excuse to "bump" into him again and chastising herself for being so desperate. She wasn't entirely sure which side was winning the battle, but the moment she saw Oliver she abandoned the Camembert versus Brie debate she'd been engaged in to focus on him. She watched as he grabbed a shopping basket and exchanged greetings with the woman at the checkout. He wore a red-and-black-plaid flannel shirt with old, soft-looking jeans and a pair of well-used hiking boots. A black T-shirt was visible at his neckline. He hadn't shaved so his jaw and cheeks were bristly with the golden-chestnut whiskers that had caught her attention during their first meeting.

He looked wild and untamed and a bit dangerous, like a cowboy who had ridden into town from parts unknown. He said something to the woman at the register that made her laugh. When he moved away she followed him with her eyes, a slightly wistful expression on her face.

Mackenzie pressed her lips together. It was galling yet oddly comforting to see someone else swayed by his undeniable hotness. Really, Oliver shouldn't be allowed out without a warning hanging around his neck. He clearly had no idea how charming he was, and now that he was single he would wreak havoc among the female population wherever he went.

He added a couple of cans of tomatoes to his basket, then glanced up and caught sight of her.

"Mackenzie." He lifted his hand in greeting, his wide, undeniably genuine smile doing wonderful things for her feminine ego.

Stupid, starved, foolish ego.

He joined her, his easy stride eating up the distance between them. She refused to regret the fact that she was once again without lipstick, her hair covered by a black beanie that made her look even more like a twelve-year-old boy than she usually did. If twelve-year-old boys had crow's-feet.

"Perfect timing. I was going to stop by later to ask if you wanted to come over for dinner," he said. "I found a fishing rod in the closet so this morning Strudel and I braved the elements to see what bounty the ocean had to offer."

"And?"

"Let's just say it wasn't the miracle of the loaves and fishes, but we have enough for two adults with good appetites and a couple of canoodling dogs."

"In that case, dinner sounds great. I can bring a salad if you like."

"Great idea. I'll see what I can rustle up for dessert. How do you feel about chocolate mousse?"

"Covetous," she said.

"Even if it's store-bought?"

"Absolutely."

Her gaze was drawn to the V-neck of his T-shirt. A scattering of golden-red hairs peeked over the top. She shifted her focus to his face, oddly disturbed by the sight.

"How's the sorting going?" she asked, switching her basket from one hand to the other.

"I've finally made it to the kitchen."

"Is this good or bad?"

"Let's just say Aunt Marion must have attended a lot of Tupperware parties in her time."

"Ow."

"On the bright side, the women at the secondhand shop know me by name now."

"Well, that's something."

He glanced toward the door. "I should keep moving. I left Strudel in the car. Always makes me feel like a bad parent."

"I know what you mean. I'll see you tonight."

He didn't move off immediately. Instead, he reached out and tweaked her beanie.

"Like your hat." His cognac eyes glinted with mischief as he walked away.

She realized belatedly that she was standing in the aisle staring after him like an excited schoolgirl.

It's called dignity, my dear. You might want to reacquaint yourself with the concept.

She turned back to the dairy case and grabbed a package of Brie and a round of Camembert. What the hell. She added a block of vintage cheddar for good measure, then worked her way up and down the aisles of the small store, occasionally catching glimpses of Oliver as he did the same. She heard him talking and laughing with the guy behind the deli counter, caught him brooding over the ice-cream freezer and wound up at the checkout three people ahead of him. She was acutely aware of him in her peripheral vision as she waited for the woman to ring up her purchases. She gave him a small, cheery wave as she collected her bags.

"Seven o'clock. Be there or be square," he said.

"A fate worse than death."

There was a bounce in her step as she carried her groceries to her car. Not because she thought his asking her over to dinner meant anything—she hadn't been rusticating out here on the peninsula so long that she'd forgotten the subtleties of socializing with the opposite sex—but because she found him interesting and stimulating and good company. No more, no less.

Rather convincing argument if she did say so herself.

CHAPTER SEVEN

SIX O'CLOCK FOUND Mackenzie dressed in her black jeans and a soft cashmere sweater with crossover ties that wrapped around her waist. She'd given in to vanity and was brushing mascara on when a knock sounded at the front door. Mr. Smith immediately bolted from the bathroom, his claws skittering on the floorboards.

"One of these days you're going to ricochet up the hall like a pinball," she called after him.

She could see a tall, broad silhouette in the glass panel as she approached and she lifted a hand to her hair. She hadn't had a chance to repair the damage the beanie had caused yet. Plus, she'd applied mascara to only one eye.

Oh, well.

"Hey," Oliver said when she swung the door open.

He was standing with one hand thrust deep into his jeans pocket, his posture stiff and uncomfortable. As though he was about to deliver bad news.

"Hi," she said, frowning.

Was he here to cancel dinner? She was surprised by the thud of disappointment she felt. She'd really been looking forward to spending time with him again.

"I have a confession to make." He sounded very serious.

"Okay. Should I brace myself? Will I need smelling salts?"

"I'm hoping it won't be that dire." He shuffled his feet, then cleared his throat. "When Brent and I went fishing as kids, he was the only one who was allowed to use the knife to clean and gut the fish."

He smiled sheepishly. She stared at him, momentarily bemused. *This* was his big confession? Then she got it.

"You want to know if I know how to gut a fish?"

"Yeah. I was going to wing it, but there's not a lot of fish there and if I stuff up it'll be pizza for dinner."

She smiled, inordinately charmed by his honesty. Most men she knew would have faked their way through the process rather than admit they needed assistance.

"I wish I could help, but I have never been fishing in my life," she said.

"Ah."

"But I have the next best thing to real-life experience. Hold on a second."

She spun on her heel and strode to the living room. Thirty seconds later she was back, iPad in hand. She displayed it triumphantly.

"It's called the internet. All the kids are using it. You ask it a question and someone, somewhere, knows the answer."

"You think someone's got a blog about gutting fish?" he asked, clearly skeptical.

"I bet there's a blog about carving toenail clippings if you looked hard enough."

She hit the button to bring the screen to life and called up a search engine. Within seconds she was trawling through the many results it produced. She clicked on a link, read a few lines, then handed him the iPad.

"There you go. Step-by-step instructions."

He scanned the page briefly. "You're a genius."

She bowed her head in mock humility. "Thank you."

He read a few more lines, then glanced at her. "This is actually pretty gruesome. I'm thinking it might be a two-person job. Someone to eviscerate and whatnot, someone else to pass the wine and provide moral support."

She smiled. Couldn't help herself. Not for a second did she believe he needed her help, but she was flattered that he was keen to start their evening together sooner rather than later.

"Going a little stir-crazy over at Tupperware Manor, are we?"

"Let's just say it would be good to talk to someone bipedal with an actual voice box, as opposed to someone with four paws and a tail."

"The tail *is* limited as a form of communication, I agree."

"You have no idea."

Her smile widened into a grin. "I'll be over in five."

"I'll prepare the sacrificial altar."

Mackenzie watched him take the stairs two at a time, allowing herself a few indulgent seconds of butt-staring—it really was a very, very nice ass—before shutting the door and heading for the kitchen.

She gathered the salad ingredients she'd bought, shoving them all into a salad bowl, then grabbed a bottle of wine and clipped Mr. Smith's lead on. It wasn't until she was standing on Oliver's porch that she realized she still hadn't applied mascara to her other eye or put on perfume or fixed her hair.

It was too late, however—Oliver was already opening the door and waving her inside, Strudel doing her best to slip past his legs and get to Mr. Smith.

"I hope you have a strong stomach," he said.

She let Smitty off the leash and followed Oliver to the kitchen. She poured them both a glass of wine while he did a very competent job of cleaning and gutting the fish. He kept up a running commentary throughout, making her laugh until her sides ached.

"You have a great laugh," he said as he dusted the fillets in seasoned flour.

"Do I?"

"Yeah."

She could feel heat climbing into her cheeks and she buried her face in her wineglass. Honestly, she so needed to get out more. It wasn't as though he'd told her she was beautiful or fascinating or something else blushworthy, after all. He'd commented on her laugh. Big deal.

He transferred the fish to a hot pan on the stove and she took the chopping board to the sink to clean it so she could prepare the salad. They talked easily as they worked, covering everything from the weather to Strudel's habit of sleep-barking to the state of the pothole-ridden Main Street in the township.

The more they talked and laughed, the more Mackenzie relaxed and let go of all the small and large concerns and anxieties that filled her days. Her recovery, her future job prospects, her life in general…she let it all fall by the wayside and simply enjoyed the fact that it was cold outside and warm inside, that she was with a witty, funny, handsome man and that right now, right this second, life was good.

They took the finished meal through to the living room where Oliver had built a roaring fire and sat on the couch, plates balanced on their laps. The dogs did their usual I've-never-been-fed-in-my-lifetime begging routine, complete with fixed, pleading stares and the occasional pitiful whine. After a few minutes Oliver caved and tossed them each a piece of fish.

"Softy," Mackenzie said.

He grinned unabashedly. "Strudel knows how to work me. She's a pro."

Once they realized they weren't getting anything more

out of Oliver, the dogs switched their attention to Mackenzie.

"Not going to work, my furry friends," she said. "This fish is too delicious to share."

It was, too—fresh and flaky with just the right amount of salt and pepper. Simple but perfect.

Like this evening, really.

Mr. Smith stepped things up a notch then, dropping onto his belly and crawling forward in the most tragic way possible.

Oliver laughed, raising his glass in a toast. "Excellent work. If there was an Academy Award for dogs, you'd have my vote, Mr. Smith."

"Smitty, come on. Have a little bit of dignity," Mackenzie admonished him.

Her dog continued to watch her with desperate, pleading eyes. Finally she sighed, cut the remaining portion of her fish into two and gave one half to each of the dogs.

"How the mighty have fallen," Oliver said.

She threw her scrunched-up serviette at him, which only made him laugh more loudly.

He left her with the bottle of wine and the fire while he sorted out dessert. She shifted to the rug before the hearth and sat staring into the flames, feeling warm and well fed and content as she listened to him rattle around in the kitchen. After a few seconds she closed her eyes and let her head drop against the couch behind her.

Funny how comfortable she felt around him so quickly. As a general rule, she took a while to warm to people, her innate caution leading her to keep her distance until she had a sense of who the other person was. She and Oliver might have gotten off on the wrong foot initially, but once she'd seen him clearly, he'd catapulted over her usual defenses with his openness and sincerity.

It probably didn't hurt that he was a very sexy, attractive man, or that there was something about him that drew her like iron filings to a magnet or ants to honey. Charm? Charisma? Presence? However you defined it, he had it. A certain light in his eyes, a quickness to his wit, an innate confidence in himself that was evident in every move he made. All of which meant he could admit to being useless with directions or ask for help gutting a fish and not lose one iota of his masculine appeal.

"Hey."

She opened her eyes to find Oliver standing over her, plate in hand. For a moment they simply stared at each other in the flickering firelight. There was something in his face—an intensity—that made her wonder how long he'd been watching her drowse. An odd little prickle of awareness tugged at her.

"It's been a while since I've done this. Tell me, is it considered a compliment when the guest falls asleep between courses?" he asked.

"If not, it should be." She sat up a little straighter and sniffed appreciatively. "I smell chocolate."

His mouth kicked up at the corner as he handed her the plate. "Brilliant detective work, Dr. Watson."

He left the room briefly before returning with his own plate and they were both silent as they ate their dessert.

"This mousse is really good," Mackenzie said.

"Thanks. I opened the package myself."

She smiled at his small joke, but for some reason she couldn't think of anything else to say. Suddenly she was acutely aware of the fact that they were alone, surrounded by all the accoutrements of a clichéd romantic evening—the wine, the fire, the dim lighting. She was sure it was unintentional—not for a second did she think that Oliver had hatched a plot to seduce her—but now the thought had popped into her head she couldn't seem to get it out.

He sat on the rug opposite her, his back against a wing-back armchair, his legs stretched out in front of him. His legs looked so long and strong, the muscles of his thighs discernible beneath the soft denim of his jeans. At some point he'd taken his shoes off and his socked feet were crossed at the ankles. Like the rest of him, they were big but surprisingly elegant looking.

Stop staring at his feet, for Pete's sake, and say something.

She cleared her throat, even though she had no idea what she was about to say. Before she could speak up, his phone rang.

"Sorry. It's probably Brent, my brother." He reached out to grab the handset from the coffee table.

He glanced at the caller ID and frowned before taking the call.

"Hello? Oliver speaking."

She heard someone speak, a woman's voice. Oliver's expression turned stony.

"I thought we agreed to do everything through the lawyers."

The coldness in his voice, the abrupt change in his demeanor—Mackenzie had no doubt whatsoever who was on the other end of the line. Her stomach dipped.

The woman spoke again. Something flickered across Oliver's face.

"Are you all right?" The words seemed dragged from him.

Mackenzie realized she was eavesdropping as avidly as a voyeur so she rose and collected first her plate then his. Without looking at him, she slipped into the kitchen. She could still hear his voice, but not every word. She busied herself at the sink, running water and washing first the dishes then the frying pan and the salad bowl. All the while, she wondered why Oliver's ex was calling, trying to work out what she'd seen in his face when he'd asked if Edie was all right. Concern? Lingering affection?

None of your business.

True, but it didn't stop her brain from churning away. Oliver was a nice guy, a lovely man and his ex had betrayed him horribly. It seemed to Mackenzie that the very least the other woman could do was leave him to lick his wounds in peace.

She banged the salad bowl onto the draining board, only registering how worked up she'd become as the sound echoed around the kitchen. There was no reason for her to get so riled over Oliver's private life. Yet here she was, feeling oddly protective of him. And maybe a little…jealous?

"Sorry about that."

She spun on her heel to find Oliver in the doorway, his mouth a hard, unforgiving line, his body taut as a bowstring.

"It's all right. Gave me a chance to tidy up a bit."

He glanced around, absorbing the fact that she'd cleaned. "You didn't have to do that."

He was so unhappy. So angry. She made a quick decision.

"Listen, you look as though you might need some time alone. Smitty and I should probably be heading home anyway."

She collected her salad bowl.

"I was going to offer you coffee."

"I can't drink it anymore, sadly. Which means you're officially off the hook. Thanks for dinner. I had a nice night."

He eyed her intently. "I don't want you to go."

She blinked, more than a little thrown by his simple honesty.

"I mean, I don't want her call to ruin a good evening. Or, more accurately, for me to let her call ruin it."

She understood what he was saying, could hear the frustration in his voice. She could remember the early days of her own divorce only too well. The struggle to redefine herself. The need to move on.

"Okay." She set the bowl on the drain board.

His expression softened marginally. "Are you allowed tea?"

"Tea's great, thanks."

"Go relax and I'll bring it in."

She returned to the living room and resumed her previous position. Her wineglass was warm from being too close to the hearth but she swallowed the remaining mouthful anyway. The dogs were in their usual tangle, sleeping cheek by jowl. Oliver entered a few minutes later with two teacups and a box of chocolates wedged beneath his arm. Some of the tension had left his face and the look he gave her was sheepish. She lifted a hand to stay the apology she suspected was forthcoming.

"Don't. I get it. It's not a problem," she said.

"Easy for you to say." He offered her the ghost of a smile before sitting and sliding the chocolates toward her.

He started talking about the local shop where he'd found them, but he was so palpably making an effort it was almost painful to watch. She waited until he'd wound down to silence before she spoke.

"Listen, if you need to vent or rant right now, let off a bit of steam, I am totally open for business," she said.

After all, he'd been on the receiving end of a pretty comprehensive gut-spill from her not so many days ago. It seemed only fair to return the favor.

"Thanks, but everyone knows there's nothing more tragic than the cuckolded husband bleating on about his ex-wife."

"I must have missed that memo. But if you don't want to bleat, that's fine, too. Just wanted you to know the option was there."

He looked at her for a moment, as though trying to assess if her offer was genuine or not. She raised her eyebrows expectantly.

He set down his cup. "Edie had a minor car accident and she needed to know where I'd filed our insurance information. Not a big deal."

Except it was, because he was desperately trying to move on from his ex's terrible betrayal. Every contact was a reminder of what he'd lost, of what Edie had thrown away.

"Okay." She studied the tense set of his shoulders for a beat. "A question for you—who are you more angry with, her or yourself?"

His gaze was arrested. As though she'd goosed a raw nerve.

"I mentioned I'm divorced, right?" she said. "I've played this game before."

He nodded slowly. Thoughtfully. "Yeah, you did."

"I spent the first year after my divorce kicking myself around for having married Patrick in the first place, it being pretty obvious by that point that it hadn't been my best move ever. It took me a while longer to appreciate the joys of twenty-twenty hindsight. No one gets married thinking it's going to fail. No one."

"I appreciate the get-out-of-jail-free card, but I'm not about to let myself off the hook for failing to notice that my wife betrayed me nearly every day of our marriage."

"Why? Was she a bad liar? Did she leave clues all over the house? Did you willfully ignore the bread crumbs she dropped for you?"

His smile had hard edges. "She was a great liar and a

consummate sneak. And I still should have known something was wrong."

She could hear the contempt for himself in his voice.

"This is not your fault, Oliver. You trusted her. You believed the two of you shared the same values. How does your trust and faith make you the guilty party here?"

The stubborn angle of his jaw told her he wasn't about to concede the point.

"So this is a pride thing, is it? An ego thing?"

"Yeah, it is." His gaze was challenging. "She played me for a fool, and I let her."

"Maybe it wasn't as cut-and-dried as that. She stayed with you for six years. No one hangs around that long without a compelling reason."

"I have no idea why she stayed for so long, since Nick was obviously the one she wanted all along."

Mackenzie processed his words. "She knew him before you were married?"

"He was her ex. In the very early days of the band, he was our manager. They had two shitty years together before they broke up the last time and we got a new manager. At least, I thought it was the last time."

Mackenzie was silent for a moment, thinking about what he'd revealed.

"Sometimes, even though you know something is a mistake, you can't stop yourself from going there," she said slowly.

She could tell from his expression he needed a deeper explanation.

"I'm not making excuses for her, don't get me wrong," she said. "It just seems to me that the why of all this is killing you as much as the fact that it happened at all."

His gaze gravitated to the fire. "Yeah. Maybe."

He looked so alone, so hurt.

"It was like that for my ex and me," she said. "We were happily divorced. So happily we became friends. Then, somehow, being friends turned into something it shouldn't have. Even though we'd been there before and we both knew it was a dead end."

"What happened?"

"I had the accident and Patrick made it pretty clear that he would *not* be around to pick up the pieces. Backed off at a million miles an hour. Not that I expected him to suddenly become someone he wasn't, but still…"

She swallowed past the lump of emotion in her throat, a little surprised by how much it hurt to publicly acknowledge Patrick's abandonment.

"He's a dick," Oliver said with feeling.

"He is. But he's a charming dick." She paused. "Sometimes, even when you know someone is a hundred different kinds of wrong for you, you get sucked into old patterns and behaviors. Maybe that's what happened with Edie. Maybe she loved you but couldn't resist him. Maybe she spent six years yo-yoing between the two of you, trying to work it out."

He was silent a moment. "That's a very generous interpretation."

"Maybe." She set her empty teacup on the coffee table and stood. "I'm going to leave you to it," she announced. She'd said more than enough.

He stood, too. "Thanks for the fish-gutting guidance."

"Thanks for the fish."

She clicked her tongue to get Mr. Smith's attention. When he came to her side she slipped his lead on, then turned to face Oliver again.

There was something she wanted—needed—to say to him before she left. Otherwise she might never have the opportunity to do so and it was definitely something he needed to hear.

"It's her loss, Oliver. You know that, right?"

"You haven't met the other guy."

She wasn't about to let him shrug off her words with a joke.

"I don't need to," she said, holding his gaze. "As you are very rapidly going to discover, there are a lot of women who would give their eyeteeth and probably a couple molars to have a man like you in their life. Don't let Edie's mistake become a judgment on you, okay?"

His cheeks were a little pink by the time she'd finished. "Thanks."

She could feel the heat in her own face but she was glad she'd said it. "I'll get off my soapbox now. Thanks for a great meal."

She stepped forward, one hand landing on his shoulder to steady herself as she pressed a kiss to his cheek. It was the second time she'd kissed him like this, the second time she'd felt the rasp of his five-o'clock shadow beneath her lips, and she had to fight the very inappropriate urge to linger over the task.

He smelled good, like warm skin and amber and spices, and his shoulder felt very solid beneath her hand.

She let her hand drop to her side. His hand reached out to catch it before she could withdraw. Their gazes locked as his fingers wove with hers. For a long beat they simply stared at each other.

"Mackenzie Williams," he said, so softly it was barely more than a whisper.

Then he leaned forward and pressed his lips to hers.

The world stood still. Her heart stuttered in her chest. She forgot to breathe. Then his mouth moved against hers and heat exploded in her belly and breasts and between her thighs. In that fraction of a second she knew how it would be between them—hot and wild and desperate.

It was too much. Too fast, too real, too confronting. She jerked backward so fast she lost her balance and would have fallen over if the door hadn't been a mere foot behind her. As it was, she cracked the back of her head against it, the pain vibrating through her skull.

"Are you okay?" Oliver asked, reaching out to steady her.

She couldn't look him in the eye, could barely force herself to lift her gaze to the middle of his chest.

"Yes. Fine, thanks. All good."

"You didn't hurt yourself?"

She could feel heat rushing into her face and chest. "No, no. I'm fine. Honestly."

She reached behind herself and gripped the knob. It twisted beneath her hand, and she stepped around the door and out onto the porch.

"Mackenzie—"

"Good night."

She didn't look back as she disappeared into the cold darkness, her mind on one thing and one thing only—escape.

OLIVER STARED at the empty doorway, trying to work out what the hell had happened.

He'd kissed his first girl when he was fourteen years old. In the twenty-five years between now and then, he'd like to think he'd improved his technique a bit. He'd definitely like to think he was a little smoother, a touch more suave than the sweaty-palmed, horny dude who had led Diane Leeds into the corner at the school dance and stuck his tongue down her throat.

Apparently, however, if tonight was anything to go by—and he figured it was—he had more in common with his fourteen-year-old self than he'd like. Because he'd misread Mackenzie so spectacularly he'd sent her running from the building.

But not before she'd banged her head against the door, she'd been so eager to escape his attentions.

He mouthed a four-letter word and pushed the door shut. The crazy thing was, he'd had no intention of making a move on her when he'd invited her over for dinner tonight. Yes, he was attracted to her, but that didn't mean he'd been primed for seduction. He'd simply been looking for some good conversation, a bit of company, a few laughs. But then she'd kissed his cheek and he'd looked into her eyes and seen what he thought was awareness—the same awareness he'd been feeling—and it had seemed natural and right and good to kiss her.

Yeah.

Mackenzie had all but left a vapor trail she'd hightailed it out of here so fast.

Good one, Romeo. Excellent work.

Clearly, kissing him had been the last thing on her mind. Not a stunning revelation when he considered that he'd spent the last hour of the evening going on about his ex. Sexy stuff, that. Nothing said *Let's get it on* like a bitching session about your failed love life and how you've been done wrong.

Oliver let his breath out on a disgusted sigh. Honestly, he wasn't fit to be out in public.

"Come on, Strudel. Bedtime."

He patted his thigh and Strudel followed him through the house as he switched off lights. She leaped onto the end of the bed when they got to the bedroom and began sniffing around for the best spot to make camp for the night. He went to brush his teeth.

There was an echo of embarrassed color in his face when

he saw his reflection. No surprises there—he'd been in the grip of a full-body blush from the moment Mackenzie had pulled away from him and the uninvited kiss.

Bloody hell, what a night.

He squeezed toothpaste onto his brush and cleaned his teeth with grim determination, unable to escape the live-action replay his brain insisted on feeding him on an endless loop: Mackenzie, jerking away from him, her head hitting the door with a resounding thud.

Stupidly, he'd thought the evening had actually been going okay, too, up until that point. Okay, Edie calling hadn't been a highlight, but Mackenzie had given him some things to think about, some new perspectives. She'd challenged him and made him laugh and asked all the right questions.

When he'd come back into the living room with dessert to find her dozing by the fire, there had been that moment when she opened her eyes and looked at him and he could have sworn he'd seen desire in her eyes....

But apparently he knew dick about desire.

He was going to have to apologize to her. Preferably tomorrow, before things got too weird between them. She probably wouldn't be signing up for dinner again anytime soon, but he would kick himself if he'd drawn a line through their burgeoning friendship with his ham-fisted attempt at seduction. Their normal lives might be a thousand miles apart, but she was the most interesting woman—the most interesting *person*—he'd met in a long time.

Spitting and rinsing, he gave his reflection one last disgusted glare before heading to the bedroom. Strudel looked at him from beneath her eyebrows as he got beneath the covers.

"Yeah, I know. I screwed up."

Strudel closed her eyes and rested her chin on his shin.

He crossed his arms behind his head and stared at the ceiling and wondered how a person apologized for an unwanted, unsolicited kiss. On bended knee? Matter-of-factly? Wryly?

It would be great to be able to pull off wryly, but luck hadn't exactly been running his way lately.

He closed his eyes. He would fix things with Mackenzie tomorrow. If it killed him.

And if he couldn't… Well, he would rue the day his libido ruined a friendship that already felt pretty damn unique.

CHAPTER EIGHT

MACKENZIE SPENT a good hour mulling over her own ridiculousness after she got home, trying to understand herself.

Oliver had kissed her. He'd looked into her eyes and said her name as though it was a mystery and a wonder to him, and then he'd laid his mouth against hers and kissed her. It had been a good kiss, too, full of potential and promise.

And she had backed off so quickly she'd smacked her head against the door.

She'd never backed away from anything in her life. She was a grab-life-by-the-scruff-of-the-neck kind of woman. A carpe diem kind of woman. And she liked sex. Not that she'd had much opportunity to enjoy it lately, all her energies having been focused on her recovery, but that was beside the point. She also liked Oliver. A lot.

She'd spent half the evening ogling his thighs and admiring his handsome face and generally basking in his reflected glory. She'd dressed nicely for him and worried about her limp hair and lack of makeup. Yet when he kissed her she'd been so overwhelmed by the experience that her only panicky thought had been to escape.

She winced as she pulled on her pajamas, thinking about how he must be feeling right now. God, she was such an ass-hat.

She climbed into bed and punched her pillow a few times. She needed to apologize to him, of course. Somehow she would have to make it clear to him that her out-ofproportion reaction was all about her and had nothing to do with him. She'd have to explain that under normal circumstances she would have been all over what he was offering.

The problem was, she was having trouble locating normal right at the moment. Her career was in limbo, her body a work in progress. She'd lost sight of so many of the things that used to be important to her, that used to define her. Maybe that was why she'd reacted so strongly. Maybe some deep, wise part of her brain had understood that she had enough on her plate right now without helping herself to a big slice of Oliver, as well. Maybe that was what her precipitous retreat had been about.

Maybe.

Not entirely convinced, she continued to chew on the subject until her tired brain finally loosened its grip and allowed her to slip into sleep.

She woke several hours later feeling hot and oddly unsettled. She flipped her pillow in search of the cool underside, remnants from her dreams licking at the edges of her mind.

A warm bed. A hot body. A man whispering in her ear. The insistent, wet pull of a mouth at her breasts. The delicate, questing slide of a hand between her legs…

Desire throbbed low in her belly. She realized with drowsy surprise that she was wet with need, her nipples hard against the soft fabric of her pajamas. She may have retreated from Oliver in real life, but in her dreams she'd apparently welcomed him with open arms.

How…confusing.

Still half-asleep, she allowed the images from her dream to wash over her. Warmth turned into heat as she remembered the dream. Oliver's strong, dexterous hands roving her body. Cupping her breasts. Sliding down her belly.

She stirred against the sheets. Her heart was racing, her breathing shallow. It had been a long time since she'd felt this way, a long time since she'd thought of her body as anything more than a damaged machine she needed to rebuild and repair.

Tentative, she slid her hand onto her stomach. Behind her closed eyelids, she imagined it was Oliver's hand as her fingers slipped beneath the waistband of her pajamas. It had been a while since she'd done this, too, but she wasn't about to question the urgings of her body. She felt too liquid and needy and ready.

She allowed herself to think about the way Oliver's face had looked tonight, lined by firelight. She thought about the way the soft, worn denim of his jeans had showcased his long, strong thigh muscles. She thought about the breadth of his shoulders, the angle of his jaw.

She remembered the taste of him, the warm, firm press of his lips against hers. She let her imagination fly as her hand slid lower—and stilled as her fingers found the ridge of scar tissue that ran between her hips and round to her right buttock.

The fantasy unrolling in her mind stalled. Her eyes opened. Suddenly, she was wide-awake.

Funny, but in the scene in her mind, her body was whole. Her hair was long, a sensual sweep over her shoulders, and she was confident and strong and empowered.

That woman didn't exist anymore. Certainly that body didn't. If something happened with Oliver, it would be this body he would sleep with, not the one in her imagination. There would be no silken, sexy hair to drape over his body and hers. There would be other issues to contend with, too. Physical limitations. She'd broken her pelvis and her hip, after all, and she still didn't have a normal range of movement.

She freed her hand from her pajamas, all the urgent heat of her fantasy draining away as she understood—finally—

why she'd retreated so strongly, so instinctively from Oliver's kiss.

She was scared.

Scared that her new body wouldn't be desirable to a man once he saw it in all its scarred, stitched and stapled glory. Scared that sex would be different, maybe even bad, thanks to her injuries. Scared that she didn't know how to be sexy in her new body. Or how to be confident or sassy or brave.

Everything in her wanted to reject the admission. She'd built a career, a life, out of being brave and bolshie and ballsy. She didn't do *afraid.*

But she knew she would be doing herself a disservice if she pretended otherwise. She needed to face this head-on, the way she'd faced learning to walk again, the way she'd faced so many of the challenges in her postaccident world.

Very deliberately, she retraced the path beneath her pajamas. She found the scar on her belly by touch, following it with her fingertips, absorbing the hard smoothness of it. There was no denying that it was not a pretty, delicate thing. Where once her belly had been flawless and soft, it was now bisected. The section where the ridge of tissue curled over her hip was puckered, an artifact of the healing process that the doctors had assured her would become less obvious with time. In broad daylight, it was nothing short of shocking, a violent slash across her body. It had saved her life, though, this slash. The surgeons had pieced her hip and pelvis back together and removed her damaged spleen and repaired her liver via it. Without it, she would be dead.

The same went for the mess on her shoulder. She ran the fingers of the opposite hand over the scar tissue there, reading the history of her injuries with her fingertips. Without this scar, she wouldn't have the use of her shoulder and arm. Her life would be infinitely more complex and difficult. Yes, it was messy and ugly, thanks to the postoperative infection that had required an extra surgery to rectify, but the bottom line was that her arm and shoulder worked.

Finally, she lifted her hand to her hair. Her fingers found the scar on her scalp unerringly, tracing the wicked curve of it across the front of her head. This scar had enabled the surgeons to repair her fractured skull and stop her brain from swelling and damaging itself. Without it, she would be lost. Pure and simple, the best part of herself—the very essence of Mackenzie Williams—damaged beyond recognition or recall.

She let her hands rest on her belly again, palms flat. Probably it was only human to be self-conscious about the changes her injuries had wrought in her body. After all, most women had been trained and indoctrinated from a young age to find fault with their own appearance. It was practically a national pastime. But she'd worked hard for this body. She'd fought alongside the doctors to keep it alive. She'd struggled against pain and expectation to become strong again. She'd survived and thrived in this body, and she refused to be ashamed of it.

A surge of defiance curled her hands into fists. If she wound up getting naked with Oliver and he balked at her scars, then so be it. He would have revealed something about himself that it would be important and good to know before she made the mistake of allowing him inside her body. And if he didn't…well, she'd cheated them both out of what had promised to be an amazing experience when she ran away from him tonight.

Next time, she promised herself. The next time Oliver kissed her, she would hang on to the pleasure and push away her doubts and insecurities. She would see this thing through.

Except, of course, that Oliver is about as likely to kiss you again as fly to the moon on the back of a winged pig.

She closed her eyes as she remembered the expression on his face after she'd retreated from him. A man would have to be pretty damned insensitive or just plain deluded to risk that kind of rejection again—and Oliver was neither of those things.

Which meant if she was ever going to kiss him again, she would have to be the one to initiate it.

She made a sound in the back of her throat. As much as it ran against the grain to admit it, the thought of taking the initiative with Oliver, of being the aggressor, made her feel dizzy with anxiety.

She stared at the ceiling, momentarily filled with despair. Not so long ago, making a move on a man like Oliver would have been an exciting challenge. Right now, it seemed scary and fraught with peril. Everything after the accident had been hard, but she hadn't expected sex and desire and romance to fall under that heading. Perhaps stupidly, she'd assumed that that part of her life would work as it always had. She was nearly forty, after all. Hardly an ingenue.

Maybe it really is a case of simply not being ready. Maybe you need to give yourself a break. Maybe being nervous and scared and self-conscious is only a stage you need to go through, like all the other stages of rehab.

She sighed and rolled onto her belly. Sometimes, the sensible voice in her head was simply too damn cool and rational and pragmatic.

Burrowing her head into the pillow, she closed her eyes and once again sought the oblivion of sleep.

OLIVER WOKE with the knowledge that he needed to apologize to Mackenzie at the top of his mind. For five minutes he lay in bed constructing the right words and phrases in his head, then he rose and headed for the shower. The sooner he got his self-appointed mission out of the way, the better.

It wasn't until he was dressed and in the kitchen waiting for the kettle to boil that he registered it was still dark outside.

He checked his phone. It was barely six o'clock. Awesome. Now he would have to cool his heels for a couple of hours while he waited for a more civilized time to call on his neighbor.

"Come on, Strudel," he said, grabbing the flashlight from his tool kit and heading for the back door.

He strode through frost-damp grass to the shed and tucked the flashlight under his arm while he struggled with the lock. It gave grudgingly and he opened the door and played the beam around the dusty interior. He immediately realized how futile his task was—there was no way he could effectively sort through the dark, overcrowded space with only the aid of a flashlight. He'd have to wait until daylight and bring each piece out onto the lawn to assess it properly.

So much for occupying himself with something constructive for a few hours. He shut the door and pushed the rusty bolt home, then contemplated the house. As though pulled by a force beyond his control, his gaze moved over the fence to Mackenzie's place. Light spilled out of the kitchen window, signaling she was up already, like himself. For a moment he toyed with the idea of throwing convention to the wind and going next door to say his piece despite the early hour. Anything to get past the moment where he had to look into her eyes and acknowledge his own poor judgment.

He teetered on the edge of temptation for a few seconds before sanity prevailed. Arriving on her doorstep at this hour smacked of desperation and preoccupation. Turning off the flashlight, he trudged toward the house.

"Oliver. Is that you?" Mackenzie's voice traveled clearly over the fence.

He stopped in his tracks, ankle-deep in wet grass. "Mackenzie."

"You're up early," she called.

"So are you."

He moved toward the fence and stepped up onto the first crossbar. Thanks to the reach of both their exterior lights, he could see her quite clearly. She stood on the other side looking at him, arms tightly crossed over her chest. She wore sunny yellow flannelette pajamas and an oversize navy cardigan, the sleeves rolled up several times to accommodate her small frame. Her hair was flat on one side, spiky on the other and her eyes looked tired.

"Hi," he said.

Not great as openers went, but it would do.

"Hi."

"Cold out."

"It is." She rubbed her hands over her biceps as though to generate some warmth. "Listen, Oliver. About last night…"

His belly tensed. *Here goes…*

"Yeah. I was going to come see you about that."

"You were?" Her cheeks were pink, her chin tilted so she could look him in the eye.

"Yeah. Wanted to clear the air. So things wouldn't get weird. If I upset you last night… I didn't mean to leap on you or anything."

"Oh, you didn't. I mean, I didn't feel leaped on. Far from it."

Her cheeks were very pink now and she seemed to have trouble meeting his gaze—reactions that perfectly mirrored his own. Jesus, since when had being an adult gotten so hard?

"In case you hadn't noticed, I'm a little out of practice with this stuff," he said. "Which I guess is why I got my signals all wrong. So…sorry about that. Won't happen again."

"Oh." She blinked. "Um, okay."

There was a beat of awkward silence and her forehead creased into furrows.

"Better go feed Strudel. She usually starts trying to gnaw her own leg off if we're up too long with no sustenance."

"Sure. Of course."

He lifted a hand in farewell. "See you around."

"Yes. See you."

He released his grip on the fence and stepped down to the ground, very aware that his armpits were damp with clammy, nervous sweat.

If he never had to have another conversation like that in his lifetime, he would die a happy man.

"Oliver?"

He took a moment to put his game face firmly in place before bracing his foot on the crossbar again and hoisting himself up so he could see her.

She was still frowning, but there was a determined tilt to her chin now.

"I didn't— Your wires weren't crossed. Me pulling away like that wasn't about you."

He nodded, even though he didn't really understand what she was getting at. "Okay."

She stared at him, her expression troubled. He waited for her to say more but she made a helpless gesture with one hand.

"I guess I'm pretty rusty with this stuff, too."

"Good to know I'm not alone. Gives me hope."

"Yes. There's always comfort in numbers, isn't there?"

They both fell silent. Against his will, his gaze shifted from her upturned face to the shadowy neckline of her pajama top. He hadn't noticed before, but his vantage point gave him a perfect view of her cleavage.

Maybe it was just him, but it seemed like a really bad

time to register that she wasn't wearing a bra under all that yellow flannel.

"I should go," he said abruptly, dragging his gaze to her face.

"Okay."

For the second time he raised a hand in farewell before dropping to the ground. He mouthed a curse as he made his way to the house. He had no idea what their conversation had been about, apart from the fact that he'd apologized and she'd accepted. But he now knew that Mackenzie had the tiniest of freckles on the upper curve of her right breast and that her skin looked smoother than velvet.

You are officially beyond help. You know that, right?

He was. Only last night he'd spent an hour staring at the ceiling, regretting the stupid impulse that had led him to kiss Mackenzie, and yet here he was, eyeing her cleavage even as she let him off the hook for his unwelcome advance.

Shaking his head at himself, he went to make breakfast. Maybe food would bring his brain back online.

He flicked the radio on when he entered the kitchen, listening to a morning talk show as he put eggs on to boil. He was slotting two pieces of bread into the toaster when his phone rang. He glanced at the screen and went still. Last night, Edie had caught him off guard because he hadn't recognized the number she was calling from. Not so this morning. He let his breath out in a rush before taking the call. Might as well get it over with, since she'd only try again later if he didn't answer this time.

"Edie."

"Hi. Sorry to call so early. I didn't wake you, did I?" She sounded guilty and nervous. As she had last night.

"I'm awake. What's the problem?"

"I'm at the house, but I can't find that file you were talking about. I've looked through both drawers in the filing cabinet."

"It's in the top drawer. Right at the back. Marked Insurance."

"I looked. It's not there."

He sighed. Edie was a self-styled incompetent when it came to business matters and he'd taken care of all the administrative aspects of their life together—the mortgage, the bills, any residual band business. He hadn't minded doing it, but he wasn't about to pander to her laziness now.

"Then I guess you'll have to look again."

It was her turn to sigh. When she spoke, her voice was so quiet he almost didn't hear her.

"For what it's worth, I miss you. I miss us. I miss Strudel and going to the bake house on Saturdays for bagels and lattes. I miss listening to you play your guitar."

The element in the toaster glowed red. Without thinking about it, he reached out and held his hand over the slots, absorbing the heat.

"Do you miss the lying?" It was a genuine question, but he was a little surprised to hear the lack of rancor in his own voice. He hoped it was a sign that her power to hurt and anger him was fading.

"You think I enjoyed that?" She sounded wounded.

"Part of you must have, Edie."

She'd kept it up for nearly six years, after all.

"I hated lying to you. I hated myself for it. Every time I promised myself it would be the last."

The toast popped up, golden-brown.

"Tell me something. Do you love him?" he asked.

There was the smallest of hesitations. He braced himself for more excuses and prevarications.

"Yes."

Honesty. A refreshing change.

"Did you ever love me?"

"Of course, Ollie. Always. How can you doubt that?"

He made a rude noise. It was a stupid question and she was smart enough to know it.

"If I'd never met Nick, if he and I didn't have this…*thing* between us, you would have been it for me, Ollie. If it's any consolation to you, I know I'm going to regret losing you." She made a sound that could have been a self-deprecating laugh. "Hell, I already do. This thing with Nick…I know it won't last. It's too damaged. And I know I'll never meet anyone like you again."

She sounded sad and broken, but he didn't have room in his heart to feel any sympathy for her. She'd destroyed six years of his life. He was working on moving past it, but he knew he'd never forgive her. She'd abused his trust too comprehensively.

His toast was going to be cold.

"I need to go," he said.

"Okay. If I need anything else, is it okay if I call?"

He didn't need to think about his answer. "No."

He wanted to put all this behind him. No way was he going to let her keep dragging him backward.

"Okay."

He hung up. The toast was hard, utterly unappetizing, and he pulled it out of the toaster and walked to the back door. He flung it outside for the birds, then toasted two fresh slices that he slathered with butter and Vegemite then sat at the kitchen table.

He felt…calm. Not angry. Not resentful. Certainly not wounded.

What a freaking relief.

It was startling after carrying around that solid burden of righteous emotions. He'd become so accustomed to their weight, to the way they alternately motivated him and depressed the hell out of him. This…this felt more normal. More like the Oliver he recognized.

At the same time, this calmness seemed too new and—dare he say it?—too temporary. He decided not to examine the situation too closely lest he jinx himself and welcome back the anger.

He was rinsing his plate at the sink when he heard the scrape of metal on concrete. Curious, he walked into the living room to look out the side window. Dressed in her workout gear, Mackenzie was clearing the gravel from the paved area in front of her house.

As she transferred a load to the wheelbarrow she'd positioned nearby, he remembered the nasty job it had been cleaning up this place—and he hadn't been flooded the way she had. He'd ached for two days after—shoveling gravel was hard work. It had taken her days to recover from their late-night battle with the water, and he could only imagine how exhausted she'd be today after hours of spadework.

"Stubborn idiot."

He knew her well enough now to know she would have convinced herself she could handle it. It would be a point of pride for her, a way of proving something to herself.

Not your problem.

It wasn't. He had more than his fair share of work to tackle on this side of the fence. The kitchen was only half-sorted, and there were still various cupboards, the attic and the rear shed to clear out.

The scrape of metal set his teeth on edge as Mackenzie hefted another shovelful. He watched as she tipped it into the wheelbarrow then paused to wipe her forehead and survey the remaining gravel. After a few seconds, she squared her shoulders and set to it again, the plucky little engine that could.

He shook his head, annoyed with himself and her. She

wasn't his responsibility. Far from it. Yet there was no way he was going to be able to listen to her toiling away, potentially exhausting herself, without doing something to help.

Which probably made him a misguided sap of the worst order.

So be it.

More than a little bemused at himself, he went to change into his work clothes.

CHAPTER NINE

MACKENZIE DUMPED a shovelful of gravel into the wheelbarrow, enjoying the feeling of using her muscles for something real instead of a series of pointless exercises on her gym equipment. It felt good to be outside, accomplishing something, instead of floating around aimlessly inside her house and her own head. Ever since she'd learned via Patrick that her job was history she'd been living in a sort of holding pattern, allowing herself a chance to regroup without the pressure of expectation.

There was only so much regrouping she could tolerate, however. She wasn't used to floating around. She was used to setting goals and going for them, hell for leather. The problem was, several days of allowing herself downtime hadn't teased a new goal or direction out of her subconscious. She still had no idea what to do now that she'd reconciled herself to the fact that high-pressure, long working weeks were not a realistic possibility for her anymore.

Hence the shovel and the gravel. The storm damage needed clearing, and even though it was something she could easily pay a handyman from the village to do, it was also something she could tackle herself, and she damn well would.

It didn't hurt that it was also a great distraction from the deeply uncomfortable, awkward conversation she'd had with Oliver. She'd embarrassed both of them last night, and while she'd tried to explain to him this morning that her rejection had been more about her than him, she was aware that she'd been woefully inarticulate. It would serve her right if he avoided her like the plague for the rest of his time in Flinders.

It was an unpleasant thought and she pushed it away, concentrating on heaving her latest shovelful into the wheelbarrow. She assessed the growing pile of gravel. The wheelbarrow was half-full, and she was conscious that if she made it too heavy she'd struggle to push it up the driveway. She set down her shovel and tried the handles. Not too bad. Another few shovelfuls wouldn't hurt.

The sound of footsteps made her glance up. Oliver appeared around the curve in her driveway, dressed in faded jeans and a long-sleeved T-shirt, a shovel balanced on one shoulder.

She was momentarily arrested by the sight he presented. Then her brain kicked in.

"No," she said, holding up a hand to halt his progress. "It's a lovely offer, but I couldn't possibly let you do that."

His gaze swept over her body and she was suddenly acutely aware of the fact that there were half-moons of sweat beneath her arms and a damp patch between her breasts.

"There's no way you can do this on your own without falling in a heap."

She blinked at his bluntness. "Wow. Pull your punches, why don't you?"

"Just stating the truth."

"I was planning on doing it in stages, if you must know. A bit today, a bit tomorrow and so on. The water-on-a-rock approach."

"So I'll help, and you'll get it done faster." He shrugged.

She breathed in through her nose, reminding herself that he was being sweet and generous and thoughtful—as well as presumptuous, bossy and overbearing. More importantly, he was here, talking to her, engaging with her, when common sense said, after the awkwardness of last night, he should be giving her a wide berth.

"You do know I'm not your responsibility, right?" she said.

"Okay. If you want me to go, I will. If you want to move all this on your own—" his hand swept in an arc over her messy, flotsam-and-jetsam-strewn concrete pad "—far be it from me to stand in the way."

He waited for her to respond, his hand resting on top of the long handle of his shovel, a challenging glint in his eye.

"Who in their right mind would want to do this all on their own?" And she was in her right mind—most of the time. "But I can't keep accepting favors from you."

"I'm sure we can think of some way you can pay me back."

He wore his poker face, his tone utterly neutral, but there was no getting away from the suggestiveness of his words. As if he could read her mind, he cocked an eyebrow.

"You could pay me in lemon tarts, for example."

"I could. Or I could barter my labor for yours. There must be something I can help you with on your side of the fence."

The tart would be easier, but she'd always feel as though she'd taken the easy option, and that simply wasn't her way.

"Good God, yes. There's still a ton of old clothes, the crawl space in the roof, the back shed…"

"Done. I'll match you hour for hour," she said, sticking her hand out to shake on their bargain.

He eyed her hand for a moment before grasping it. His skin was warm, his palm and fingers much bigger than hers.

"You drive a hard bargain, Williams."

"Oh, yeah, I'm a real hard-ass," she said drily.

They both knew he'd had her whipped the moment he appeared. As she'd already noted, no one in her right mind would choose to take on the thankless task of moving so much debris on her own.

He surveyed the work she'd already done and, without another word, began shoveling gravel into the wheelbarrow.

"I was going to empty that, actually," she said doubtfully. "It's getting really heavy."

"That won't be a problem, because you won't be pushing it."

"Won't I?" She gave him a look.

"Nope."

He didn't cease shoveling the whole time. She toyed with the idea of embarking on another tussle of wills with him, just for the fun of it, then decided to save her energy. No doubt they'd find plenty of things to disagree about as the day wore on.

Instead, she added her efforts to his, piling the barrow high. Once it was full, he pushed it to the top of the driveway and upended the load.

"We can rake it out later. Let's concentrate on clearing the area first," he suggested as he returned.

"Aye, aye, Captain," she said, giving him a salute.

He gave her a quizzical look. "Am I being too bossy?"

"Not yet. Skating close, but I'll let you know when you get there."

"I can hardly wait."

He smiled at her and the last of this morning's awkwardness evaporated as she found herself smiling in return. Maybe she hadn't completely ruined things between them with her scaredy-cat routine last night.

"Hey," he said after a few minutes of working. "I heard something on the radio this morning that will make you feel better. Apparently some researchers have done a study and discovered that people who sit down all day die younger. So you may have dodged a bullet when they gave your job away."

"Great. I'll add that to my list of requirements for my job search. 'Must not be sedentary.'"

There must have been something in her tone because he threw her a look. "Still beating yourself up on that one, huh?"

"Not beating myself up, as such, but I'm not feeling too inspired at the moment. So maybe there is such a thing as having too many options." She was aware that he was working twice as fast as her.

Well, she was pacing herself. Contrary to his belief, she wasn't foolish or reckless with her well-being. She valued her hard-fought-for stamina too much to blow it all in one day.

"What did you want to be when you were a kid?"

His question was so out of left field she stopped and stared at him.

He grinned. "Sometimes when I'm having trouble with a song I go back to the inspiration. Doesn't get better than childish dreams."

There was something incredibly appealing about the warmth in his eyes. For the hundredth time she found herself wondering how any woman could cheat on this man.

"I wanted to own a candy shop when I was a kid," she said. "And when I got a little older, I wanted to be a flight attendant."

He laughed, clearly amused by the idea of her pushing a food-service cart up the aisle. "You would totally suck at that."

"No kidding."

"So why did you choose TV?"

They'd filled the wheelbarrow again and she pondered

his question as he pushed it up the driveway and dumped the load.

"I saw this documentary when I was about to finish high school—*Baraka.* It's a nonnarrative feature, an amazing journey around the planet exploring humanity and nature…." She remembered the impact the film had on her when she'd first seen it.

"I think I saw that. Is there a scene with monkeys bathing in hot springs in the mountains somewhere?"

"That's the one. I was so inspired, I saw it nearly a dozen times before embarking on the biggest documentary glom the world has ever seen. Nature, current events, history, I was insatiable. I'd registered to study business at university, but I changed my preferences at the last minute and took film and media classes instead."

"How did the high-achieving parents take that?"

She was surprised that he recalled her throwaway comment regarding her parents. "They were worried. With good cause. As I discovered after I graduated and started doing the rounds with a proposal for my passion project—a documentary about Dr. Mary De Garis—there's not a lot of money or interest in documentaries. Especially ones about obscure pioneering feminists in the medical field." She pulled a face. "In hindsight, it probably wasn't the best put together proposal, either. A little too much idealism, not enough commercialism."

"So your dreams were crushed?"

"In a way. But I was so persistent, one of the producers I tried to get interested in the project was impressed by my 'formidable pestering powers.' That's a direct quote, by the way."

"Makes you wonder how he formed such a wrongheaded impression of your personality."

God, she truly appreciated this man's wit. It was a challenge to keep a straight face and stay on topic. "It does, doesn't it? Anyway, he offered me a job as a production assistant, and I was away."

Oliver paused, leaning his shovel against the wheelbarrow. "So deep inside the hard-nosed producer is a passionate documentary filmmaker?"

He grasped the bottom of his top and lifted it over his head, revealing a black tank top underneath.

"Um, I wouldn't say that," she said, more than a little distracted by the play of muscles in his arms and shoulders as he folded his shirt neatly and draped it over the railing of the porch. "I've always enjoyed the challenge of my work."

"Not even a little itch to be behind the camera more directly?"

The sun chose that moment to come out from behind a cloud, gilding him in sunlight, and she lost the power of speech entirely. He had a very, very good body. Shoulders to weep over, arms to sigh over, a chest that made her fingers curl into her palms with the need to touch. Then there was his fine ass and awesome thighs….

She was staring, and she suspected that her mouth was slightly agape, too. Somehow she got a grip on her galloping, unruly libido and prodded her brain into action.

He'd asked her a question. She needed to answer it—and then she needed to check that she didn't have drool on her chin.

"I don't think so," she said, a vague enough answer since she couldn't really remember his question.

"How you doing? You need to take a break?" he asked, his concerned gaze scanning her face.

"No, no. I'm fine," she said, even though she was uncomfortably aware that she was suddenly very hot.

She waited until he'd turned away before fanning the front of her top and rolling her eyes at herself. Honestly, anyone would think she'd never seen a good-looking man up close before.

But it wasn't only that Oliver was extensively easy on the eyes. He was also *lovely,* pure and simple. Sweet and funny and generous and smart. He remembered throwaway comments she'd made and teased her and seemed genuinely interested in her and her life.

And you pushed him away last night when he kissed you.

She muttered a four-letter word beneath her breath as she drove the shovel into a pile of gravel. She didn't have a long list of wholehearted regrets in her life—the accident, moments during her marriage—but her knee-jerk reaction last night was on its way to qualifying.

If only she'd been better prepared. If only she'd been more conscious of where things had been going with her and Oliver…

But she hadn't, and the moment was gone and she needed to move on.

One of those concepts that definitely came under the heading Easier Said Than Done.

As they toiled, no matter which way she turned, Oliver was in her line of sight, either directly or peripherally. He was a hard worker, giving the task his all, and soon he was gleaming with sweat. His tank top clung to the planes of his chest, and his jeans slipped down his hips an inch or so. Every now and then he stopped and wiped his brow with his forearm and she was treated to a flash of hairy male armpit.

She wasn't sure what planet she'd been living on, but never had the differences between a man's body and her own been so compelling. Her own chest and underarms were smooth as silk, thanks to Mother Nature and the regular attention of a razor, respectively. Oliver's hairier, rougher body had her mind and heart racing. She wanted to press her face to his chest and inhale the smell of him. She wanted to wrap her hands around his big biceps. She wanted to lick the point where his neck became his shoulder, right in the little hollow between his collarbone and trapezius muscle. She wanted to slide her hand down his flat belly and inside the waistband of his jeans. She wanted—

She gave herself a mental slap. She was out of control, like one of those oversexed, humpy dogs that went to town on unsuspecting houseguests. Next thing she knew, Oliver would be shaking his leg, trying to remove her from his person.

"Maybe we should take a break," she said, mostly out of desperation. Energywise, she was holding up well, but mentally she was a mess. A turned-on, confused, aroused mess.

Oliver stopped and considered the walkway. They'd cleared over half of the gravel, an effort she was more than happy with.

"Sure. We've made a good start."

"Do you want a cold drink? I've got orange juice or mineral water."

"Water would be great."

She headed into the house, aware of him following her, his heavy tread echoing down the hallway. In the kitchen, she served them both water. He leaned against the sink, she against the opposite counter. He swallowed his in one big gulp, his Adam's apple bobbing. She told herself not to stare and had to resist the urge to roll the cold glass across her chest to cool herself down.

It hit her suddenly that there was no way she could handle another hour of watching him do manly things in faded jeans. Not without an icy shower.

"You know what? Maybe we should call it a day. We got so much done I can probably chip away at what's left over the rest of the week."

Oliver rinsed his glass and set it on the drain board.

Now that they were in closer quarters, she could smell the strong, spicy scent of his deodorant, along with a faint hint of clean, male sweat.

"If you're whacked, I don't mind doing the rest alone."

"There is no way I could let you do that."

"I knew you were going to say that."

Her weakening resistance sent up a silent cheer. He wasn't going to fight her. Hallelujah.

"When were you thinking of tackling the shed?"

"Want to pencil me into your busy schedule?" His smile was teasing.

"Something like that."

"Let's see how you feel tomorrow. If you're not too sore maybe we can tackle it then."

"Sounds like a plan." She swallowed the last of her water and took the three steps necessary to take it to the sink. She was conscious of him standing a couple of feet away as she rinsed her glass and set it beside his.

"Your hair's gone all curly on the ends," he said.

She went very still as she felt the brush of his fingers on the nape of her neck. Sensation washed through her—heat and awareness and an almost animal sense of yearning.

It had been so long since she'd lain skin to skin with a man. So long since someone had touched her with anything other than clinical detachment.

Oliver was standing barely two feet away. All she had to do was take a step and she'd be so close to him she'd be able to feel his body heat.

There were a lot of good reasons to ignore that impulse. The concerns that had kept her awake in the small hours hadn't dissolved overnight. As aroused as she was, as aware of him as she was, she still felt a panicky sense of uncertainty when her imagination moved beyond contemplating what she wanted to do to him to what he might like to do to her. It was one thing to assert she was proud of and reconciled to her damaged body, and another thing entirely to practice what she preached.

Out of the corner of her eye, she saw his hand drop to his side. She turned her head.

His gaze met hers. Her breath got caught in her throat as she read the carnal intent in his eyes. He wanted her, still. Even though she'd been such an idiot. All she had to do was reach out and he could be hers. All that beautiful, intoxicating masculinity.

She didn't move. Her arms felt leaden, her feet glued to the ground, weighted by indecision and doubt. Eyes locked to his, she willed him to understand and to make the first move for both of them, breaking this Mexican standoff, forcing her past her own fear.

Kiss me, she willed him. *Kiss me and make it all better.*

The moment stretched. Oliver's gaze dropped to her mouth.

He took a step backward. "Let me know if you don't feel up to working tomorrow, okay?"

Disappointment slammed through her as he headed for the door.

Do you blame him, after last night? Why on earth would he risk you flinging yourself against the nearest hard surface to escape him again? Why would he put himself in that position?

She didn't blame him, but it didn't stop her from feeling seriously disgruntled as she followed him to the foyer.

On the surface, it was such a simple equation. He was a healthy, single, consenting adult, and so was she. There was nothing in the world stopping them from acting on the attraction between them. And yet he was about to walk out the door, and she was about to let him.

"Thanks for your help," she said as they reached the entryway.

"Don't be too grateful. I plan on working you hard tomorrow."

"Bring it on." She managed to produce a smile.

His gaze dropped to her mouth one last time before he turned away. "You'll have to tell me about Dr. Mary De Garis one of these days."

"It would serve you right if I held you to that," she said as he exited.

He didn't say anything, simply lifted a hand in farewell. She watched until he'd disappeared around the curve in the driveway, then shut the door.

If only he'd kissed her. There was no way she would have pushed him away this time.

If only you'd kissed him.

But she hadn't. She'd choked, pulled up short by her self-consciousness.

She went to the bedroom and stripped before stepping into the shower in her en suite. All the while she thought about Oliver, about that heated, taut moment that had stretched and stretched and finally broken beneath the weight of her uncertainty and doubt. A year ago, she would have bridged the distance between them and let him know what she wanted. She wouldn't have hesitated. Not that she'd thought she was some sort of irresistible sexual goddess before the accident, but she'd been around enough to know when a man wanted her and to act on that awareness if the feeling was reciprocal.

Bowing her head, she let the water flow over her back. She hated being afraid. Hated to think that she'd let fear be the deciding factor. Hated to think that this was something else the accident had taken away from her.

She didn't want to be the sort of woman who let self-doubt rule her world.

Then don't be.

She lifted her head.

It was such a simple thought. If she took the time to pick it apart, she could find a dozen different ways to debunk it. But maybe she needed to stop thinking so much and start acting. Maybe she needed to seize the bull by the horns and simply get over herself.

She laughed, the sound half scared, half amused as it bounced off the tiles. Before she could talk herself out of it, she reached for the razor. She shaved her legs and under her arms, then got out of the shower and patted herself dry. She rubbed vanilla-and-orange-peel-scented lotion into her body and spritzed perfume onto her breasts. Then she brushed her teeth and wiped the condensation off the mirror and reached for her makeup bag, going all out with the eyeliner and mascara.

She walked into her bedroom and spent considerable time pawing through her underwear drawer, looking for something that wasn't cotton and practical. She found a matched bra-and-panty set made from see-through black mesh, the panties high cut with lace detail in strategic places.

Sexy. She hoped.

She pulled the underwear on. Then and only then did she turn to face the full-length mirror on the back of her bedroom door.

Her gaze gravitated immediately to the ugly scar that ran between her hips and around her right side. Her focus lifted to the twisted mess that ran from her left shoulder and around her upper arm. Finally, her gaze came to rest on the dark puncture scars on her rib cage, relics from where her fractured ribs had broken through the skin.

None of it was pretty. The scars weren't old enough to have faded, despite her religious use of rose-hip oil to promote healing. The scar on her belly… There was no way a man could avoid contact with it if he was in bed with her. It would be a very present part of any action that took place.

She forced her gaze away from her stomach, focusing instead on her breasts. They'd always been small but the rest of her was, too, and she'd never had a problem with that. Cupped in sheer black mesh, they looked perky and dainty and, yes, sexy. She moved on to her legs. Before the accident, she'd worked hours in the gym to tone them, but rehab had given her muscles that ordinary gym exercises never could. Her legs would never be long and fantasy inspiring, but they were slim and strong and they looked good to her.

So, nice legs and breasts, with some not-so-great bits in between. Given that she'd been minutes from death out on that dark, rainy road, she figured a bit of not-so-great was a light price to pay for being alive. As she reminded herself every morning, she was lucky to be here.

She met her own gaze in the mirror, her chin lifting in challenge.

Was she really going to do this?

She glanced at her body again, then remembered that moment in her kitchen when Oliver had been standing just out of reach, golden and hard and gorgeous.

So damned good…

Yes, she was going to do this.

She turned to her wardrobe and pulled out her skinny jeans and a snug-fitting black sweater. Not siren stuff, but most of her fabulous clothes were in Melbourne. With her black stiletto ankle boots she was almost certain she could pull off foxy.

Technically, she wasn't supposed to be traipsing about in high heels—her back and pelvis simply weren't up to it—

but she needed the added confidence they gave her and she figured the short walk next door wouldn't kill her. Plus, she didn't plan on being on her feet for long.

She grinned at her own bravado as she zipped the ankle closure on her boots. The smile faded as she stood and smoothed her hands down her thighs and inspected her reflection one last time.

She tweaked the neck of her sweater to show more cleavage, then nodded. She looked good. Her eyes were nightclub sultry and there was color in her cheeks. The sweater hugged her breasts, the jeans molded her thighs. The boots gave her a little bit of extra height and made her legs appear that bit longer.

She was ready. Well, as ready as she'd ever be.

Butterflies did a river dance in her belly as she tip-tapped her way to the front door. Smitty kept pace with her, his face turned upward, his expression questioning.

"Sorry, buddy, but this is a solo mission."

She was about to leave when she remembered something important. She swiveled and walked back to her bedroom. Yanking open the bedside drawer, she rummaged around, hoping against hope that the box of condoms she'd bought eighteen months ago was still there.

It was. Better yet, the expiry date was good. She extracted one condom and slid it into her pocket, then added another for good measure. Just in case.

Feeling brazen and bold and terrified as all get-out, she left the house.

CHAPTER TEN

TRAVERSING TWO GRAVEL driveways in stilettos prevented Mackenzie from dwelling on the slightly sick/excited feeling in the pit of her stomach, but there was no denying the swoop of adrenaline that washed through her as she climbed the stairs to Oliver's front porch.

She shook her hands, blowing out a breath.

He's a good guy. Trust him. And trust yourself.

She knocked. A beat of silence followed. Her throat was so tight with nerves she wondered how she would keep breathing. Then footsteps sounded on the other side of the door. She closed her eyes for a brief moment, reaching for courage. The door was swinging wide when she opened her eyes.

Oliver stood there in his tank top and jeans, his feet bare. Her gaze dropped to his hips. The stud on his jeans was open, as though she'd caught him in the act of undressing.

"Mackenzie." His gaze traveled over her face before dropping to scan her body. A small, confused smile tilted his mouth. "You heading out?"

She opened her mouth to tell him why she was there—an expurgated version, anyway—but nothing came out. Nerves squeezed her diaphragm and chest. She felt a little dizzy.

I don't think I can do this.

She could feel her courage draining away. Driven by desperation, she reached out and clenched her hand into the fabric of his shirt. Then she used her grip to yank him toward her. His eyes widened as they bumped chests. She was already lifting her head, her mouth finding his unerringly, instinctively. Her free hand landing on his shoulder for balance, she closed her eyes and kissed him with all the urgency and need in her soul.

For a horrible, too-long moment his mouth was still against hers, then his arms came around her and his lips opened. The hot, knowing slide of him inside her mouth made her knees weak with lust.

He tasted like coffee and desire, and his stubble rasped against her face as he angled his head and deepened their connection. One of his hands slid down her spine to cup her backside, curving around it possessively before pulling her into more intimate contact with his body. She felt his hard-on against her belly, a thick, firm ridge that made her moan with anticipation.

She needed this. Needed him. She wanted the mindlessness of sex, the beauty of being in the now, the carnal joy of giving in to her animal self. Her hands grasped at his tank top, searching blindly, desperately for the hem. Once she found it she slid her hands onto the firmness of his belly, her inner muscles tightening as she felt the shiver of need that rippled through his body. His skin was still slightly damp from their yard work and she rubbed her hips against his as she remembered how *good* he'd looked, working and sweating on her behalf.

Vaguely aware they were still on his doorstep, she urged him backward, not stopping until she had him pressed against the hall wall. Utterly focused on getting him naked, she kicked the door shut and started tugging his shirt up his torso. She needed to touch and see and lick him. *Now.*

He broke their kiss, his hands finding hers to halt their progress.

"Mackenzie," he said, his voice thick and low. "I haven't had a shower—"

"Thank. God," she said, kissing him again.

She wanted him hot and sweaty. She wanted him exactly as he was.

He laughed but let her have her way, ducking his head and lifting his arms obligingly so she could tug the top over his head. She let it fall to the ground, eating up his shoulders and chest and belly with her eyes. Her gaze zeroed in on the hollow at the base of his neck that she'd wanted to lick earlier and she leaned close and tasted him. Salt and heat and man. She wrapped her hand around his biceps and pressed herself against him as she tasted him again.

He muttered something under his breath and the next thing she knew she was moving backward, and then she was the one with her back against the wall on the other side of the hall and he was pinning her there with his body weight.

"Are you trying to kill me?" he asked her as he looked into her eyes.

"I was trying to seduce you."

"Mission accomplished."

He kissed her, his body shaking with barely controlled need. His hands covered her breasts, his fingers plucking at her nipples as he pressed his hips against hers. She'd never been so turned-on in her life, every inch of her skin screaming to be in contact with his. Desire was an ache between her thighs, insatiable and demanding.

Her hands fumbled at his fly, dragging the tab down. His body jerked as she slipped her hand inside his jeans and underwear and wrapped it around his erection. He was incredibly hot and hard in her hand and she made a needy sound in her throat.

His hands found the stud on her jeans and she bit his lower lip encouragingly as he lowered the fly. His warm hand smoothed south, slipping beneath the elastic of her panties. Way, way, way at the back of her brain she was aware that this was one of many moments where he might hesitate or, worse, retreat as he encountered the evidence of her injuries. That part of her was silenced as his fingers slipped lower, delving between her thighs.

"Mackenzie," he whispered as he discovered how wet and ready she was.

Her hand tightened around his erection as he found her, his finger working in delicate circles. She could feel her climax rushing toward her, even though they'd barely started. It had been so long and he was so damn hot....

But she wanted him inside her when she came, wanted to have the hardness in her hand filling her, stretching her. She released her grip on him and started pushing at his jeans.

He broke their kiss, his lips trailing across her cheek to find the sensitive skin beneath her ear. "Not here," he murmured against her skin.

"Yes," she insisted, pushing his jeans lower on his hips.

She wanted him now. Couldn't bear to wait even as long as it would take to find a bedroom. Pushing him away, she locked eyes with him briefly before concentrating on his jeans, dragging them down his legs. It seemed only natural to follow them down, to press her face against his flat belly before taking him in her hand and pulling him into her mouth.

He swore, his hand coming to cup the back of her head. He tasted like sweat and need and she closed her eyes and savored him. After a few seconds he pulled away from her. He gripped her beneath the arms and encouraged her to rise.

"You're not getting off that easy," he said.

He grasped the waistband of her sweater, pulling it over her head in one swift move. His gaze swept from breast to breast.

"You put this on for me?" he asked, tracing the edge of her lacy bra where it curved over her breast.

"Yes."

"Good choice." He reached behind her and her bra was suddenly loose around her torso. "But this is much, much better."

The next thing she knew, he had the straps down her arms and she was naked from the waist up. He made an appreciative noise before lowering his head to pull a nipple into his mouth.

The sharp pull of his mouth, the wet heat, the sight of his head over her breast… She cried out, her hands gripping his shoulders as she hung on for dear life.

"You taste good," he said as he lifted his head. He kissed her again, the force of his desire tilting her head back. She felt his hands at her hips, then the tug of denim against her skin as he pushed her jeans and panties down her thighs.

She was naked now, bared utterly to him, and a rush of anxiety cut through her arousal. There was no way he could fail to notice the brutal scar across her hips now. It was center stage, waiting for its moment in the spotlight.

The thought had barely registered before he ducked in front of her, tucking his shoulder beneath her body. Suddenly she was airborne, flailing for purchase, one of his strong arms clamped around her waist, the other gripping an ass cheek in a provocative, primitive way as he lifted her in a firefighter's hold.

"Been wanting to do that for a while," he said as her shock turned to laughter.

He headed up the hall, turning into the first room. He leaned forward, then she was tumbling onto a bed. He wasted no time following her, his gaze sweeping over her in hungry appraisal.

Again, she tensed, waiting for him to hesitate or backpedal or comment.

"You look good enough to eat," he said.

Then he lowered his head and licked his way down her belly before pushing her thighs open. She forgot to breathe as he licked the seam of her sex, her fingers fisting in the sheets. She almost levitated when he opened his mouth and kissed her, a fully, earthy caress that made her forget everything.

From that moment on she was gone, lost in her body and what he was doing to her. The flick of his tongue, the gentle, insistent pressure, the build of tension inside her…

Her hips lifted as she sought more, and he obliged by sliding a finger inside her, then another. She was so close it hurt, her arousal a painful, desperate ache. Any second now she was going to break….

"No. I want you," she panted, her fingers clamping down onto his shoulder as she tried to ease him away.

He lifted his head, his eyes dark with passion.

"Get up here," she ordered, curling her fingers in his hair and encouraging him upward.

His mouth curved into a slow, knowing smile as he relinquished his position and came on top of her. His hips settled between her thighs and she reached for him, positioning him at her entrance.

"Wait." A chagrined expression came over his face. "Condom."

"Front pocket of my jeans."

A slow smile curved his mouth. "You don't do anything by halves, do you?"

"Not if he's worth doing."

He laughed, and then she was watching his perfect, rounded ass as he hightailed it out the door in search of her jeans. Five seconds later he was back, the silver square of a condom in hand. He knelt on the bed between her thighs and she watched through half-closed eyes as he smoothed the latex onto his erection.

She couldn't be one-hundred-percent certain, most of her blood being south of her navel right now, but she was pretty sure it was about the sexiest damn sight she'd ever seen. He stretched over her, his weight balanced on one elbow. She felt the warm, hard press of him at her entrance, her hips instinctively lifting to welcome him inside.

At the last second a bolt of panic made her grip his shoulder.

"What's wrong?"

"It's been a while since I've done this. I have no idea if everything still works the way it should."

His mouth tilted at the corners. "We'll join the dots," he said confidently, and then he flexed his hips and slid inside her, a hot, hard invasion that stole her breath and made her cry out.

He swallowed the rest of her cry with a kiss before withdrawing almost to the brink before driving home again. The delicious movement of his body inside hers was too much, too good, too fine. She rocked with him, finding his rhythm, closing her eyes and getting lost in the world behind her eyelids. He was so heavy and male and she loved the way he felt, the weight of him and the urgent, demanding stroke of his body inside hers. Tension rose inside her and instinctively she tried to bring him in deeper, arching her back, widening her thighs. Pain shot through her hip, sharp and undeniable, and she instinctively tried to pull away from it, pressing her thighs tight to his. He stilled immediately.

"Mackenzie?"

The pain was fading already and she gripped his backside, silently urging him to continue.

"What just happened?" he asked, stubbornly refusing to move.

"My range of movement isn't what it used to be."

His face was concerned as he studied hers. "Okay. What if you were on top?"

"No, no. This is fine. I can handle it."

She needed him to keep going, in the same way that she needed oxygen. She tilted her hips, trying to coax him into moving.

"It's not supposed to be an endurance test."

She gave a wordless cry as he withdrew, the loss of him a profound, unwelcome shock.

"Oliver, I swear..." She curled her fingers into the muscle of his hip, trying to stop him from leaving.

His arm came around her as he rolled onto his back, lifting her at the same time so that she wound up on top, sprawled across his body.

"Do your worst," he said as he grinned at her.

She stared at him, momentarily thrown by the easy, casual way he'd made things right for her, even when she'd given him permission to simply plow on, regardless.

"Thank you," she said simply, because his generosity deserved recognition.

"Don't mention it," he said as he slid his hands onto her backside.

His erection surged against her belly, a potent reminder that the best was yet to come. Slipping her knees either side of his hips, she gripped him and arranged herself. In this position she could control the extension of her hip and there was nothing but pleasure as she slid onto him.

His hands gripped her as she started to move, his eyes dropping to half-mast. She concentrated on the feel of him inside her, on the needful pressure of his hardness against her softness, her gaze running over his chest and belly and face.

He was so damned hot, his body so beautiful, and the way he felt inside her…

She held her breath as her climax hit her, her head dropping back as she rode it out.

"Yes. Come for me, Mackenzie." Oliver's voice was low and deep, his hands a welcome anchor as he thrust into her.

She opened her eyes in time to see him come, the tendons standing out in his neck, his lips drawn back in an almost snarl. She stared, transfixed, then gasped as he slipped a hand between their bodies and found her with his thumb. Two, three, four strokes and she climaxed again, his name a sob on her lips.

She fell across his chest afterward, her face pressed into his neck. She could smell his deodorant and something she suspected was simply him and she nuzzled closer as her body slowly came down to earth.

His hands smoothed over her arms, her back, her hips, a steady, calming, hypnotic caress. She felt warm and sated and safe and she let her eyelids drop closed. After a few minutes he pressed a kiss to her temple and she slipped off him, allowing him to do something with the condom before pulling the covers over them both. He encouraged her onto her side facing away from him, then curled his body around hers, one arm sliding around her rib cage. The last thing she registered before drifting into sleep was the brush of his lips at the nape of her neck.

IT WAS DARK when Oliver woke with the sweet scent of vanilla surrounding him. A warm, soft body was curled into his side, a slim leg tangled with his.

Mackenzie.

God, Mackenzie.

She'd been incredible. So hot and tight and ready for him. The way she'd launched herself at him when he'd opened the door, pushing him against the wall and sliding her hand inside his jeans…

And when she'd taken him into her mouth…

It had been all he could do not to disgrace himself on the spot. Ever since he'd met her a part of him had wondered what she'd be like—what they'd be like together. And now he knew.

Unforgettable. Undeniable.

Tightness stole into his chest as he blinked at the ceiling. Mackenzie stirred beside him, her lips pressing briefly against his shoulder, a small, unconscious gesture of affection that made his armpits prickle with sudden, clammy sweat.

She was incredible. Sexy beyond his wildest fantasies, earthy and lusty and so damned responsive… One part of him wanted to lose himself inside her all over again—and the other part was freaking out for exactly the same reason.

He'd had one-night stands before, a long time ago in his band days. This was not how a one-night stand felt.

Because what had happened with Mackenzie had been about more than sex. It had been about connection and affection and true intimacy. It had meant something. It had been real.

His heart thumped against his breastbone as flight-or-fight adrenaline pumped through him. Suddenly the quilt felt too heavy, Mackenzie's weight against his side a burden. Moving carefully, he eased away from her before standing and exiting the room. He found his jeans in the hall and pulled them on before making his way to the kitchen.

The power button for the kettle glowed softly in the darkness and he used it to orient himself while his eyes adjusted. When he could make out the dim outline of the cupboards and the fridge, he hit the button to bring the water to boil and found the tea bags and a cup in the cupboard. Then he sat at the kitchen table, hands wrapped around the hot mug, trying to get a grip.

He shouldn't be feeling this way about anyone so soon after the breakdown of his marriage. Edie was still so much in his head. There was still so much to deal with. He didn't have the mental real estate available to take on something big and important and significant right now.

Something he maybe should have thought about before he pushed Mackenzie's bra off her shoulders and pulled one of her small, tight nipples into his mouth. Definitely something he should have thought about before he'd lost himself inside her sleek, strong body.

But he hadn't. He'd gone along for the ride when she'd barreled over the threshold because he'd wanted her, hadn't stopped wanting her, from the moment he'd first met her. Even when he'd decided she was rude and beyond redemption, a part of him had been mentally undressing her. She fascinated him. She compelled him. She aroused him. And now he'd touched her and kissed her and held her and tasted her and swallowed her cries of release and felt her body arch against his own… And he was pretty damned sure he would never be able to forget any of those things for as long as he lived.

It had been that good. *She* had been that good.

He shoved the mug away.

This was crazy. He was a mess. A liability to any woman right now, but particularly to Mackenzie, who was dealing with her own crap. The last thing she needed was some crazy, unstable guy in her life. She needed someone rock steady and solid as she navigated the next challenging phase of her recovery, as she redefined who she was and what she'd do with her career. She didn't need a guy who woke in a cold sweat and snuck out because he couldn't handle the intensity of what he'd experienced in her arms.

Dude. Take a deep breath and a big step back. You had sex with the woman. You didn't sign a bloody marriage certificate. You didn't enter into a binding agreement. She hasn't asked for anything from you, and you haven't offered it. It was just sex. Great sex, yes, but still just sex. Get. A. Grip.

His rolled his tight shoulders. Maybe he was getting too far ahead of himself. Reading too much into one experience, racing ahead to imagine a disaster that was unlikely to ever occur. Mackenzie hadn't indicated by word or deed that she wanted anything more from him than a good time. Not that there had been much time for rational discussion after she'd pushed him against the wall and pressed her body against his, but still. She was a smart, sophisticated woman, and she'd come to him knowing that his life, his business, was in Sydney, and that his personal situation was messy and complicated right now. It stood to reason that she wouldn't be expecting or demanding anything from him.

He waited for the tightness in his chest to ease. In vain. It took him a moment to understand that it wasn't Mackenzie's expectations or assumptions he was worried about managing, but his own.

He'd recognized something in her, something fundamental and special. He was drawn to her, in every possible way—and he knew, in his gut, that he was in no fit state to handle the intensity of his own feelings.

They were too overwhelming, too confronting, when he was only now recovering his equilibrium after Edie's betrayal.

Shit.

He put his head in his hands. He shouldn't have slept with Mackenzie. Shouldn't have let the genie out of the bottle.

"Hey."

He lifted his head. Mackenzie stood in the kitchen doorway. There was enough light for him to see that she was dressed, her shoes dangling from the fingers of one hand.

"I wanted to let you know I was going home. So you didn't think I was sneaking off or anything."

"You don't have to," he said, more because he felt he should than because it was how he honestly felt.

"Smitty needs his dinner." She hesitated. "And you look like you could do with some space."

He opened his mouth to deny it, but he didn't want to lie to her.

"I don't know that I'm a great bet at the moment," he said.

He could tell by the look on her face that she understood he was talking generally and not only about tonight.

"I guess that depends on what a person is looking for."

He stared at her, unable to separate what he wanted from what he needed.

"It's okay, Oliver. I get it. You live in Sydney, I live in Melbourne. You're here trying to put your life back together. And so am I, I guess. There are no strings or obligations between us."

It was exactly what he wanted to hear, but his chest remained tight. She entered the room properly and came to his side. Her hand was warm as it landed on his shoulder. She leaned down and dropped a kiss onto his forehead.

"Thank you for a great time."

He watched in tense silence as she disappeared through the door.

"Mackenzie. Wait."

She was waiting for him in the darkness of the hallway. He could smell the vanilla sweetness of her and the urge to pull her into his arms was almost undeniable.

He resisted it, leading her silently to the front door. She rested a hand on the door frame for balance as she slipped on her boots, Strudel sniffing around her ankles with interest.

"Will you be okay getting home?" he asked awkwardly as she straightened.

She laughed. "Yeah, I think so. Good night, Oliver."

She made her way down the stairs, then she was swallowed by the darkness of the night. He listened to the crunch of gravel beneath her boots and didn't shut the door until he heard hers close.

Strudel was already waiting on the bed when he returned to the room. He pulled off his jeans and slipped between sheets that smelled of Mackenzie and sex. He rested a hand on Strudel's soft head and closed his eyes and told himself that everything would look clearer in the morning.

With a bit of luck.

MR. SMITH WAS WAITING by the door when Mackenzie let herself in. She gave him a small smile and waited patiently while he did his happy dance, giving him a reassuring pat. He trotted after her as she walked to the kitchen to put out some food for him. She propped her hip against the counter as she watched him eat, trying not to think about the scene she'd walked away from next door.

Oliver, sitting in the dark at his kitchen table, head in his hands, shoulders hunched.

It had taken every ounce of pride she possessed to make a gracious exit from his house. And then some.

Thank God he hadn't been beside her when she woke up. She'd been so warm and sated and pleased with herself, there was no telling what she might have said.

That he was a wonderful lover, powerful and intuitive and generous.

That he made her feel beautiful and sexy and happy and wild.

That his easy, casual acceptance of her flawed body had felt like a benediction and the most precious gift she'd ever received.

Thank God, also, that she'd chosen to dress before she went looking for him. The thought of having to pull on her clothes after that chat in the kitchen made her toes curl in her shoes.

Mr. Smith gave his bowl one last, snuffling lick before sitting on his haunches and looking up at her.

"Outside, little guy?" she asked, crossing to the French doors to let him out.

No lights were on next door and she guessed Oliver had gone to bed. Now that the coast was clear.

Don't. Don't do it to yourself. You knew going in what it was. Like you said to him, you knew it wasn't forever. It was just sex. It doesn't matter how he reacted afterward. You're not in a relationship. It's nothing to do with you.

Except it was. Of course it was. It was everything to do with her. Something had happened when they were skin to skin. Something intense. At least, it had been intense for her. Intense and tender and funny and hot and mind-blowing, all at once.

Not what she'd expected, by a long shot. Not what she'd been looking for, either. But it had happened. For her, anyway.

Oliver, apparently, had had a very different experience. The kind that induced a man to retreat to the coldest, darkest room in the house and put his head in his hands.

Mr. Smith bounded up the deck steps and trotted into the house. She locked up and made her way to her bedroom. She stared at her bed, thinking of that other bed next door, the one where Oliver had made her come twice and then held her so lovingly afterward. He'd even kissed the nape of her neck before she'd drifted into sleep. She hadn't imagined that.

I don't know that I'm a great bet at the moment.

Oliver's words came to her, along with the troubled, guilty, confused expression in his eyes. Some of her regret and hurt drained away as she saw past her own feelings and put herself in his shoes. Oliver was such a good guy, so rational and laid-back, it was easy to forget that a mere handful of months ago his life had been turned inside out by the one person he should have been able to trust above all others.

He might put on a good show, but he wouldn't be human if he wasn't raw and hurting and confused right now. There wasn't a doubt in her mind that she was the first woman he'd slept with since the breakup with Edie. Was it any wonder, really, that he'd retreated to a quiet space to try to get his head together? If his experience of their time together had come even close to being as intense as hers, Mackenzie could forgive him for feeling overwhelmed. Hell, *she* felt overwhelmed. She'd isolated herself here on the coast in an attempt to win her life back. She hadn't expected to find Oliver. She absolutely hadn't expected it to feel so… *right* when she'd given in to their mutual attraction.

So. Maybe she wouldn't make an excuse to avoid helping him tomorrow, as she'd half planned on the walk home. Instead of avoiding him and protecting herself, maybe she would take a chance—another chance!—and show Oliver that while last night had changed some things, it hadn't changed everything. They still liked each other, after all. It was possible that the sex, as spectacular as it had been, had been a mistake, but she refused to write off their burgeoning friendship because they'd made the mistake of falling into bed at a shitty time in both their lives.

She liked him that much. She really did.

It had been a night for revelations, apparently.

Feeling infinitely better, she began her preparations for bed.

CHAPTER ELEVEN

SHE WOKE FROM A DEEP SLEEP with a single, vivid image in her mind's eye—two women standing side by side, one dressed in the sober, neck-to-ankle garb of a hundred years ago, the other in the clothes of today. The first woman was Dr. Mary Clementina De Garis, the second more amorphous and ill defined. It took Mackenzie a moment to understand she was simply a placeholder, a representative of the young women who aspired to be doctors today.

A buzz of excitement fizzed in her belly as she pieced together the fragments her subconscious had revealed overnight.

The old and the new. The trailblazer and the women who followed in her footsteps. An engaging, challenging examination of past and present culture.

She would find a young female medical student. Maybe even more than one. And she would follow them as they completed their training. She would contrast their experiences with those of Mary De Garis, who had had to fight every step of the way for acceptance and credibility. Mackenzie would look at the milestones for women in medicine. She would examine female medical achievements.

Her gut told her it was a good idea. It made her old project less of a dry examination of a woman's life and more an exploration of women's roles in Australian society over the span of a century. It gave Mary De Garis's life context, shining a light on her achievements by showing how much things had changed.

Perhaps most importantly, it made Mackenzie's passion project commercially viable because suddenly she had a hook. She threw the covers back and almost bounded out of bed, she was so energized by her re-visioning of her old project. Shoving her feet into slippers, she made her way to the study, stopping only to let Smitty out for his morning ablutions.

She dragged open the filing cabinet, searching through the neatly labeled files there for the backup she'd made of her old computer hard drive several years ago. The De Garis project had been with her so long it had been stored on floppy discs before she'd converted it to CD a few years ago. At the time, she'd felt foolish, preserving old research and ideas that she'd long since given up on. Now she blew a kiss to Past Mackenzie. She'd had good instincts, it turned out.

The file wasn't there, and she turned to the cupboard and considered the half-a-dozen file boxes stacked in there. She'd brought all this stuff to the beach house when the storage locker in the underground garage beneath her apartment had reached the overflowing stage. There were many more boxes like this in Melbourne, and it was only when she'd rifled through those stacked in the cupboard that she accepted that the De Garis file must be among them. Damn.

She would have to make a trip up to Melbourne to retrieve them. Not the end of the world, but she dearly wanted to look over what she had in order to start planning her first steps forward with this new project, and she wanted to do it *now.* She grinned, wiping her dusty hands on her pajama pants. It had been a long time since she'd felt this stimulated and excited about a creative project. Wait until she told Oliver that his back-to-basics songwriting technique had borne fruit.

The thought gave her pause, but only for a second. Last night had been awesome and awkward in equal measures but she'd already decided she could live with that. She was standing by the decision she'd made in the small hours: Oliver was a friend worth having, even without benefits.

She fed Smitty and herself and dressed in cleaning-out-the-shed clothes—yoga pants, a sweater and sneakers—and headed next door, Smitty leading the way double-time. If she was going to be spending hours in Oliver's yard, there was no reason Smitty should miss out on some quality time with his favorite girl.

She was approaching Oliver's porch when she heard the mellow tones of an acoustic guitar. Oliver, of course, playing a lovely, rolling melody that made her want to hum along. Her steps slowed as he began to sing in a pleasing, slightly raspy baritone.

"Left town 'cause of her, couldn't leave me behind. Drove through the country, regret on my tail. Looking for a place to work out why we failed..."

The song washed over her, sad and hopeful in equal measures. She knew, absolutely, that this was an original composition, something he was still creating. She had to blink away tears when he reached the chorus.

"I thought she was the best of me, now I know she set me free. I'd rather look life in the eye than live a quiet suburban lie. It's true what the wise men say, tomorrow is another day. Another day, yeah...another day..."

She waited until the guitar fell silent before climbing the steps. She knocked, and a few seconds later the door swung open. Oliver stood there in his jeans and sweater, his face bristly with stubble, his hair bed-messy, his guitar in one hand.

"Morning," she said.

She knew from the expression on his face that he'd guessed she'd heard him playing. She smiled.

"I like it, for what it's worth. Reminds me of Ben Harper."

His eyes were very steady on hers. "I didn't think I'd see you today. You're a brave woman."

"Not that brave, really. Are Smitty and I too early? We can go for a walk and come back."

"I just need to grab a shower. If you don't mind waiting..."

She had a flash of him standing naked beneath the shower spray and had to blink a couple times to get rid of it. That kind of thing wasn't going to help anyone with anything.

"Sure. I can wait. No big deal."

He stood aside to allow her to enter before leading her into the living room. The fire glowed in the grate, a fine layer of ash on the logs, and a crumb-strewn plate and coffee mug rested on the small side table.

"Been up for a while," Oliver said, obviously interpreting her expression.

A laptop was open on the sofa, a complicated-looking software program filling the screen. She knew enough from sitting in on sound mixes that she was looking at a recording program.

"Oh, good, you got it down," she said without thinking.

His smile was endearingly shy. "Yeah. Very roughly." He shrugged.

"I mentioned it was good, right? Thoughtful and a bit sad but mostly optimistic."

He stared at her for a long beat, a muscle in his jaw flickering as though he was working to contain strong emotion.

"Last night meant something to me, Mackenzie. I want you to know that." His voice was all gravel and bass.

Any lingering misgivings she'd been hanging on to dissolved. How could she regret having been naked with this man?

"Me, too."

His smile broadened. Maybe it was her imagination—her ego—but he looked relieved.

"I'll go grab that shower."

"I'll be waiting."

"Help yourself to toast or coffee. Sorry, tea." He started toward the kitchen, as though he was going to make her a cup himself.

"Shoo. I can make myself tea. You go make yourself presentable, you reprobate."

He glanced down at himself, one hand rubbing his bristly jaw.

"Fair enough."

He left the room, Strudel following him into the hall but stopping short of trailing him to the bathroom. Clearly the poor girl was torn between two loyalties—the man who fed her and the boy dog who captured her attention.

"I know which way I'd be leaning, Strudel," Mackenzie said as she wandered into the kitchen and made herself tea. She looked out over the lawn as she drank it, pretending that her mind was not alive with images of Oliver naked in the shower.

Water cascading down the strong column of his spine. Bouncing off his firm, muscular ass. Sleeking down his flat belly.

She tipped the dregs of her tea down the drain. There was no point getting herself all worked up over something that wouldn't happen again. Because that was what the little conversation in the living room had been about—Oliver drawing a line under what had happened politely but firmly, and her agreeing.

Her newly reawakened libido might regret the decision, but her head and heart didn't. Who in their right mind set themselves up for almost certain disaster? Not her. She had enough good sense to dodge that bullet.

The shower stopped with a groan of the pipes. Oliver would be out any minute now. Composing herself, she went into the living room to wait for him.

OLIVER SHRUGGED INTO a T-shirt and topped it with a sweater before pulling on jeans, very aware that Mackenzie was waiting for him. He hadn't expected to see her today. Not after last night. He wouldn't have blamed her for giving him a wide berth, either. Yet she'd still turned up, ready to fulfill her part of their bargain.

If he didn't like her a hell of a lot already, her classy, honest actions this morning would have sealed the deal.

He took his boots into the living room to put them on and found Mackenzie ministering to both dogs, who were offering her their bellies for rubbing.

"Got you hard at work, I see," he said as he donned the boots.

"No rest for the wicked. Hadn't you heard that?"

"I'd heard a rumor." He stood and gave her an assessing look. "Do you feel okay after yesterday's workout? Because we don't have to do this today if you're not up to it."

She blinked a couple of times and it hit him suddenly how he must have sounded—as though he was checking if she was able to function normally after a few hours in his bed.

"Because of the yard work," he quickly tacked on. "I meant because of the yard work. Obviously."

She bit her lip, then gave up trying to hide her smile. "I'm okay, on both counts. But thanks for asking."

His face burned with embarrassment. Which served him right for being such a yokel.

"Maybe we should get started before I have to have my foot surgically removed from my mouth," he said, heading for the door.

They walked through the overgrown grass to the shed, the dogs disappearing into the thicker vegetation toward the rear of the lot.

Mackenzie stood to one side as he wrangled with the rusty bolt before opening the door wide. She joined him on the step to inspect the contents.

"Okay. That's a lot of old furniture," she said.

"It is. Feel free to back out if you're freaking out right now."

She gave him a look. "What do you think I am, some kind of wimp?" She pushed up her sleeves. "How do you want to do this?"

He couldn't help grinning. She was small but feisty. A true force to be reckoned with.

"Bet you gave those doctors hell when you were in hospital."

"I was a model patient—once we'd all agreed that no one was going to tell me what I couldn't do."

"Poor bastards."

She punched him in the arm. "You're supposed to be on my side."

He fought the urge to sling his arm around her and drop a kiss onto her lips.

"I am."

She made a noise to signal she wasn't so sure, but he knew she wasn't really pissed. Just as he knew what her body would have felt like against his if he'd given in to the urge to kiss her.

It occurred to him belatedly that maybe there were worse

things than Mackenzie avoiding him after what had happened between them—like spending quality time with her and having to keep his distance now that he knew exactly how soft her mouth was and how round and perky her breasts were and how silken and tight she was—

He turned away, aware that he was already half-hard. He'd made his decision where Mackenzie was concerned. He wasn't messing up her life with his own confusion. No matter how attractive he found her.

Between them they decided to carry each piece of furniture onto the lawn so they could assess and photograph it for potential listing on eBay or valuation by a dealer. He did everything he could to minimize Mackenzie's workload, assigning her the task of cataloging and photographing their finds, but she insisted on helping him shift the bulkier items.

"You're pretty strong for a girl," he observed as they set down a chunky Edwardian-era card table. Especially for a girl who had been put back together again by surgeons.

"Rehab, baby." She pulled up her sleeve and flexed her biceps for him. It was noticeable and he gave an appreciative whistle.

"Few more inches, you might actually be dangerous," he said.

"I'm dangerous now. You just don't know it." She threw him a challenging look as she walked toward the shed.

He had to agree with her—she *was* dangerous. To his peace of mind, as well as his resolve. The tight bounce of her bottom, the gleam in her eye. The arch of her slim neck, the tilt to her mouth.

She was sexy and smart and real, and a part of him wanted to snatch what she offered—pleasure and desire and distraction and laughter—and hang on for grim life.

But he hadn't forgotten that sense of panic from last

night. The feeling that he'd grabbed a tiger by the tail. Until he had his head on straight, he had no business even looking sideways at Mackenzie.

They worked until midday, talking and laughing, sharing stories from their working lives and childhoods. He learned that she'd tortured her brother when they were younger by throwing her least favorite vegetables under his chair at the dining-room table when their parents weren't looking, letting him take the blame for the failure to eat. He told her about the time he and Brent wrote a stream of outraged letters to the purveyors of X-ray glasses, complaining that despite having handed over a significant sum of pocket money, they were unable to see through walls.

At lunchtime, Oliver and Mackenzie drove into town to buy sandwiches and vanilla cakes from the local sweetshop. Mackenzie insisted she was happy to keep working into the afternoon, pointing out they were very close to finishing. She was right—the clock hit two as they photographed the last piece and returned it to the shed.

"I think I owe you dinner as well as lunch," he said as they walked to the house.

"What you owe me is three more hours on the end of a shovel. Don't think I wasn't keeping track."

He noticed that she hadn't responded to his invitation, which he chose to interpret as a "thanks, but no thanks." Probably a good decision, all things considered.

"Someone's going to have a great time restoring all that furniture," Mackenzie said as they entered the kitchen.

"Not me, thank God. I'll be more than happy to see the back of it."

"Amen."

Mackenzie busied herself at the sink, washing her dusty hands and forearms.

"I'll grab you a towel," he said, heading for the bathroom.

She was washing the last of the soap off as he returned, and she glanced toward the doorway expectantly. There was a smudge on her nose and a cobweb in her hair. At some point she'd stripped off her sweater to reveal a slim-fitting black T-shirt, and the soft fabric outlined her breasts and belly faithfully. Because he wanted to touch her so badly it hurt, he fell back on the devices of adolescence, tossing the towel at her so swiftly and forcefully it hit her in the chest before she could intercept it.

"Hey!"

"Sorry."

"Like hell."

He grinned. She dried her hands, shaking her head.

"You didn't really expect me to take that sort of unprovoked attack lying down, did you?" she asked, her head tilted to one side, her eyes bright.

"It was an accident. Bad timing." He kept his expression deadpan.

"Yeah? Wait till you see my timing with a towel flick."

She held the towel by one corner and twisted her hand in the air, coiling the towel on itself.

"I wouldn't do that if I were you," he warned her.

"Lucky you're not me, then."

She flicked the towel at him, but he was ready for her, his hand flashing out to grab the end before it could connect. She gave a war cry, securing her grip on her portion, refusing to relinquish her weapon as he tried to tug it free. He laughed and began hauling her toward him instead, using the towel to reel her in.

"I warned you," he told her.

Despite her laughing efforts to dig her heels in, she was soon within reach.

"Give up yet?" he asked.

"Do *you* give up?"

"Never."

He gave one last, hard yank, jerking her forward a final step so that there was less than a foot separating them.

"Now what do you say?" he asked, looking into her eyes.

"That you play dirty."

"Do I?"

His gaze drifted over her face—her neatly arched eyebrows, her upturned nose, the delicate shape of her jaw. It came to rest on her mouth, where it had wanted to be all along.

She was smiling, and the urge to lean forward and taste her happiness was like a hand in the middle of his back, pushing him forward. He didn't move, and the smile slowly faded from her lips. "I guess this is going to keep happening, huh?" she said.

He recognized it as a fundamental truth. Immutable. As long as there was air in his lungs, he would be attracted to Mackenzie, and he would want to kiss her and touch her and get naked with her. It was as simple and basic as that.

"I'm having a hard time remembering why I shouldn't kiss you again," he said.

"If it helps any, I'm all for it. I'd even go so far as to say that I am an enthusiastic advocate of more kissing. Not to mention any ancillary benefits that might flow on from said activity."

How was he supposed to resist this woman? Especially when he didn't even want to try.

His gaze found her mouth again. She tilted her face toward him. He leaned forward, and so did she. She tasted clean and good and sweet and he angled his head, wanting more. The towel fell to the ground between them as they stepped into each other's arms. He made a satisfied noise as her breasts pressed against his chest and his hand slid onto the curve of her backside.

It wasn't long before kissing wasn't enough. He slipped his hands beneath her top, filling his palms with her breasts. Mackenzie freed the stud on his jeans and made short work of his fly. He groaned against her mouth as she found him, her hand gripping his erection firmly before stroking up and down his shaft. Only the knowledge that he didn't have any condoms stopped him from throwing her to the floor there and then. That, and the awareness of her physical limitations. He settled for sliding a hand past the waistband of her yoga pants. His fingers glided over soft skin and silken hair before sliding into wet heat. She made an inarticulate noise, her hips curling forward to welcome his touch. He found her with his thumb, small and perfect and hard for him, and started teasing her.

She clenched her hand around his erection as she strained toward him. She broke their kiss, pressing her cheek to his, her body taut as a bowstring as she panted with need. He slipped a finger inside her and she groaned, the sound vibrating through her body and into his, an expression of pure need. He could feel how close she was and he backed her against the table and bent his head to her breasts, suckling her through the thin fabric of her T-shirt.

Her hand slipped from his pants to grasp his hip, her other grasping his shoulder. Her whole body trembled as she hovered on the edge of release.

"Come on, baby," he urged her.

Her breath came out in a warm rush as she climaxed, her fingers biting into his shoulder and hip as she lost herself in pleasure. After long seconds, her grip loosened. He drew back enough to see her face.

Her eyes were tightly closed, her lips rosy from his kisses. She was breathing hard, her chest rising and falling. Slowly she opened her eyes.

Something hard and irrevocable hit him in the chest as

he looked into her eyes. He had the odd sense that for a split second, the world stopped. There was only him and her and the sweetness of her climax and the hazy pleasure in her eyes and the need to be inside her....

Then she closed her eyes again and let her head fall forward against his chest.

"This is crazy," she said, so quietly he almost didn't hear her.

It was. They'd only just met. They lived in different parts of the country. They had too much going on in both their lives.

But when he was with her, he wanted to touch her. He wanted to make her shudder with need, and he wanted to make her laugh, and he wanted to be challenged by her, and he wanted to ask questions until he knew all there was to know about her.

Maybe it wasn't smart. Maybe it wasn't even rational or remotely explainable. All he knew was that he'd spent nearly twenty-four hours freaking out over something that had made sense to him only when he set his mouth against hers again.

This was happening, whether they liked it or not. And right this second, it felt unstoppable and absolutely inevitable.

He leaned forward and laid his cheek against hers. Closing his eyes, he inhaled the scent of her perfume and shampoo and the warmth of her skin.

"I don't know about you, but crazy is feeling pretty bloody good right now."

He felt rather than saw her smile. Easing away, she dug her hand into a hidden pocket in her pants and pulled out a small foil pack, pressing it into his hand.

"Just in case," she said with a butter-wouldn't-melt smile.

"Have I mentioned I love how organized you are?"

She took his hand and towed him toward the door. "Tell me later."

She didn't say anything more as she led him to the bedroom. The moment they got there, he pulled his sweater over his head, then his T-shirt. Her gaze went to his chest before dropping to his crotch. He savored the gleam in her eye. She wanted—needed—this as much as he did.

He pushed his jeans down, stepped out of them. Mackenzie started to undress, quickly catching up to him as she flung her yoga pants to one side and stripped off her top. She was wearing plain cotton bikini panties with an equally plain bra and she slipped both off as he pulled the sheets back. They met in the middle of the bed, legs tangling.

They kissed and stroked and teased each other until Mackenzie pushed him onto his back and straddled his hips. Her sex pressed against his erection and she gazed at him, her mouth slightly open, her eyes smoky with desire. He cupped her breasts, flicking her already-tight nipples with his thumbs. She arched her back, pushing her breasts more firmly into his hands.

She started to move, stroking her sex along his erection, hands planted either side of his shoulders. He could feel how wet she was and how hard he was and he got even harder. She closed her eyes, an intent expression on her face as she concentrated on the slide of their bodies.

After a minute she opened her eyes again. She locked gazes with him before collecting the condom from where he'd left it on the bedside table. She tore the packet open with her teeth before stroking it onto his erection with firm, sure hands. Then she rose to her knees and took him in hand. His hands found her hips as she sank onto him.

"Mackenzie."

She started to move and it was all he could do to stop

himself from coming on the spot, she was so damned hot and tight and wet.

Mackenzie rode him with her eyes closed and her head tilted back. Her breasts rose and fell, rose and fell as her movements became increasingly urgent. He watched her through half-closed eyes, his hands gliding over the warm silk of her skin, fighting the growing need to grab her hips and thrust into her soft, yielding warmth.

Finally it was too much for him and he gave in to instinct, driving himself into her, need an urgent tattoo in his blood. She gave a small, inarticulate cry, her head dropping forward, her hands clutching at his shoulders. He felt her pulse around him…and was gone.

For long seconds there was nothing but the pleasure of release, then Mackenzie slid off him and dropped to the pillow next to him. He grabbed a tissue from the box beside the bed and took care of the condom before pulling up the covers and stretching out an arm. Mackenzie took the cue to rest her head on his shoulder, curling her body into his side.

He closed his eyes and let himself enjoy the perfect simplicity of the moment. Her body warm from the exertions of their lovemaking. The *thud-thud* of her heart close to his own. The hush of her breath across his chest.

A feeling welled inside him, almost painful in its piercing sweetness. It took him a moment to recognize it as happiness.

Mackenzie rose onto one elbow, her blue gaze traveling over his shoulders and chest before scanning his face. She reached out and ran her fingers across his chin.

"Don't think it to death, okay? We've both had a shitty time. Let's just enjoy some good stuff for a change."

There was only one possible response to her suggestion.

"Okay."

She ran her fingers across his chin again, her gaze following the action.

"Your whiskers are like glitter. Gold and bronze and chestnut."

"Glittery whiskers. I'll add that to my Facebook profile."

She smiled faintly. The sheet slipped off her shoulder, exposing her upper arm and the curve of her breast.

"You're the first man I've slept with who has longer hair than me, you know that?"

"Is that a fact?" He tugged on her fringe.

"I used to have long hair. Before the accident." She said it wistfully.

"It suits you short."

"Does it?" She didn't sound convinced. "Every time I look in the mirror I feel like I'm looking at a little boy."

"Trust me, there's nothing boyish about you." His gaze shifted to the curve of her breast.

"You talking about these little ladies?" she said, glancing at her chest.

"I believe I was. Among other things."

She pushed herself up so that she was kneeling beside him. "You like them, huh?"

The covers pooled around her waist as she slid her hands onto her breasts, plumping them for him.

"I do. Quite a bit, actually."

"You don't think they're too small?" She considered her breasts and almost absently ran her thumbs over her nipples.

He grinned, well aware of what she was doing but more than happy to go along for the ride.

"I think they're about right. They say more than a handful is a waste."

"But you have pretty big hands." She pinched her nipples this time and he watched as they hardened into pale pink peaks.

He was getting hard again. Such was her power over him.

"Your breasts fit perfectly into the palm of my hand." He demonstrated, cupping her warm flesh.

"Huh. I guess they do."

There was a mischievous glint in her eye as she noted the tent his erection made beneath the covers.

"You're a vixen. A wanton, lascivious vixen," he said.

"I think you're supposed to sound more disgusted when you call me names like that."

"Are you kidding me? Wanton, lascivious vixens are my favorites."

She slid her hand beneath the covers and wrapped her fingers around his erection. "I can feel that."

She'd only brought the one "just in case" condom, so they drove each other crazy with their hands and mouths instead, taking their time, learning each other's sweet spots. Afterward, she sprawled across his chest, limp and sated, her cheeks a rosy-pink.

"Wake me if I get too heavy," she murmured as she drifted into sleep.

He was on the verge of sleep himself, but he smiled as he thought about the way she'd teased him, the sass of her, the way she made him feel.

This was good. He knew it in his bones. It might be too soon, he might be too messed up, but it was happening and he wasn't about to throw it away. As Mackenzie had said, they'd had enough shit in their lives. Why shouldn't they enjoy some good stuff for as long as it lasted?

The voice at the back of his head wanted to pick a fight with his logic, but he didn't want to listen. Right now, he was happy, and it felt good. It seemed to him that only an idiot would question that.

CHAPTER TWELVE

MACKENZIE WOKE ALL AT ONCE, aware that something was wrong. It took a moment to work out that it was because she wasn't in her own bed. Again.

So much for her "dodging a bullet" game plan.

Tentative, she reached toward the other side of the bed and found a warm, solid back. Oliver hadn't retreated to the kitchen this time, then.

Or, he hadn't retreated *yet.*

The thought made her belly tight. Granted, they'd agreed that they would accept this for what it was—whatever that may be or may become. Still, she didn't want to feel like an unwanted guest twice in as many nights. If Oliver felt the need to create some space for himself again, it would be kinder to both of them if she simply offered it to him. She should slip from the bed and quietly get dressed and leave as though it was her choice.

She didn't move. She told herself it was because the bed was warm and the night was cold, but she knew it was a lie.

She didn't want to leave. Didn't want to walk away from the way Oliver made her feel.

Beautiful. Sexy. Wanton.

Not once in any of their encounters had he said or done anything or indicated in any other way that her scars even registered on his radar. She knew that couldn't be true, but she was everlastingly grateful for his low-key acceptance. Unless he was the best actor she'd ever met, the only conclusion she could draw was that her scars and the limitations of her body simply didn't matter to him. He wanted her, scars, dodgy hip and all. On top of all his other charms and attractions, it was pretty heady stuff.

She weighed the demands of her still-fragile vanity against her heartfelt desire to avoid a repetition of last night's debacle. It was a titanic struggle, but after a tense few minutes her pride won out.

Moving quietly, she slid to the edge of the bed. She stood, blinking in the dim light, trying to work out which of the dark shapes on the floor were her clothes. She bent to pick up the first indeterminate shape and quickly worked out that it was her yoga pants. She did a slow circuit of the bed, adding items of clothing to her haul as she identified them. She was on Oliver's side, bending to pick up her bra when a large, warm hand wrapped around the back of her thigh. She gave a small start and nearly dropped her bundle.

"What are you doing?" Oliver asked, his voice a husky murmur in the dark.

"Getting dressed so I can go home."

There was a small silence, then he curled his hand more fully around her thigh and tugged her backward.

"Come back to bed."

She hesitated, and he tugged on her leg again.

"Come back to bed and I'll give you a foot rub."

She smiled, even though she was pretty sure he couldn't see it in the dark. "How do you know I like having my feet rubbed?"

"A good guess."

She let her clothes fall to the floor and allowed him to pull her onto the mattress, shaping her body to match his as he made room for her on his side of the bed. She tried not to read too much into his actions beyond the fact that he wasn't ready for her to go home yet.

He smoothed a hand down her back, his fingers stopping here and there to knead the small muscles either side of her spine. "Tell me about Mary De Garis," he asked idly.

She was so surprised by his request she sat up to stare at him, even though she could only see the outline of his head against the pillow.

"What's wrong?" he asked.

"I went searching for my De Garis project files this morning. Talking about it with you yesterday gave me an idea for a new take on it. A sort of modern twist to make it more relevant."

"Ah. That must be why I'm getting such strong Mary De Garis vibrations off you."

She nudged him with her elbow, amused despite herself. "Do not pretend you're suddenly psychic."

"I could be."

"And I'm Zsa Zsa Gabor." She settled in again. "Why?"

"Why what?"

"Why do you want to know about her?"

He turned his head to look at her. "Because you said she was your passion project."

He said it as though it should be the most obvious thing in the world that what interested her naturally interested him. But she'd been married to a man who put his own needs and wants first, second and third. It took her a moment to get her head around the idea that Oliver was prepared to invest his time and energy in something simply because she was fascinated by it.

In that second it hit her that she was navigating very shaky, dangerous ground with this man. He was so lovely and sexy and sweet, it would be very, very easy to slip from liking and lusting into some far more life-changing emotion, despite all the little warnings she kept issuing herself along the way.

"I'll get you started. Mary De Garis was a woman, and she wanted to be a doctor…." he said encouragingly.

It was on the tip of her tongue to tell him he didn't really want to know, that he wasn't really interested. That was how well her ex-husband had trained her. She caught herself, however, and decided to take Oliver at his word.

"Okay. She was born in 1881 in Charlton, and she was one of the first thirty-five women to graduate from medicine at Melbourne University…."

She sketched Mary's life for him in broad strokes, answering his questions, filling in details when he wanted more information. When she'd finished he wanted to hear about her new idea, so she told him about that, too, this morning's excitement bubbling up inside her again.

"How long will it take you to make it?" Oliver asked.

"To do it properly, probably two years. Maybe three, so we can get a true sense of the women's journeys through med school. These kinds of documentaries are long-haul, big-commitment projects."

"Well, have at it. The sooner you get started, the sooner you'll be giving your acceptance speech. 'I'd like to thank the Academy for recognizing this film….'"

"Can I have a kilo of your faith in me, delivered fresh to my door every morning, please?"

"What's wrong? Don't think you can go the distance?"

She knew he was playing devil's advocate, deliberately goading her, so she didn't bother rising to the bait. "There's no money in it, for starters. I'd be living on the smell of an oily rag. And if I ever want to jump back into drama production I'll have to start kissing ass at the bottom of the ladder all over again."

"How much money do you need?"

She thought about her lifestyle, about her apartment and the beach house and her European car. She'd been paid well in her career—of course, she'd earned every penny—and everything she owned was hers free and clear. If she wanted to, she could live frugally without sacrificing much. After all, there was only her and Mr. Smith to provide for.

"Correct answer," Oliver said very softly, and she knew that he'd guessed what she was doing in the privacy of her own head.

She rolled onto her belly and rested her chin on her folded hands, contemplating his profile.

"How did you get so wise?" she asked quietly.

"Am I wise? I don't feel it, I can tell you. I only know that life is short and time passes anyway, so you might as well do something you believe in as something you don't."

"Does that mean you're going to do something with that song you recorded this morning?" she asked.

It took him a moment to answer. "Maybe. I need to see if there's more where that came from first."

"Then?"

"Maybe I'll record an album. Stick it up on the internet to see if anyone wants to listen to the midlife-crisis ramblings of a nineties pop star."

"Me, me, pick me," she said, holding her hand in the air like a child in class. Inside, she was deeply pleased to hear that he'd been doing a little stargazing of his own. It was good to move forward. Good to dream.

He started to say something, only to be interrupted by the ferocious growl of her stomach.

"Wow," he said.

"Lunch was a while ago."

"It was."

"And being on top is strenuous work."

"Tell mc about it."

"Do you have anything to eat?"

"A couple of pieces of slightly stale bread?"

"That's not going to cut it."

He slipped an arm beneath her, encouraging her to roll on top of him. "I had a feeling you were going to say that. We could send the dogs out for pizza."

She settled on top of him, loving the feel of his hair-roughened legs against hers. "There's a reason why dial-a-dog pizza didn't take off, you know. The dogs always eat it before it gets home."

She kissed him again, then rolled off him and threw back the covers.

She heard the rustle of sheets as he leaned across and flicked the bedside light on. "Where are you going?"

"To my place, where there is food in abundance."

"Huh."

She glanced at him over her shoulder as she began collecting her clothes again.

"You're invited, in case you were wondering."

"Why didn't you say so?" he said, rising with flattering alacrity.

They dressed hurriedly and gathered the dogs, then raced next door where she turned the heating up high before making them scrambled eggs and ham on toast. Later, they showered together, then Oliver made good use of the stash of condoms in her bedside drawer.

Afterward, she kept waiting for him to make noises about returning to his place, but he seemed content where he was, taking up more than his fair share of her bed, his big body sprawling across the mattress.

Gradually it sank in that he wasn't going anywhere. She knew she should be alarmed by the notion—or at the very least wary—but she wasn't. She was, simply, glad.

"IT'S THAT ONE. Number sixty-five," Mackenzie directed.

Oliver turned into the spacious parking spot, stopping

his wagon in front of a large storage cage that looked as though it was filled to the brim with boxes.

"Tell me that's not yours," he said, even though he already knew it was. This was the allocated parking spot for her apartment, and it made sense for the locker to be hers, too.

"Don't be a chicken. It's perfectly manageable."

Her tone was serious, but her eyes were laughing with him. It had been a week since they'd cleared out his shed, a week full to the brim of Mackenzie, and he'd had enough of her to know he could never have enough.

She was no walk in the park. She had a temper, and she was impatient. She loved a good debate, and she was competitive, as he'd discovered to his detriment when they played chess last night.

She was also incredibly smart and sharp, and she knew how to laugh at herself and the world, and she was strong, with an inner resilience he was slightly in awe of. He found her face captivating and her small body more so, and when they were in bed—or the living room, or the kitchen, or the shower—he gained enormous pleasure from making her crazy.

In short, he was hooked. And despite his initial misgivings, it didn't feel like a bad place to be. It felt *right.* As though it was meant to be.

"It's probably worth checking the apartment first," Mackenzie said as she opened the car door. "There's another filing cabinet in my home office."

"You have a lot of offices," he said as he exited the car.

"That's because I used to work a lot. Early starts. Late finishes. There's always more to do on a TV production. Auditions to watch, rushes to assess, story lines and scripts to read over. *Time and Again* is pooh-poohed by some of the more high-brow one-hour dramas, but we produce the equivalent of a feature film *every week.* Those are no small apples."

"No, they are not," he said, nodding, his face serious to let her know he understood the import of what she was saying.

She laughed. "Did I just have a too-many-coffees moment?"

"Not at all. Please, tell me about your plans for world domination."

She rounded the car and grabbed a fistful of his sweater, pulling him close and kissing him.

"The only thing I plan to dominate around here is you. If you'll let me."

"Consider this my white flag," he said, pulling her into his arms.

He kissed her more thoroughly, his hands slipping beneath her coat. He loved her breasts and he palmed them, teasing her nipples through the thin wool of her top. She gave a small moan, her hips pressing forward.

The sound of a car starting had her stepping back. She gazed up at him, her eyes cloudy with need.

"How do you keep doing that to me?" she asked.

"You started it."

He was only half-joking. She had only to look at him in a certain speculative way and he could feel himself growing hard.

"Let's go upstairs," she said, throwing him just such a look.

He smiled to himself and beeped the car locked, following her to the elevator. She swiped her security pass through the card reader to the right of the control panel, then punched the button for her floor.

The lift transported them smoothly, the doors opening seconds later to reveal plush charcoal carpet and a discreetly lit corridor. He knew enough about Melbourne to understand that South Yarra was a very desirable suburb, situated as it was a stone's throw from the city center, and he'd already guessed from the exterior of Mackenzie's building that this was a classy, glossy, expensive place.

A funny little tickle of something he couldn't quite name itched behind his breastbone as she led him to a shiny black door. She unlocked it, and he followed her into a small foyer that led into a huge, open-plan living and dining area. He took in the sculptural modern furniture, the pieces of art, the bold colors and, most importantly, the view—a no-holds-barred, untrammeled panorama of the Royal Botanic Gardens, lush and green and beautiful—and admitted to himself that he was more than a little intimidated. He'd never doubted for a second that Mackenzie was good at what she did, but this apartment was something else.

"You want something to drink? There's no milk, but I could make you a black coffee and there should be some mineral water." She entered the kitchen, a severely modern creation in black granite and stainless steel that opened onto the living area.

"I'm fine, thanks."

He crossed to the freestanding wall unit that created a screen between the living and dining sections of the room. It was filled with books, their spines a kaleidoscope of colors. He pretended to scan them as he absorbed the fact that it was likely Mackenzie could buy and sell him twice over. He caught himself doing a mental tally of his net worth—the house, his car, his investments, the royalties from the band, his share of the studio and his aunt's place—and gave himself a mental slap.

So what if Mackenzie had more money in the bank than he did? It didn't change who she was or who he was. In fact, her success was very much a part of who she was. Integral, even.

His gaze ran over a bold, abstract painting on the wall and it occurred to him that one of the reasons he was feeling so disconcerted was that this place was nothing like Mackenzie's beach house. This apartment was all hard edges and bright colors, a sophisticated inner-city pad. The beach house had crinkly linen couches and soft, neutral colors and the warmth of wooden floors. He'd met Mackenzie there, grown to know and like and admire her there, but this place made him feel as though he didn't know her at all. Or, at least, that he only knew a part of her.

"Wow. I used to drink a lot of coffee."

He glanced to where Mackenzie stood in front of a floor-to-ceiling pantry. Half-a-dozen glossy black blocks of vacuum-sealed coffee beans marched along the top shelf.

"The working-life equivalent of Dutch courage, right?" he said.

She nodded, but she was frowning. He continued to watch her as she opened the fridge to assess the contents. He could see bottles of Diet Coke and a few jars of olives, as well as what looked like either vodka or gin.

"I used to drink a lot of Coke, too. And martinis, apparently."

She sounded as though this was news to her. As though she was inspecting some other Mackenzie's apartment.

"When was the last time you were here?" he asked.

"Nearly four months ago. I stayed here for a week after I got out of rehab, then I moved to the beach house. So I guess it's been nearly a year since I've lived here, really. Although my cleaner has been giving it the once-over every month for me."

She sounded a little bewildered. He followed her as she left the room, traversing a short hallway that opened onto two rooms, the doorways opposite one another. A quick glance to the left told Oliver it was the study, complete with frosted-glass desk and formidable-looking ergonomic chair. He guessed the other room was her bedroom, a guess that was confirmed when he followed Mackenzie inside. A large king-size bed sat beneath a broad, wide canvas made up of gray swirls, the whole set against a severe white wall. The carpet was snowy-white, and one wall was nothing but floor-to-ceiling windows, exposing the room to the world.

It was stunning, but he couldn't help wondering how a person got undressed at night, since there didn't appear to be any curtains or blinds.

"How do you…?" he asked, and she flipped a switch next to the bed.

The windows instantly became an opaque gray, utterly impenetrable.

"Ah. Fancy." And also a little sterile for his tastes.

But, hey, he didn't have to live here.

Mackenzie walked to an opening to the left of the bed. He assumed it was the doorway to an en suite bathroom—there was no way this apartment didn't have an en suite, and he bet his worker's cottage in Newtown that it was dripping with marble—and when he ducked his head around the corner he saw that he was both right and wrong. It did lead to a bathroom, a gleaming white marble space, but it was also a walk-through closet, complete with a shoe display worthy of Imelda Marcos.

Mackenzie was contemplating the shoes, a faintly wistful expression on her face. She selected a pair of deep purple suede shoes with a wicked-looking heel, her hands smoothing over the leather almost reverently.

"Can't wear any of these anymore."

He scanned the shoes again and realized they all sported varying degrees of high heels.

"Maybe that will change," he said, because he understood that women were funny about shoes. It was a thing, and he didn't fully get it, but he knew enough to tread carefully.

"Nope. My orthopedic surgeon told me that if I wanted to end up in a wheelchair by fifty, wearing high heels was a surefire way to get there. I'm pretty sure he wasn't yanking my chain." She put the shoe back, giving it one last pat. "Which means these guys are all going to have to find new homes."

He moved to her side and slipped his arm around her shoulders. She gave him a faint smile.

"Guess we should start looking for that file, huh?"

"There's no rush." They'd already agreed to stay the night in the city. The dogs were keeping each other company back in Flinders, ably assisted by two big, juicy bones and a local dog walker who had agreed to look in on them a few times. There was no schedule to adhere to. Not today, at least, although a part of him was constantly aware that his stay in Flinders was drawing to a close. The freelancer covering his workload at the studio was contracted till the end of July, which meant he had only ten more days before he was due home. He could push to extend the contract, of course, but Rex wouldn't be happy, and Oliver wouldn't blame him. He'd been covering email and bouncing things back and forth with Rex, but there was no denying that his partner had made a huge concession, allowing him this downtime to get his shit together.

All of which meant his time with Mackenzie was drawing to a close. Something neither of them had addressed, even obliquely.

"You know, you don't have to actually help with the search. You could head into the city, check out the sights, leave me to it while I burrow through my boxes."

It was a genuine offer, but he wasn't about to take her up on it. He'd rather be with her, sorting through files, than wandering around the city on his own.

"This may shock you, but I have been to Melbourne before," he said.

"It does shock me. Most Sydney-siders never bother. Which is why they remain safe in the delusion that Sydney is the better city."

He grinned. The Melbourne-Sydney rivalry had been alive and well for centuries, and he wasn't about to fall down in his duty to do his bit to preserve it.

"You're so right. A handful of rattly old tramcars and some graffiti-covered laneways are more than a match for Sydney Harbor, the bridge and the Opera House."

They continued to trade playful insults while they searched through the boxes in the study. When they had no success there, they descended to the parking garage and began a systematic search of the storage locker.

Two hours later, they were both dusty and hungry and speeding rapidly toward being done with searching—and the research still had yet to be located. Oliver was about to suggest they stop for a break when Mackenzie swore and pushed the box she was looking through away from herself.

"You okay?" he asked.

"No. Why on earth did I keep all this stuff? When will I ever need the scripts from a show that isn't even on air anymore? Or a contract from ten years ago? Or my dental X-rays from 2005?"

She looked very cute, sitting there with dust on her cheek, frustration pleating her forehead.

"I think we have to face the fact you're an administrative hoarder. It happens. It's nothing to be ashamed of," he said.

She made a rude noise but her mouth kicked up at the corner. "You think you're so funny, don't you?"

"I don't think, I *know.*"

The strident ring of a phone interrupted whatever response she was about to make and they both reached for their hip pockets at the same time.

"Me," Mackenzie said as she slipped her phone from her jeans. Her smiled faltered as she checked the caller I.D.

"Who is it?"

"My boss. My ex-boss, I mean."

Only yesterday he and Mackenzie had been discussing the fact that even though she knew beyond a doubt that her role had been handed to someone else, she had yet to hear the news from the powers that be at Eureka Productions. A fairly typical scenario in television, Mackenzie had told him. Now, apparently, her boss had found time in his busy schedule to destroy Mackenzie's hopes. Big of him.

"Hi, Gordon." She answered the call, crossing an arm over her body, bracing herself for what she knew she was about to hear.

Oliver moved closer, resting a hand on her shoulder. He could hear someone talking, but couldn't distinguish the words.

"Thanks, but I'd already heard the news," Mackenzie said crisply.

He smiled faintly, understanding that she wasn't letting her boss off the hook easily. Oliver squeezed Mackenzie's shoulder. Good on her for giving the bastard a hard time, even if it wasn't going to change the outcome.

More talk came down the line. Mackenzie shifted her weight impatiently.

"I understand that, Gordon, but I'm won't pretend I'm not disappointed. You know how much I put into that show. I wouldn't even have been on that road if I hadn't been driving to a location shoot."

Gordon spoke again and Mackenzie's body tensed

beneath Oliver's hand. She glanced at him, surprise in her eyes.

What? he mouthed.

"That's very generous of you," Mackenzie said slowly. "You're aware I wouldn't be able to start for at least another three months, right? And I'd need time to build up my stamina to work a full schedule again."

She listened intently, her gaze focused on the wall.

"Well. That's a very attractive offer. I've got to admit, you've caught me on the hop a little. I thought you were going to fob me off with a game show."

There was a new light in Mackenzie's eyes as she wound up the call, promising to get an answer to Gordon in the next few days. She bit her lip as she slipped the phone into her pocket.

"They offered you something else?" Oliver guessed.

"Yeah. A new drama series they're developing. A one hour. They just got the green light from the network." She seemed a little dazed.

"One hour is good, yes?"

"One hour is the next step. What I was hoping for after I'd paid my dues long enough on *Time and Again.*"

"So this is a good thing?"

"I guess." She didn't looked thrilled or excited, though. She looked…confused.

"You don't want it?" Now he was confused. This opportunity seemed perfect for her—or at least the Mackenzie who lived in that stark apartment upstairs.

She sat on the nearest box, her expression troubled. "If you'd asked me a month ago, I'd have leaped at this opportunity and held on with both hands."

He suddenly understood why she was torn. Over the past week, she'd dusted off her old dreams and reinvested in them. She'd written up ideas and phoned industry friends and put out feelers. She was excited about her Mary De Garis project.

"You don't want to give Mary up?"

She pulled a face. "That's stupid, though, right? I mean, Gordon is offering me a gold-plated opportunity. I'd be an idiot to walk away from it. He even said that they know it will take a while for me to get up to speed, but they're happy to do whatever it takes because they want me on this project."

"Pretty flattering."

She laughed, the sound incredulous. "I cannot tell you what I would have done to hear him say those words twelve months ago."

"Could you do both? Mary on the side, this other thing during the week?"

She thought about it for a moment. "Before the accident, yes. No question. Not now, though. I'd struggle with managing full-time work on its own, to be honest. Even if a one-hour drama is less demanding than a soap, it will still get crazy at times." She glanced at her hands where they rested in her lap. "How strange that I even have to think about it."

"You don't have to decide now. He's given you a few days, right?"

"Yeah."

"So, use them. Weigh the pros and cons."

Her eyes wrinkled slightly at the corners as she considered him. "You're being wise again."

"I have my moments."

He dusted his hands on the seat of his jeans and glanced around. "You want to take a break and come back to this or keep plowing on?"

She checked her watch. "Shall we go another half hour then find somewhere to grab lunch?"

"Sure."

He returned to the box he'd been working with, once again flicking through its contents. He'd become so habituated to flicking past things he almost missed the envelope tucked in between two dog-eared folders.

"This disc we're looking for...would it be with an envelope full of pictures of a woman with scary eyebrows?"

Mackenzie was on her knees pawing through another box, but her head snapped up. "That's Mary. You found her!"

She came to his side and inspected the portrait he was holding. The woman in it was very young, her face soft, her hair escaping from it's neat updo.

"Those eyebrows aren't scary. They just haven't been airbrushed or plucked because Dr. De Garis had better things to do with her time." Mackenzie beamed at him. "Thank you."

She slipped her arms around his neck and kissed him. She smelled good, and he encouraged her onto his lap. They kissed long and lazily, enjoying each other. Then Mackenzie shifted against him and instantly kissing wasn't enough. He slid his hand onto her breast, teasing her nipple with his thumb.

"Don't start something you don't plan to finish, Oliver," she murmured against his mouth.

He pinched her nipple firmly enough to make her squirm. "Sorry, did you say something?"

She retaliated by sliding a hand between their bodies, stroking him through his jeans. He let her taunt him for a few minutes before lifting her bodily off his lap.

"Let's go check out your view again," he said.

They kissed in the lift going up, and when they entered Mackenzie's apartment she started to strip as she made her way to the bedroom. Her top, her jeans, her socks and shoes, until she was wearing nothing but silky dark green panties and a balconette bra as she entered her bedroom.

"Do you have any idea what you do to me?" he said, unable to take his eyes off the rounded curves of her backside.

She didn't say a word, simply gave him a Cleopatra smile before unbuttoning his shirt and pulling it off his shoulders. She tackled his belt next, then pushed his jeans down his hips. His erection sprang free, and she sank to her knees to push his jeans the rest of the way down. She looked up at him, a wicked, knowing glint in her eye, and he barely had a chance to appreciate the picture she presented before she pressed a kiss to his belly and inhaled audibly.

"You smell so damn good."

She pulled back, focusing on his erection. He grew harder as she licked her lips, running her fingers through the springy hair at the base of his shaft. She was enjoying teasing him, and he was enjoying being teased.

She wrapped her fingers around his shaft and guided him into her mouth, teasing his head with her tongue before taking all of him. Sensation assailed him—heat and moisture, the knowing flick of her tongue, the firm grip of her hand.

She drew back, licking the length of him.

"You taste good, too. Like clean skin and hot man."

He was beyond speech. It was all he could do to remain standing as she went to town on him, using her hands and lips and tongue to drive him wild. He could feel his climax building, could feel the heat of it in his belly. He wanted to come like this so badly, but he wanted to be inside her, too, giving her as much pleasure as she was giving him.

Even though it almost killed him, he eased away from her. She looked up at him, slightly dazed, her mouth wet and pink.

"Get on the bed."

He didn't need to ask twice. She blinked, the dazed look

leaving her face, then she stood and shimmied out of her panties and bra. She lay down on the bed and lifted her hips obediently when he slipped a pillow beneath her backside. They'd discovered that the small increase in height made it comfortable for her when he was on top, something he'd been more than happy to exploit to the full. He was all for equal opportunity, but sometimes a man just needed to be in charge.

Mackenzie watched as he smoothed on a condom, then welcomed him home when he stretched out on top of her.

As always, the first slide of his body inside hers was transcendent. The rightness of it, the sense of connection. Then the insistent, greedy ache of his arousal required that he start to move, and before long he was lost in the rhythm of it and the tidal pull of desire.

She came quickly, her breath coming in choppy pants, and even though he was close, he held on, his teeth gritted. He kept stroking into her, then he stroked her with his hand, a counterpoint to the thrust of his hips inside her. She came a second time and finally he let himself go, his face pressed into her neck as his body shuddered into hers.

Her body was damp with sweat and he paused to lick between her breasts before withdrawing from her. She gave a small shudder, shifting her hips restlessly.

"Want to hear something funny?" she said as he stood and headed for the bathroom to lose the condom.

"What?"

He padded to the bed, stopping in his tracks when he realized that instead of opaque glass he was staring out at the view.

"I forgot to blank the window," Mackenzie said.

"No shit."

The glass went opaque as he returned to the bed and Mackenzie gave him a sheepish smile.

"Sorry about that."

"Don't worry, I've already thought of a way you can make it up to me."

She smiled drowsily. "Let me guess." She rolled onto one elbow and lazily smoothed a hand over his chest. Her gaze grew thoughtful and he knew without asking that she was thinking about the call from her boss.

"How's that list of pros and cons going?" he asked.

"I think I'm still freaking out. This little voice in the back of my head keeps telling me what a great opportunity it is and asking how I could possibly not take it. But the new ideas I have for Mary are so clear in my mind, I can practically *see* how this documentary is going to look."

"You want to talk it through?"

She considered for a beat, then met his gaze. "Not just yet. I need to process a little more. Get past the shock and my first panicky reaction to grab on to what Gordon's offering, no matter what. Is that okay?" She looked worried, as though she though he would be wounded because she wasn't discussing it with him.

"Of course."

Her expression softened. "Thanks. For everything. For finding Mary and being so great about searching through all those boxes—"

"Not to mention for being so awesome in bed."

She laughed, her breath warming his chest. "I can't believe I haven't mentioned that, like, a million times already. Very remiss of me."

He trailed a hand down her side. "Did I mention I've already thought of a way you can make that up to me?"

She allowed him to draw her closer. "I seem to have a lot of making-up scheduled."

"I know. Better get started."

They fooled around a little, teasing one another. After a

few minutes he nuzzled a kiss into her neck, then lifted his head. “Where did you want to go to dinner?”

“Right. Dinner.” There was an odd note in her voice that caught his attention.

“What’s up?” he asked.

“How would you feel if we didn’t stay the night in the city and we went back to the beach instead?”

“Sure. If that’s what you want.” He wasn’t invested either way, and it would be no hardship to say goodbye to this apartment.

Her gaze scanned his face, worried. “You really don’t mind? You didn’t have your heart set on a big-city meal and bright lights?”

“Nope.”

She looked relieved. “Good. Because I really don’t want to spend the night in this place.” She glanced at him. “Does that sound nuts?”

She’d surprised him. This was her place, after all. Her primary place of residence. “Why don’t you want to stay?”

“It just doesn’t feel…right. I can’t explain it any better than that. The coffee, the Coke, the shoes. This carpet, that window. I feel as though they belong to another life. To another me.” She made an embarrassed noise. “That really does sound nuts, doesn’t it?”

She was frowning and he reached out to smooth her brow.

“You haven’t lived here for a while, that’s all.”

“I guess. Although, when I look around, I wonder if I ever lived here. I was always so busy working. Those books out in the living room—I’ve probably read about ten percent of them. I think I’ve used the oven only half-a-dozen times. When I bought this place after the divorce, I thought it would be great for dinner parties, but I was always too snowed at work to host any sort of party.”

She sounded bemused, and he was reminded, again, of what a profound impact the accident had had on her life.

"Maybe you can have a dinner party when you move back." He felt an odd pang as he imagined Mackenzie hosting a party in her fabulous apartment at some unknown future time. It was a million miles away from the world they shared together at the beach.

"Yeah, maybe." Her gaze was troubled as she looked at him. She started to say something, then shook her head.

"What?"

"Nothing." She shifted to the edge of the bed. "If we leave now, we should be home in time for dinner."

She stood. He watched as she started to dress, turning away to pull on her jeans. The bumps of her vertebrae looked incredibly fine and fragile as they marched down her back. He wondered what she'd been about to say, and why she'd chosen not to say it.

Something about her apartment or Gordon's job offer, maybe?

Something about him?

Oliver knew he should ask, but he wasn't ready for what she might say if it was the latter. Not yet.

There was still time yet. Ten more days.

Following her lead, he started to get dressed.

CHAPTER THIRTEEN

SMITTY WAS WAITING by the door when they arrived at her cottage. Mackenzie prepared herself for the happy dance, but instead he whined anxiously and trotted up the hallway, glancing over his shoulder to see if she was following him. She realized Strudel was missing and threw Oliver an uncertain glance as he followed her inside.

"Something up?"

"I don't know."

They found the dogs in the living room, Smitty standing over Strudel, his tail down. Strudel glanced at them from beneath her eyebrows but didn't move, the tip of her tail barely twitching in welcome.

"Hey, sweetheart. Are you okay?" Oliver said, crouching to run a hand down her body.

She turned her head to lick his hand briefly before closing her eyes again. It was so removed from her usual buoyant behavior that Mackenzie felt a spike of alarm.

"Maybe the bone didn't agree with her?" she wondered out loud.

She glanced around, looking for it, and spotted a gelatinous mess by the French doors.

"Oh. It looks like she's thrown up."

Oliver followed her gaze, his face creased with worry.

"Has she ever done that before?" she asked.

"Not since she was a puppy. She used to eat the filling

from her toys and then throw it up a few days later. But she hasn't done that for over a year."

Mackenzie joined him by Strudel, patting the dog's silky coat.

"What do you want to do? Take her to the vet?"

"Is there one nearby?"

"I'm not sure. I've been to a clinic in Rosebud a few times, but I don't know if there's anything closer." She checked her watch. It was nearly seven. "But they probably wouldn't be open now, even if there was one nearby."

As though she sensed their dilemma, Strudel pushed herself to her feet and started wagging her tail in earnest, nuzzling her snout into Oliver's hand.

"Okay," he said slowly. The look he gave Mackenzie was baffled.

She shrugged. She had no idea what to do, either. "This is where a basic grasp of English from you two would be really handy," she said to the dogs.

Oliver ran his hands over his dog, pressing on her belly, checking her paws and eyes. Strudel tolerated the inspection happily enough, waiting patiently for it to be over.

"Well, I'm a sound engineer, not a vet, but she seems okay to me."

"She's not quite herself, though, is she?" Mackenzie said.

"No." He scratched under Strudel's chin. "Why don't we keep an eye on her, and if she's still lethargic in the morning, I'll take her to the vet?"

He didn't voice the other option—that her condition might deteriorate even further—but they both knew the possibility was there.

Mackenzie was aware of a low level of anxiety within herself as she made spaghetti for dinner, something she'd like to attribute to concern for Strudel but that she suspected had been present since their arrival at her Melbourne apartment.

It had been unsettling, walking into a space that had felt more like a museum celebrating her former life than her home. The furniture, the food in the cupboards, even the toiletries in the bathroom had looked familiar but strange. She'd always been proud of the decor—she'd paid an interior designer enough to create it for her—but all she could think when she stood in her living room was that the couch looked incredibly uncomfortable and that the sculpture by the window was dangerously sharp.

The whole experience had been jarring. As though she'd spied an old family snapshot and not recognized herself.

Gordon's phone call and subsequent job offer hadn't helped, either. Despite having had several hours to digest what had happened, she was still no closer to making a decision—yet another marker of how everything in her life had shifted since the accident. Home wasn't home anymore, and apparently her ever-present ambition had mellowed.

At least, that was the way it felt right now. But maybe Oliver was right. Maybe she had only to move into her apartment and it would become home again. The same with Gordon's job offer. If she took it, she'd essentially be slipping back into her old life.

It should have been a reassuring thought. It was what she'd been striving for through months of arduous rehab, after all. But it didn't feel reassuring. It felt…empty. Hollow.

They settled in for a quiet night, turning in early after watching half a movie. Mackenzie was aware of Oliver getting up twice in the night to check on Strudel, but both times he returned to bed and assured her everything was fine.

Strudel wasn't interested in her breakfast the next morning, however, sniffing her bowl disinterestedly before returning to the cushion and settling down to sleep again.

"I could defrost some chicken to see if she'll eat that," Mackenzie offered.

"Thanks, but I'm going to take her to the vet," he said.

She would do the same in his shoes. She stayed with Strudel while he went next door to shower and change, patting the schnauzer soothingly.

"You're okay, aren't you, girl?" she crooned.

She hoped she was correct, because she didn't even want to contemplate how horrible it would be if there was something wrong with Strudel.

Oliver was back quickly, his hair wet.

"I'll come with you. Give me a couple of minutes to dress," she said.

"It's okay. I have no idea how long we'll be and there's no need for both of us to waste a day."

If it *was* a waste, of course. Mackenzie fervently hoped it was.

She was tempted to insist, wanting to be there for him, but he seemed impatient to go and she didn't want to overstep the mark. They were only temporary lovers, after all.

"Well, call me the minute you know anything, okay?" she said.

"Give me your number and I'll save it into my phone."

She blinked in surprise at the request. They'd been living in each other's pockets for nearly three weeks now, and yet they hadn't even exchanged phone numbers. It seemed almost unbelievable given the times they lived in.

She pulled her scrambled thoughts together. "It's O-4-3-0—"

"Wait. Damn. My phone's dead."

She walked to the bench and grabbed her phone from her bag.

"Take mine. I'll charge yours while you're gone, and you can call me on your number."

They both had the same phone model, so there would be no issues with her charger fitting his phone.

"You're sure?"

"Of course."

She helped him herd Strudel out to his car, then stood on the front porch with Mr. Smith and waved them off as they reversed into the street.

"Please, Universe, let Strudel be okay," she said, casting her gaze heavenward.

If she wasn't— She didn't want to think about it. Oliver had suffered enough loss and unhappiness in his life recently. He was due some luck.

Tense with worry, she went inside to pace and fret.

OLIVER KEPT ONE eye on the road and the other on the rear-view mirror as he drove, constantly checking to insure Strudel was coping okay. She seemed fine, her tongue lolling as she gazed out the window for a bit before settling down and going to sleep.

He told himself she was probably fine and that he was being a fussy helicopter fur parent, but his gut was still uneasy.

If something was wrong with his dog…

No. He couldn't let himself go there. He'd take this one step at a time, save the freaking out for when it was needed. *If* it was needed.

Mackenzie had drawn him a map to help him find the vet clinic and he found his way there with only one wrong turn—quite the achievement given his navigational handicap. The woman behind the counter gave him a brisk smile when he approached, Strudel padding obediently at his side.

"We need to see a vet. I don't have an appointment, but I think this is an emergency," he told her.

"Okay. Have you been here before?"

"No."

She passed over some forms for him to fill out and told him it would be a fifteen-minute wait. He sat on one of the uncomfortable plastic chairs and filled out the form with one hand, the other resting comfortingly on Strudel's shoulder. She was still just a baby, really, only eighteen months old. Surely there couldn't be anything serious wrong with her?

He'd just handed the clipboard with the form to the receptionist when Mackenzie's phone buzzed in his pocket. He checked the screen, wondering if he should simply let it go through to voice mail. He didn't want to invade her privacy.

Then it occurred to him that it might be her calling him, and that if she was worried about her privacy she wouldn't have lent him her phone.

"Who the hell is Mackenzie and why does she have your phone?" his brother said the moment the call connected.

"Brent. How did you get this number?"

"How do you think I got it? I rang your phone, and *Mackenzie* answered it and gave me this number. Which is *her* phone, apparently."

"If you don't mind me saying so, you're a little excited," Oliver said drily.

"So would you be if you rang me and a strange woman answered the phone."

"Unclench. Mackenzie is my neighbor. Our neighbor, technically, since you own half the house."

"That still doesn't explain why she has your phone."

Oliver sighed. The receptionist was giving him a look to let him know she didn't appreciate being forced to eavesdrop on his conversation. Signaling to her that he'd be outside, he and Strudel exited to the parking lot.

"My phone was dead and I needed to take Strudel to the vet, so Mackenzie offered me hers."

"Mighty generous of her."

"She's a nice person." Oliver could feel his brother burning to ask the obvious but Oliver wasn't about to make it easy for him.

"How old is this Mackenzie person?" Brent asked.

"I don't know for sure. About my age, I'd say."

"Is she married?"

"Nope."

"You're sleeping with her, aren't you?"

"Not really your business, mate."

"I'm going to take that as a yes. Wow. You don't muck around, do you?"

Irritation ate at the edges of Oliver's temper.

"In case you'd forgotten, Edie is the one who screwed up our marriage, not me." Yeah, okay. So there were some vestiges of anger about his marriage hanging about his psyche. And how like his brother to find those buttons and push them. "Was there a reason you called, other than to interrogate me about stuff that has nothing to do with you?"

"You can't tell me you're getting jiggy with some unknown woman four months after your marriage ends and expect me to not have an opinion."

"First, I didn't tell you anything—you guessed and assumed. Second, it's been nearly five months. And I don't need your permission or approval to have a private life."

It came out sounding angrier and more serious than he'd intended and he could feel his brother's surprise radiating down the line.

"Okay. Calm down. I only want to make sure you're not jumping into anything crazy."

Oliver glanced through the glass panel in the clinic door,

willing the vet to call him in so he'd have an ironclad excuse for bailing on this conversation.

"I appreciate the concern, but you need to stop worrying about me, okay? I'm fine. In fact, I'm better than fine. I'm good."

"Guys do weird things when they get divorced, Ollie. Trust me, I've seen it. They buy stuff they can't afford and hook up with women they shouldn't hook up with—"

"Mackenzie isn't like that, okay? She's smart and she's funny and she has the second-coolest dog in the world. So put your smelling salts down, I don't need an intervention."

There was a small pause. "You sound pretty serious about her."

Oliver let his breath hiss out between his teeth. Then he laughed, because it was either that or throw Mackenzie's phone across the parking lot in exasperation.

"Let's get this out of the way. Yes, I am serious about her. She's special. She makes me feel good. I think you'd like her. Happy now?"

"Mate, it's been *four months*."

"Five months, and I'm not turning my back on something good because the numbers are wrong. Mackenzie and I are good together. I know what I'm doing."

"Ollie, listen to me. There is an extremely high likelihood that thanks to what happened with Edie your head is still up your ass in some capacity right now. Anything you get into is going to be swayed by that. There's a reason people have mourning periods, you know. To give themselves time to decompress."

Oliver glared at the road. "Since when did you have a psychology degree?"

"Simply stating the facts, that's all."

"You know what? I need to go."

He should have ended this conversation ages ago. Like

the moment Brent started the I-know-best older-brother routine.

"You know I'm right."

And there it was, right on cue.

"I'll speak to you later, okay?"

"Ollie, don't hang up. Just listen to me, okay? Statistically most guys remarry within a year of getting divorced."

"So?" His brother loved statistics. No wonder he was an accountant.

"So you probably want to be sure that you're jumping into something because you really want it, not because you've gotten comfortable living your life a certain way."

Oliver snorted his disbelief. "Right. I'm so desperate to have a joint bank account and someone leaving the toilet seat down again that I'm going to latch on to the first passing woman."

"Can you honestly say there isn't a part of you trying to replace what Edie took away from you?"

Oliver wanted to reject his brother's words in the same way he'd rejected everything else Brent had said, but he could hear the very real concern in his brother's tone. As much as it galled him to admit it, were Brent and Sandra ever to break up, Oliver would be pretty worried, too, if Brent started waxing poetic about another woman so quickly. As irritating as his brother's fussing was, it came from a good place.

"If you'd met Mackenzie, you'd understand." Oliver thought for a moment, trying to articulate his feelings. "When I'm with her, it feels right, you know? Am I a little freaked out by how fast it's all happened? Yes. But life doesn't work to schedule."

Brent was silent for a long beat. "Does she feel the same?"

The million-dollar question. Oliver squinted into the sun.

"We haven't talked about it."

Another silence. "Okay. It's your life." Brent said it with all the weighted doom of someone handing out a death sentence.

"Stranger things have happened, you know," Oliver said quietly. "Who says that because I wasn't looking for it, this isn't the best thing that's ever happened to me?"

"For your sake, I hope you're right."

Out of the corner of his eye, Oliver saw the vet come out and talk to the receptionist.

"I have to go. Did you need anything?"

"Yeah. I wanted to let you know that Sandra's offered to load all the furniture on eBay so we can sell it off. If you send her the pictures and descriptions, she'll take care of it."

"Great. Tell her thanks from me."

"Okay."

Oliver ended the call and shoved the phone into his pocket. His brother's timing was awesome. As if he didn't have enough on his plate right this second with Strudel being under the weather.

He shortened the dog's lead and reentered the clinic.

"Sorry about that," he told the receptionist.

"You're fine. All taken care of?" she asked.

Her gaze was curious and he wondered how much she'd heard.

"Thanks, yeah."

"The vet will be with you in a minute."

Oliver resumed his seat, signaling for Strudel to sit at his feet.

He felt rattled and off balance after Brent's call. He should have told his brother to pull his head in rather than feed his curiosity. Oliver didn't need to justify himself to anyone.

He picked up one of the magazines piled next to his seat,

then put it down again. Brent's words kept echoing through his head, setting his teeth on edge.

There is an extremely high likelihood that thanks to what happened with Edie your head is still up your ass in some capacity right now.

And: *You probably want to be sure that you're jumping into something because you really want it, not because you've gotten comfortable living your life a certain way.*

He shifted in his seat, forcing himself to consider his brother's words, even though they made him uncomfortable. Was it possible he was simply seeking to replicate what he'd lost? Was he simply one lonely, pathetic half of a whole, looking for another half—*any* other half—now that Edie had revealed their marriage to be a sham?

He was relatively certain the answer was a resounding no. Being married had suited him in many ways, but he hadn't loved being married *that* much. He wasn't lying awake at night missing arguments over the remote control and who left the lid off the toothpaste and whose turn it was to empty the dishwasher. His attraction to Mackenzie was because of who she was, not some sort of limpet instinct on his behalf.

"Strudel Garrett?" a male voice said.

Oliver shot to his feet, wondering how long the other man had been standing there, waiting for him to notice him.

"Sorry. This is Strudel. I'm Oliver."

"Nice to meet you. I'm Jacob. Come in."

Strudel tried to dig her heels in when Oliver led her toward the examination room and he had to coax her then lift her onto the examination table.

"So, what seems to be the problem?"

Now that it was the moment of truth, Oliver felt both foolish and anxious. Recited cold, Strudel's symptoms didn't seem that ominous, and he suspected he was about to be given a reassuring chat and sent home with some information brochures. And yet he couldn't let go of the fear that something really was wrong.

He listed Strudel's symptoms dutifully, explaining how rarely she threw up and how bouncy she usually was. He even mentioned that Mr. Smith had been concerned, as though a dachshund's behavior could corroborate his own observations. A definite low point in the conversation.

Jacob hmmed and aahed, listened to Strudel's heart, then got a curious look on his face.

"Interesting."

"In a good way or a bad way?"

Jacob held up a finger to indicate he needed silence, shifting his attentions from Strudel's heart to her abdomen.

"Right. Well, that would do it," the vet said, slipping the stethoscope from his ears.

"What?"

"Your dog is pregnant."

MACKENZIE HAD A SHOWER after Oliver left, then proceeded to do laps of the house—kitchen to study to exercise room and back—anxiously waiting for Oliver's call.

She had his phone charging and was so eager for his call she pounced on it when it rang, inadvertently taking a call from his brother.

The other man sounded deeply suspicious until Mackenzie explained the situation in detail. Clearly, he thought she'd lifted Oliver's phone. She did what she could to reassure him, then resumed her pacing.

After Oliver had been gone an hour she started to create excuses to call him, even though he'd assured her he'd let her know as soon as he had any information about Strudel. She managed to sit on her hands for another twenty minutes, then—finally—Oliver's phone rang and her number flashed on the screen.

"How is she?"

"She's fine."

"Really? Oh, that's great." She sat in the chair with a thump. "I'm so relieved."

"She's also pregnant."

"What?"

"Tell me, is Mr. Smith still in possession of the crown jewels?"

"Um, yes. He is. I was going to breed him. Wire-haired dachshunds are really hard to come by…." Guilt washed over her. She hadn't even thought to mention that he was packing heat. Most bitches were spayed these days. And Smitty was very rarely out unattended. With many male dogs, a warning wouldn't have been necessary since the fact that they weren't neutered would be readily discernible at first glance. But Mr. Smith was so furry and so low to the ground Oliver could be forgiven for not noticing his small but apparently very efficient man parts.

"I see."

"I take it Strudel hasn't been spayed?" she asked, even though she knew it was stating the bleeding obvious.

"No, she has not." He sounded pissed.

"It might not have been Mr. Smith," she said. Then she realized it sounded as though she was calling Strudel a strumpet. "I mean, has she been around any other dogs lately?"

"Mackenzie, I caught them in the act."

"Oh, right. Now I remember." She and Oliver had even had a fight about it, after he'd deposited Mr. Smith on her side of the fence.

"When is she due?"

"The vet isn't sure. But if we use the first week we arrived as a guide, she's due in five weeks or so."

"Wow. That soon."

"Yep. That soon."

He was definitely pissed.

"Are you guys coming home now?"

"We'll be there in half an hour or so."

"Good. I'll see you then."

Mackenzie winced as she ended the call. Then she went in search of her dog.

"Mr. Smith, you are in so much trouble. Oliver is going to kill us, you know that, right?" she told him when she found him. "Why couldn't you keep your furry little paws to yourself?"

Mr. Smith looked up at her with his bright button eyes, his mouth slightly open. The picture of innocence. Except she knew better.

"Prepare yourself for some major sucking up, my friend. You need to charm Oliver within an inch of his life."

She was waiting on the porch of Oliver's place when he turned into the driveway, her reprobate dog unhappily locked up next door. She wasn't about to wave a red flag in front of Oliver while he was on the warpath.

"Hey," he said as he exited the car.

"Hi," she said, way too brightly. "How was the drive?"

"Uneventful." Oliver shot her a curious look before letting Strudel out of the car.

"Hey, girl. How are you? You're going to be a mummy, are you?" Mackenzie scratched Strudel's chest and fondled her ears. She shook the bag she'd brought with her. "I brought you some rawhides and a couple of pig's ears to chew on. And a nice warm blanket for you to sleep on."

She saw Oliver frown out of the corner of her eyes.

"You didn't have to do that."

"Well, she's a VIP now, isn't she?" While her dog was a VNP—very naughty pet.

"It's okay, Mackenzie, I'm not angry," he said.

She glanced at him quickly. "Aren't you?" She really hoped that was true, because she was painfully aware that they had only a handful of days left and she didn't want anything to ruin their limited time together.

If it was limited. But now was definitely not the time to broach *that* subject.

"I was at first. But it takes two to tango, right?"

"I think it must have been more of a pole vault in this case, but yes. I guess it does."

"I wasn't planning to breed her, and they are going to be weird-ass puppies, but what the hell. We can't do anything about it now."

"No."

"I'm going to set her up in front of the fire," he said, moving past her and climbing onto the porch.

"Sure. Okay."

"You want to come in?" Oliver's eyes crinkled at the corners as he smiled at her, waiting for her response.

Relief washed over her. They were okay.

"I'll go get your phone."

"See you in five, then."

She crunched her way up the driveway, inordinately relieved that Oliver's sense of humor extended to animal husbandry. She wasn't sure that she would be quite so understanding in his position. Mr. Smith jumped on her the moment he walked in the door, balancing on his hind legs, letting her know in his special way that he was glad she was home—even though she'd only been gone give minutes.

"Yes, yes, you're very cute, but you're still in big trouble," she told him.

He sat and looked at her with such a wounded expression she almost believed he understood her. She bent and rubbed his chest.

"I know you were only doing what comes naturally. But if you tell Oliver I said that, you're in big trouble."

Stars skittered across her vision as she straightened. She closed her eyes briefly and they continued to dance behind her eyelids.

"Shit."

In the months immediately following the accident she'd suffered from some skull-splitting migraines. They'd tapered off as she recovered, however, and the worst she'd had in recent months had been bad headaches that she'd been able to keep at bay with over-the-counter medicine. The stars were not a good sign, though. If they presaged a migraine, within thirty minutes she would be in her own personal hell, nauseous and in pain and unable to endure light.

Please let it be a false alarm.

She walked carefully to her bedroom and into the en suite, keen to do an inventory of what painkillers she had on hand. To her dismay, she quickly discovered that she was out of the prescribed migraine medication she'd been given when she left rehab. Panic fluttered behind her breastbone. An over-the-counter painkiller wouldn't even put a dent in a migraine. She returned to her bedroom and did a quick rifle through the prescriptions in her bedside drawer. Sure enough, she had one for the medication she needed. The problem would be filling it before the migraine set up camp in her head. Already she could feel her neck becoming stiff, and the stars danced every time she moved too quickly. If she drove into town, there was every chance she'd be stranded there.

There was really only one option. Prescription in hand, she made her way next door.

"If Mr. Smith has come to grovel and beg for forgiveness, he's more than welcome," Oliver said the moment he opened the door.

"I need a favor," she asked.

Pain stabbed behind her temple and she pressed her fingers to her forehead.

"Hey. Are you okay?" He stepped closer.

"I think I have a migraine coming on. I thought I had some meds, but I'm all out and I need to get a prescription filled...."

His gaze dropped to the piece of paper in her hand.

"You need me to go get it? Not a problem."

"Okay. Thanks. That would be great. Listen, I need to go lie down."

"I'll walk you home," Oliver said, stepping onto the porch.

"You don't need to do that."

His arm came around her as they started down the steps. "Yeah, I do."

They slowly traversed the driveways, his body warming her side, his arm strong around her. He didn't say anything, a gift for which she was supremely grateful because she was starting to feel as though she was going to lose her breakfast any second and every fiber of her being was focused on walking and not throwing up.

He walked her all the way to her bedroom, helping her undress and slip between the covers.

"Can you take anything else until I get back?"

"I don't know if I should mix things. I'll tough it out until you get back."

He brushed the hair from her forehead, his expression concerned. "I'll be back in ten. Hang in there."

"Okay."

He was so worried for her she couldn't help but be

touched. She reached out and caught his hand. "I'll be fine. It's just a headache. Believe me, I've survived worse."

"I know, superwoman. But that doesn't mean it's fun to see you in pain." He lifted her hand to his mouth and kissed her palm. "Be back soon."

She closed her eyes as he left the room. The pain was starting to build, but she knew that he would be returning soon and the knowledge that she could rely on him, that he had her back, took the edge off her panic.

It was a novel feeling, knowing that someone else was looking out for her, even in the smallest of capacities. In three years of marriage, she'd never felt that way with Patrick. He had a childish fear of illness or disability in any form—witness his abandonment since her accident. Oliver, though...Oliver was solid. Oliver was real and generous and lovely.

To think, if she hadn't had her accident, if he hadn't caught his wife cheating, if she hadn't decided to isolate herself at the beach to go hard on her rehabilitation and if his aunt hadn't left him her house...if it hadn't rained like a demon and if their dogs hadn't fallen for each other...she might never have met him. She might never know what it was like to kiss and make love and to hold and be held by him.

Pain made her breath hiss between her teeth. Nausea washed over her. She rolled onto her side and reminded herself that Oliver would be back soon.

Any minute now...

CHAPTER FOURTEEN

THERE WERE TWO traffic lights between his place and the only pharmacy in town and Oliver was tempted to run them both when they changed on him at the last minute as he drove. He resisted the impulse—just—then scared the hell out of the pharmacist when he insisted she fill the prescription on the spot rather than make him kick his heels for ten minutes in long-standing pharmacist tradition. He made it to Mackenzie's place in fifteen minutes and didn't bother to knock before letting himself into the house.

She was on the bed where he'd left her, curled on her side, eyes closed, forehead creased with pain.

"How are you doing?" he asked quietly.

She didn't open her eyes. "Not great."

"Do you need water to take these?"

"Yes, please."

He went to the kitchen for a glass of water. He helped her sit up, more than a little alarmed at how hot her back felt and the fact that she still hadn't opened her eyes.

"Thanks—" She lurched forward suddenly, trying to scramble out of bed.

But it was too late—she threw up on herself and the bed, her small body bent almost double. When the spasm had passed, she cracked her eyes to survey the damage.

"Did I get you?"

"It doesn't matter."

"Shit."

"I think you'll find that's usually a different color."

Her mouth twisted unhappily. "This is not a laughing matter. I just threw up on you."

"But you mostly didn't. Come on, let's get you cleaned up."

He hooked an arm beneath her shoulders and helped her out of bed and into the bathroom.

"Could you stand a shower?" he asked.

"Yes. But can I have my tablet first?"

"Yes. God, sorry. Will you be able to keep it down?"

"I'll have to."

He made sure she was steady on her feet before grabbing the glass of water and handing her a tablet. Then he helped her strip and got her into the shower.

"You all right in here for a few minutes?" he asked.

She was very pale, her slim body hunched as though she could protect herself from the discomfort if she could make herself compact enough.

"Yes. Thanks, Oliver. I'm sorry to be dumping all this on you."

"Shut up," he said gently.

She smiled faintly before resting her shoulder against the shower wall and letting the water run down her back. He returned to the bedroom, working quickly to strip the bed. He found clean sheets in the hall cupboard. By the time he heard the shower fall silent he'd remade the bed and kicked the soiled linen into the hall.

"You shouldn't have," Mackenzie said.

She stood in the bathroom doorway, a towel wrapped around her torso. More wet than dry, hair plastered to her skull, her eyes clouded with pain. A surge of protective affection rose inside him. Mackenzie was such a fighter and fiercely independent, but right now she was intensely vulnerable and he was humbled that she was so willing to put her trust in him.

"Come to bed."

She walked obediently to his side and he toweled her dry. She stood placidly, her brow slightly furrowed.

"How we doing now?" he asked.

"Bearable. If I can lie down for a while, I think I should be okay."

"Where do you keep your pajamas?"

"Second drawer down."

He found a T-shirt and a pair of pants and helped her dress, then helped her into bed. She sighed as the covers settled over her.

"Oh, that's nice. Clean sheets." She opened her eyes and touched his knee. "Thank you for taking such good care of me, Oliver."

Something jabbed him in the chest as he looked at her. Something painful and sharp and sweet and good, all at the same time. The urge to take her into his arms was almost overwhelming.

"Would it disturb you if I stayed awhile?" he asked.

"No. That'd be nice." Her words were a little slurred and he guessed the meds were kicking in.

He toed off his shoes and took off his jacket, then lay down beside her. She curled on her side and he wrapped his arm around her middle.

"This okay?"

"Yes."

She wriggled a little closer. They lay snuggled together for what felt like fifteen minutes and slowly he felt the tension ease out of her body.

"Feeling better?" he guessed.

"Yes. Thank God." She sounded drowsy, almost as though she was tipsy.

"Let me guess. You're not supposed to operate heavy machinery on those pills, huh?"

"Something like that."

He tightened his grip for a moment, pulling her closer. Unable to help himself. She felt strong and fine and infinitely precious cradled against him.

"Can I ask you something?" Her voice was slow and lazy and contemplative.

"Sure."

"You can be honest, because I probably won't even remember this tomorrow. Do they ever bother you? You never look at them, you never say anything, but it's not as though they're not obvious. They must register. Right?"

It took him a moment to understand she was talking about her scars. It hit him that this was something that had been playing in her mind for a while, even though he suspected she would never have raised the subject if she wasn't dopey from the pills.

He hated the thought that she'd been worried about something so trivial, that beneath her surface confidence and assurance this had been eating away at her. If he had known, he would have said something long ago. Mackenzie's scars were a part of her, testaments to her grit and courage. He couldn't imagine her any other way. It was that simple.

"They don't register, for the most part," he said, choosing his words carefully. "You have to understand how the male brain works. When there's a naked woman in the room, there are better things to focus on, if you know what I mean. But I do wonder sometimes if they hurt."

"They don't hurt. Not anymore. My hips hurt, sometimes. And my back. And I can't lift my left arm past shoulder height. But otherwise I'm good as new."

He pressed a kiss to her shoulder. "You're better than new."

"So are you."

Her hand slid over his, squeezing warmly. Words—affectionate, committed, emotional words—filled his head. Crazy and impulsive. He opened his mouth, but common sense stopped him before he could say what was in his heart.

It was too early to even be thinking like that. He needed to take a deep breath and remind himself that there was no need to rush into anything. They had time. Even though he would be returning to Sydney soon, Melbourne was only an hour's flight away. He could visit every weekend if he wanted to. Or Mackenzie could come to him. His returning home was not the end of this. Of them.

"It would be really easy to fall for you, Oliver Garrett," Mackenzie said. "So easy."

He went very still, but she didn't say anything further. After another minute or so her body loosened even more and he realized she was asleep. He lay beside her, breathing in her scent, thinking about what she'd said and what he hadn't.

Was it possible to fall in love so quickly? It seemed to him that the answer had to be yes, because he was in love with Mackenzie. Fiercely so.

She challenged him, aroused him, fascinated him. She made him laugh, she made him think. She made him want more.

More of her. More happiness. More hours in the day. More laughter.

He could hear his brother's cautious voice in his head, warning him to be practical and prudent, but he ignored it. His gut told him this was right, and so did his heart.

He waited until Mackenzie was deeply asleep, then eased from the bed and left the room, closing the door behind him. Mr. Smith waited in the hallway, his head resting mournfully on his front paws. He glanced at Oliver without lifting his head, giving him an even more lugubrious air.

"She's fine, buddy. Don't worry." He leaned down and scratched beneath the dog's chin. "You're a good dog. But that doesn't mean you're off the hook for messing around with my girl."

Mr. Smith settled his head back onto his paws, his gaze once more going to the closed bedroom door. Oliver left him to his watchdog duties, heading home to check on Strudel.

She seemed fine, if a little sleepy, but the vet had warned she might be lethargic in the early stages of her pregnancy. He fed her some liver treats and changed her water, then drifted from room to room, seeing half-a-dozen things he could do but not feeling inspired to do any of them. Finally he gave in to need and went to Mackenzie's place, taking Strudel with him this time. The dogs skittered off to do whatever they did when they hung out on Mr. Smith's cushion in the living room, and he let himself into Mackenzie's bedroom.

She was still asleep, and he took off his shoes and joined her on the bed, wrapping an arm around her. She murmured in her sleep, then settled again. He pressed a kiss to the nape of her neck.

"I love you," he said very quietly.

He expected it to sound preposterous, like a teenager making a rash declaration.

It didn't. It sounded…right.

He closed his eyes and let himself fall asleep.

MACKENZIE WOKE FEELING disoriented and woozy. It was very dark, and a heavy arm lay across her belly. Oliver, sleeping beside her.

She tried to ease out of the bed without disturbing him but his arm tightened around her middle.

"All good?" he asked.

"Yeah. I think so. My head doesn't feel as though it's going to split in half, anyway." She glanced at him, even though she could only make out the shape of his face in the dark. "Thanks for staying with me."

"Thanks for letting me stay."

It hadn't even occurred to her to send him away. Even though she'd been sick and pathetic and helpless. She trusted him. It was that simple. And having him near had made her feel infinitely safe and cherished.

"You want a glass of water?" he asked.

"I can get it."

He slid his arm free as she sat up and swung her legs over the edge of the bed. There was a moment where her head was a little swimmy—a side effect of the pain meds—then the world righted itself and she was fine.

She made her way into the kitchen, aware of Oliver following her. She smiled at him as she opened the fridge door.

"I'm not going to keel over, if that's what you're worried about."

"Never thought it for a second."

She pulled out a carton of juice and found two glasses. Her stomach rumbled as she poured them both a drink.

"I can take a hint. You want some eggs on toast, or maybe a sandwich?" he offered.

"You don't have to make me dinner on top of everything else."

"Shut up," he said, pushing her toward one of the stools on the other side of the counter.

"That's the second time you've said that to me today."

"And yet you're still talking."

She smirked at his joke and slid onto the stool, nursing her juice.

"How's Strudel?"

"Asleep on Smitty's cushion." He gestured with his chin and she glanced over her shoulder. Sure enough, the dogs were sleeping next to the sofa.

She rested her elbows on the counter, keen to give voice to the thought that had been sitting front and center of her mind once the fog of her medication had dissipated.

"I've made a decision."

Oliver stilled. "And?"

She loved that he didn't need to ask what she was talking about.

"I want to explore the possibilities with Mary," she said firmly. It would mean the next few years would be a little dicey, income-wise, but she could manage.

A slow smile curved his mouth. Then he lifted his juice in salute. "Good decision."

"It feels good."

Especially because as a self-employed documentary producer, she would be able to base herself anywhere—Melbourne...Sydney...

Soon she would run that aspect of her decision past him, see how he responded. But not this morning. She wasn't confident she could mask her disappointment right now if he didn't say what she desperately wanted to hear.

The dogs chose that moment to patter into the kitchen in search of sustenance. Not for the first time it struck her that they made a very mismatched pair, Strudel knee-height and nicely proportioned, Mr. Smith ground-hugging and overly long.

"I can't believe she's going to have Mr. Smith's babies. You have to send me pictures of the puppies when they're born."

He glanced at her as he cracked eggs into a mixing bowl. "You can see them for yourself when you come to visit."

She blinked. Then she shook her head. "Sorry, I'm a bit thick at the moment."

"I'm asking if you want to come visit me in Sydney after I go home."

"Yes."

She said it without hesitation.

"And if I can visit you here in Melbourne."

"Yes."

"You don't want to think about it for a moment? Maybe phone a friend?"

"No."

His mouth curled into a wide, unashamed grin. "Well, then."

"Just what I was thinking."

They locked eyes, both of them smiling. He abandoned the eggs and moved around the counter to kiss her. She rubbed her cheek against his and looped her arms around his neck.

Suddenly she felt crazy to have ever doubted him, to have doubted *them.* So what if it had been only a few weeks? So what if his life was in upheaval?

What was happening between them felt *right.*

"Why do you always smell so good?" she asked.

"Why do you always feel so good?"

They kissed until her stomach rumbled again.

"Yes, ma'am. Coming straight up," Oliver said.

He made them both creamy scrambled eggs with toast and they ate on the couch. An old Cary Grant movie was on and they watched it and talked about their favorite movies and books. After a while she was struggling to stay awake and Oliver insisted she go to bed.

"Only if you come with me," she said.

He did, and she made him roll away from her so she could spoon herself to his back.

When she woke again it was morning and she could hear the shower running in the en suite. She lay still, mentally shaking off the last of the pain medication. Then she joined Oliver in the shower and managed to convince him that yesterday's migraine had not incapacitated her one iota.

They had a late breakfast and lounged around reading the paper and sharing the crossword puzzle. Oliver went next door to grab his guitar after lunch, and she looked through the De Garis files on her computer while he strummed away.

As days went, she figured they didn't get any better. They decided by mutual consent that some fresh air and exercise might be beneficial to all, and they set off for the beach at a slow pace. Mackenzie stood on the windswept sand and let the cold air cleanse her, breathing in big mouthfuls of the stuff.

"Good?" Oliver asked, glancing at her.

"Perfect."

He'd forgotten his scarf again and she gave him half of hers as they walked along the wet sand. This time, she knew she wasn't imagining the sense of connection between them.

"I was thinking we should do something special for dinner. Maybe go out, if you're up to it," Oliver suggested.

"I'm up to it. There's a place in Red Hill that does great French. La Petanque. I'll give them a call when we get back and see if we can get a booking."

The sky started to cloud over after half an hour so they whistled the dogs to heel and started back.

"I bought some Italian hot chocolate at the shop the other day," Oliver said as they made their way up the sand to the bush track. "Want me to bring it over to you and we can see if it's as thick and creamy as the packet promises?"

"Be still, my heart. You officially secured your status as the perfect man."

"And all it took was a packet of hot chocolate?"

"Plus a night of Florence Nightingale duties."

"Chocolate and spooning. You're easily bought."

She used the scarf to reel him closer and stood on tiptoe to kiss him. "You have no idea."

They reached the single-file section of the track and Mackenzie fell behind to allow him to take the lead.

"You need to make your elephant sound again," she told him.

"You know it's a mating call, right?"

"I had my fingers crossed."

He laughed, then made her laugh with a series of ridiculous animal sounds, none of them remotely elephantine. She had tears in her eyes by the time they emerged at the end of their street.

"Did you win the lottery while we were at the beach and not tell me?" Oliver said.

She followed his gaze to the bright red Ferrari parked in front of her house. Her steps slowed.

"Someone you know?" Oliver asked.

"Yes. Patrick. My ex-husband."

It took her less than a second to get past her surprise.

There was only one reason that Patrick would come calling out of the blue like this: he wanted something.

Tightening her grip on Smitty's lead, she went to see what it was.

IT TOOK OLIVER a moment to catch up with Mackenzie. He'd known she'd been married before, but she hadn't mentioned that her ex-husband had the kind of money that allowed him to drive around in a car worth a quarter of a million dollars.

Oliver wasn't really a car guy—if he had a choice, he'd prefer to drop that kind of money on a 1959 Les Paul standard guitar—but he was man enough to feel a twinge of envy as they approached the Ferrari. Sleek and low, it looked as though it could break the sound barrier and then some.

"Does he often show up like this?" he asked.

"Patrick isn't big on planning. So, yes. He probably woke up this morning and remembered I existed and decided he must see me right now, this second, for whatever reason."

Mackenzie sounded more amused than annoyed, as though she'd long ago reconciled herself to her ex's peccadilloes.

Oliver stopped at the top of Mackenzie's driveway. She came to a halt also, throwing him a questioning look.

"You don't need me hanging around, getting in the way," Oliver said.

He did his best to sound casual, as though her ex-husband dropping into her life unexpectedly wasn't a big deal to him, because he knew it shouldn't be. But the truth was that he was feeling more than a little rattled.

He knew she had a life beyond the cottage and Mr. Smith and the time they spent together, in the same way that he had a life that involved the studio and all the other elements that made up his day-to-day. But until this moment that other life hadn't seemed real to him. Mackenzie had seemed utterly his, accessible and attainable, their relationship a clean and simple meeting of minds and hearts. They'd been living in a cozy little bubble, sharing their beds and cooking meals together and monopolizing each other's time and energy.

And now the real world had intruded, in the form of a Ferrari-driving ex-husband.

"You don't need to disappear because Patrick is here. We're not changing our plans to accommodate him."

"Call me crazy, but I don't think he'll be thrilled to sit around drinking hot chocolate with some strange dude from next door after driving all this way to see you," he said.

"Mackenzie. Thank God. I was about to call the police and tell them to launch a search party."

Oliver turned to see a tall, dark-haired man striding toward them, a broad smile on his face. For a moment he didn't quite believe what his eyes were telling him, because the blue-eyed, ruggedly handsome man bearing down on them had twice been voted Australia's most popular actor and could usually be found smiling from the magazine racks at the supermarket.

Not once in any of the conversations he'd had with Mackenzie had she mentioned the fact that her ex was the television actor *Patrick Langtry.* She'd simply referred to him as Patrick.

"I checked around the back, just in case you'd fallen down an old mine shaft or into a wormhole to another dimension or something," Patrick said as he covered the final few feet.

"Patrick—"

Mackenzie barely got the word out before she was scooped into a bear hug, her face crushed against her ex-husband's shoulder. Patrick loosened his grip enough to drop a kiss onto her mouth before letting her go again.

"You look great, Mac. Really fantastic. My God, when I think of how you were last time I saw you… Those doctors are miracle workers," Patrick said.

Oliver shoved his hands deep into his coat pockets. It was either that, or give in to the need to reach out and forcibly move the other man back a foot or so out of Mackenzie's personal space.

"Can I talk now? Is it safe?" Mackenzie said, her expression wry.

"Go right ahead," Patrick said easily.

Mackenzie gestured toward Oliver. "First off, this is my friend Oliver. Oliver, this is Patrick. He doesn't usually talk quite this much but I'm guessing he's had too many coffees on the road here."

"Three. But who's counting? Good to meet you, Oliver."

Oliver found himself the focus of Langtry's intense pale blue gaze as they shook hands.

"Yeah, you, too."

"You a local, Oliver, or down here visiting with Mac?" Patrick asked.

"*Patrick.* Does the phrase 'none of your business' mean anything to you?" Mackenzie said.

Again, she seemed more amused than irritated.

"What? I'm being polite. Making conversation," Patrick said, smiling and shrugging helplessly as though he had no idea what he'd done wrong.

"Oliver is here from Sydney to sort out his aunt's estate," Mackenzie said.

"Not Marion? When did she go?" Patrick appeared genuinely dismayed.

Oliver felt an unreasonable niggle of irritation that not only did this handsome, charismatic guy feel free to kiss and manhandle Mackenzie and call her *Mac,* but he also knew Marion.

"She died at Easter last year," Oliver said. "Pneumonia."

"I'm really sorry to hear that. She was great fun. A real hoot."

Patrick sounded utterly sincere, but Oliver figured that came naturally. The man was an actor, after all.

Mackenzie turned toward the house. "Come on. It's too cold to stand around outside."

Oliver hesitated, but she hooked her arm through his and all but forced him to walk with her toward the house. He was aware of Langtry noting the gesture and couldn't help feeling pleased that Mackenzie had indicated they were more than friends.

Stop being a territorial dick. Next you'll be competing with Mr. Smith to mark the yard.

"Who wants coffee, who wants tea?" Mackenzie asked as she entered the house.

Oliver followed her inside, Langtry on his heels.

"Have you got any of that French Earl Gray tea you had last time I was down?" Patrick asked.

"I have no idea. I'll have to have a rummage," Mackenzie said. "What about you, Oliver?"

"Tea's good for me, too, thanks."

Oliver could feel Langtry studying him, no doubt wondering if Oliver had registered his familiarity with Mackenzie, her house, her dog and her tea supply. Apparently, Oliver wasn't the only one feeling the urge to piss in a few corners.

Mackenzie headed down the hall, her back very straight. He couldn't help thinking of how fragile she'd been last night, and how trusting. The possessiveness working its way through his bloodstream dissipated as he remembered the things she'd asked him last night, and the way she'd fallen asleep in his arms.

Patrick Langtry might be almost offensively good-looking; he might drive the ultimate big boy's toy; he might have charisma and charm to spare; but he was Mackenzie's ex. He'd had his shot to make her happy and had failed and Mackenzie had moved on. It was stupid to get into a dick-stretching competition with someone who wasn't even a contender.

Mackenzie threw Oliver a warm smile as he joined her in the kitchen.

"Would you mind grabbing that tin at the back of the pantry?" she asked, pointing to the highest shelf.

"Sure."

He grabbed the tin in question and handed it to her.

"You're a lifesaver."

"Wait till you see my next trick."

"Okay, I will." She reached out and brushed a speck of lint off his coat, a world of affection in the small gesture.

The last of his stupid jealousy drifted away. Which was good, because he wasn't a jealous kind of guy. Certainly it wasn't an emotion that had had a lot of airplay in his life to datc.

"You need any more help here?" he asked.

"Thanks, but I'm good for now. You go grab a seat."

She sent him on his way with a small tap on the butt, making him smile.

Langtry had already made himself comfortable on the couch and was flipping through a magazine. Oliver took the armchair and girded his loins to make small talk and whatever else was required of him until the other man got in his fast car and went on his way.

CHAPTER FIFTEEN

MACKENZIE WAITED FOR the water to boil, one eye on the kettle, the other on the two men in her living room. They were talking about Oliver's work in Sydney, Patrick asking polite questions, Oliver answering them equally politely.

It was very, very strange seeing Patrick and Oliver in the same space. Revealing, too. She'd always been powerfully aware of Patrick's charisma—the man wielded it like a weapon, it was hard to ignore it—but it was a little surprising to realize that Oliver more than held his own on that score. He had the edge on Patrick, actually, because not only was he good-looking with a lovely body and an engaging, compelling way about him, he was also sincere. When he asked a question, he waited for the answer because he genuinely wanted to know. With Patrick, there was often the sense that he was simply going through the motions of social niceties before he could hear the sound of his own voice again.

Meow. Saucer of milk, table two.

Mackenzie shrugged. She figured she was allowed to be a bit pissy with her ex. In the years since their divorce, they'd slipped into an easy friendship consisting of phone calls and emails and occasional dinners. They'd listened to each other's woes and offered each other advice and enjoyed each other without the burden of forever hanging over them. They had become so comfortable she hadn't hesitated to offer him the role on *Time and Again* when she took over the show. But letting their friendship become something more had been a mistake. That didn't excuse Patrick from his shitty behavior since her accident, though. At the very least, he'd owed her some kindness and consideration. The kind of compassion you'd show someone you cared about on a very basic level. And yet Patrick had been nowhere to be seen when it counted.

She filled the teapot with water and added it to the tray she'd prepared before taking it in to the men.

"Smells fantastic," Patrick said as she passed him a cup.

"This is very civilized," she said as she added milk to Oliver's cup. "I feel like an extra in *Downton Abbey.*"

"I don't think the extras would have been given hot tea to drink," Patrick said.

"True."

They talked about his drive down the peninsula and the weather before touching on industry gossip. Mackenzie felt herself being drawn in, even though she was very aware that none of it would mean anything to Oliver.

"Enough scuttlebutt, we'll send Oliver into a coma."

"Sorry, mate. Lifestyles of the rich and famous and all that," Patrick said lazily.

Mackenzie's back went up instantly. She wasn't sure if it was the look in Patrick's eyes or the way he'd said it, but there'd been something subtly, sneakily dismissive in his manner. As though he was drawing a circle around himself and her and leaving Oliver on the outer.

"Oh, Oliver knows all about that. Probably had more underwear thrown at him than you in his day, right, Oliver?" Mackenzie said.

Oliver glanced at her and she could see the question in his eyes. Immediately, she felt stupid. Oliver didn't need her to defend him. Clearly he felt no compulsion whatsoever to compete with Patrick or try to one-up him. Which was admirable and infinitely more mature and likable than the way her ex was behaving.

"Do tell," Patrick said, settling back into the couch as though he was there for a good, long stay.

Oliver's smile was self-deprecating. "Ancient history, hardly worth talking about. And there wasn't that much underwear."

Patrick glanced from her to Oliver and back again. "So, what, no one's going to let me in on the joke now?"

"I was in a band in the early nineties. We had a bit of success."

Patrick studied Oliver through narrowed eyes. "You know, I thought I recognized you when I saw you. What was the name of the band?"

"Salvation Jake."

"Yeah? I went to that gig you guys did at the first Big Day Out."

Oliver shook his head. "That was a while ago—ninety-one, right?"

"Ninety-two. That was an awesome concert."

There was new respect in Patrick's eyes but Mackenzie wanted to squirm in her seat for trotting out Oliver's history, as though his fifteen minutes of fame made him more worthy or important.

He was worthy and important all on his own. No fame required.

She settled for standing and collecting everyone's teacups. "Anyone want anything else to drink? Something to eat?"

The sky had continued to darken with cloud-making the interior dim, so she flicked on the overhead light as she walked into the kitchen. Unless Patrick cut to the chase soon, he'd be driving home in the dark.

She dumped the dishes in the sink and nearly leaped out

of her skin when she turned and found Oliver had followed her into the kitchen.

"Sorry," he said, touching her shoulder. "Didn't mean to scare you."

"I didn't hear you, that's all."

"My years of ninja training paying off at last." He glanced toward the living space, then lowered his voice. "Listen, I might leave you guys to it."

"Oh, no, you don't have to do that."

"Yeah, I do. The guy came down to talk to you, and he's not going to spill his guts while a total stranger is sitting here."

He was right, but that didn't mean she was happy about his assessment.

"But we were going somewhere special for dinner."

"Tomorrow night will be as good."

"I was looking forward to putting on makeup and getting all gussied up."

He leaned in and gave her a quick kiss. "Tomorrow night. Lots of gussying. Tons of it."

He was being generous, bowing out. She caught his hand in hers.

"Sometimes you're too nice, you know that?"

"That's a problem?"

"No. That is not a problem."

Except that it made it extremely hard for her to keep her head where he was concerned.

"Give me a call when you're done, okay?"

"I will."

She waited at the counter while Oliver went to say goodbye to Patrick and collect Strudel, then she walked him to the door.

"I'm really sorry," she said.

"Forget about it. It's not a big deal."

It wasn't, but it was. She threw her arms around him and pressed her face into the place where his neck became his shoulder. He smelled lovely—like fresh air—and she kissed him before opening her mouth and tasting him. He tasted good, too, and she felt the stir of desire.

"Okay, now it's becoming a big deal," Oliver said.

He tipped her chin up and kissed her, his tongue stroking hers with lazy, carnal intent. She clutched at his coat, wanting to be closer.

"Mackenzie." There was laughter in his voice and his eyes when he pulled back to look into her face.

"I know. Sorry. You go."

"Call me, okay?"

"I'll come over."

"Even better."

He and Strudel exited to the porch and she watched them for a moment before shutting the door.

He was such a good man. Solid and real and open and—

She shook herself. She had an ex-husband to get rid of, and the sooner she did it the better.

OLIVER CLEANED OUT the fireplace grate when he got home, carrying the ashes outside to the garden. He glanced over the fence as he climbed the rear steps. Mackenzie had drawn the curtains with the approach of night and all he could see was a thin strip of light where the curtains met.

He wondered what her ex wanted. From Mackenzie's demeanor, she didn't seem to think it would be anything too onerous or serious. Obviously, the guy hadn't come looking for money. So what else could it be?

Unbidden, the memory of the way Langtry had pulled her into his arms and kissed her on the lips upon arrival flashed into Oliver's mind. There had been a lot of familiarity in that embrace. A lot of assumptions, too.

They were married. They have history. Get over it.

Mackenzie had told him herself that they should never have gotten married. She'd said that she and Patrick had a fundamental disconnect. That she'd been worn down by all the times her ex had put himself and his own needs first and hers second.

She also said that she fell into an affair with him because she couldn't help herself. Because he was charming and "sometimes even when you know someone is wrong for you, you get sucked into old patterns and behaviors."

The thought curdled his gut. He turned away from it, grabbing a pot and banging it onto the stove. He pulled the fridge open and grabbed anything that looked as though it would turn into soup—potatoes, onions, carrots, half a head of cauliflower, sweet potato.

Working methodically, he peeled and chopped his way through the lot, tossing it into the pot with water and some powdered chicken stock. All the while he kept his mind on the matter at hand, and every time his thoughts wavered toward Mackenzie he yanked them back into line.

He trusted Mackenzie. He trusted what they'd started together. He trusted the way she made him feel, and he believed that feeling wasn't one-sided. He would not sit over here in his cold house and dwell on the worst thoughts thrown up by his primitive lizard brain. He refused to.

Besides, Mackenzie would be calling soon to let him know Captain Bleached Teeth was gone and normal services would resume. Any second now.

He built and started a fire, the actions second nature after weeks of it being his primary source of heat. He fed the dog and checked on his soup and started reading one of the thrillers he'd kept from the boxes he donated to the thrift shop.

An hour later, the soup was ready and Mackenzie still

hadn't called. He abandoned the idea he'd had in the back of his mind that they'd eat soup by the fire and rub each other's feet and instead ate a bowl on his own with only Strudel for company.

The phone rang as he was cleaning the kitchen.

"It's me," Mackenzie said. "This is turning into a bit of a thing, I'm afraid. Patrick's had an offer for a movie and he wants me to look over the contract and the script. It'll mean breaking his contract with *Time,* or at least pushing them pretty hard to give him a few months off the show, so he wants to be sure before he makes any hard-and-fast decisions."

"Fair enough," he said, even though what he was really thinking was that Patrick must have an agent who could do all of the above for him *and* get paid for the privilege.

"We were thinking of grabbing some Chinese from the place in town for dinner. Do you want to come eat with us?" Mackenzie sounded both hopeful and apologetic.

"Strudel and I just had dinner. But thanks for the offer."

"This kind of sucks," Mackenzie said quietly.

"It's one night."

She made a dissatisfied noise.

"I'll see you tomorrow, okay?" he said.

"Okay. Give Strudel a pat for me."

"Done."

He hung up and walked to the sink. The yard outside was pitch-black and all he could see was his own reflection in the glass. Not wanting to look into his own eyes, he returned to the living room and took up his book. Twenty minutes later he heard the low rumble of the Ferrari starting up. It seemed to take a long time for it to return—more than the drive into town and back to pick up food.

Pull your head in. What are you, a stalker now?

He abandoned the book and picked up his guitar. He

started fiddling with the song he'd composed but knew straightaway that he wasn't in the right frame of mind. Everything felt wrong—the bridge, the chorus, the lyrics. He played a few classic Rolling Stones songs, then found himself fingering Tracy Chapman's "Fast Car."

Yeah.

He started watching the clock at nine, calculating how long it would take for Mackenzie to eat some Chinese food and then read a script. He had no idea how many pages the average movie screenplay ran to, but he figured that it couldn't take longer to read a movie than it took to watch one. Which meant she should be well and truly done by now.

Can you hear yourself? You don't own her. If she wants to stay up all night doing a bloody live read-through of the thing it's none of your business. Calm the hell down.

He was way too wound up to be able to let it go, though. He kept thinking about the way Patrick had sprawled across Mackenzie's couch, as though he was utterly at home. And maybe he was. Oliver had no idea how long Mackenzie had owned the beach house. Perhaps it had once been shared marital property. Perhaps Mackenzie and Langtry had once enjoyed long weekends and summers together beneath its roof.

He shot to his feet, sick of his thoughts, wishing he could take a break from his own head. Somehow he found himself at the window, looking out at Mackenzie's place. He could see shadows moving behind the curtains. Mackenzie walking into the kitchen, maybe. Langtry following her…?

"What are you doing?" He said it out loud, because he needed to hear the words.

What *was* he doing, standing here at the window, projecting half-a-dozen ugly possibilities onto a perfectly ordinary situation?

Two people having dinner and discussing a work matter.

Nothing could be more innocuous, even if they had once been married. And even if that marriage had extended into a postdivorce affair.

Sometimes, even when you know someone is wrong for you, you get sucked into old patterns and behaviors.

"Jesus."

He stalked away from the window, glancing around the room, desperately seeking distraction. His gaze fell on Strudel, asleep by the fire.

A walk. He'd take her for a walk. Great idea. Get some fresh air, blow this craziness out of his head.

He strode to the bedroom and pulled on his coat, then wrapped his scarf around his neck. Strudel blinked at him blearily when she heard the clink of her lead, then shook herself to alertness as she understood a walk was in the offing. She waited patiently while he clipped her lead on and followed him out the door.

His breath steamed in the night air as he walked past Mackenzie's house. The Ferrari was covered with a fine sheen of condensation and he had to resist the urge to write something profane and childish on the misty paintwork. *Go home, wanker,* or something to that effect.

He turned his back on the house and the car and walked, willing the cold and the dark and the rhythm of his stride to loosen the knot in his gut.

He wasn't a jealous person. Never had been. For him jealousy had always signaled weakness, fear. A lack of belief in yourself. That wasn't the way he saw himself. He had his own business, was on the way to owning his home—at least, he had been before the divorce. Now, he and Edie would either have to sell, or he could buy her out.

Or maybe she and Nick would buy him out.

Acid burned in his gut. He didn't want to think about Edie and Nick while he was trying to keep thoughts of

Mackenzie and Langtry at bay. Mackenzie was not Edie. Mackenzie was straight up and fierce and direct. She called a spade a spade. She would curl her lip with scorn at the thought of sneaking around behind her partner's back. She'd see it as a cop-out, as the actions of a scared, indecisive, weak woman. And Mackenzie was none of those things.

Sometimes even when you know someone is wrong for you, you get sucked into old patterns and behaviors.

He swore. If there were a brick wall handy right now, he'd bang his head against it. As it was, all he could do was grind his teeth together as his brain kept feeding him worst-case scenarios.

Because Mackenzie might not be interested in Langtry, but there was nothing to say that he didn't want to pick up where he'd left off. And Mackenzie might be angry with him, she might be hurt because he'd dropped her so callously after her accident, but she'd admitted herself that she had a weakness where he was concerned. She'd said Langtry was charming—and he was. Most of Australia agreed with her. The guy was good-looking, wealthy, famous. A walking, talking female fantasy, basically. Oliver was willing to bet that if the other man turned it on and applied himself, there weren't many women who would say no to him.

Langtry could be working his magic right now. Using his shared history with Mackenzie to push all the right buttons. Wooing her, slowly but surely.

For Pete's sake, stop. Just stop. Mackenzie is not interested in her ex. She's interested in you. She's sleeping with you.

He knew the voice in his head was right, but the worm of doubt kept working away in his gut. For six years he'd been a dupe. He'd swallowed Edie's lies because he simply hadn't believed that anyone was capable of that kind of deceit.

He knew differently now. People were weak. People said

one thing and then did another. People made mistakes, then kept on making them, over and over. Was Mackenzie immune from any of that? Was he? Wouldn't he be exactly the same gormless idiot all over again if he simply sat back and let this happen?

Somehow, he'd found his way back to his street. The Ferrari was ahead, a screaming testament to Langtry's success and desirability. What kind of a chance did Oliver stand against a guy like that? How could he possibly compete?

There was so much adrenaline charging around in his system he felt sick. He stopped outside Mackenzie's house and stared at the soft light showing through the glass panel in the front door.

He could simply walk up and knock, say he'd been out for a walk and thought he would join them for coffee.

Or he could sneak along the side of the house and take a look through the kitchen window. Just to check what was going on.

For freak's sake, can you hear yourself? Are you insane? What is wrong with you?

He didn't know. He felt possessed. As though there were two Olivers at war within him—the Oliver who was in love with Mackenzie, who believed in her, who was already planning a future with her, and the Oliver who had been badly burned by Edie's lies and was still recovering from six years of deceit and betrayal. One part wanted to believe, to trust, while the other wanted to make sure that he would never, ever put his faith in someone or something without being absolutely certain that it wouldn't turn on him.

Nothing in life comes with that kind of guarantee. Nothing.

Strudel strained against the leash, keen to return home, but he remained staring at Mackenzie's front door, rooted there by his suspicion and jealousy and doubt.

Headlights flashed across him as someone turned into a driveway farther up the street. It was enough to make him move, and he turned away from Mackenzie's place and trudged up the driveway to his aunt's house.

Strudel resumed her spot by the fire the moment they entered, but he was too agitated to sit. He hated the way he was thinking, yet he couldn't stop it, couldn't push the ugly image of Mackenzie in bed with Langtry out of his mind.

Langtry touching her. Kissing her.

He thumped his palm against the side of his head, trying to dislodge the picture, but it was stuck there, held in place by pride and anger and hurt and self-doubt.

Call her. Call her and listen to her voice and remind yourself of who she is and who you are.

Relief flooded him. He could totally call her without coming across as some kind of possessive, jealous stalker. Even though that was how he felt right this second. He pulled his phone from his back pocket and dialed her number. The phone rang. He moved to the window so he could see her place.

The phone rang, and rang. His grip tightened on the handset. He stared at her house, willing her to pick up. Finally, it went through to voice mail.

What the...?

He glared at her empty, dark kitchen window, a sudden, violent rage ripping through him. What was she doing that she couldn't answer the phone? What were *they* doing? How could she do this to him?

For long seconds he stood raging at the window, literally shaking with the force of his own fury. He wanted to smash the glass in front of him. He wanted to pick up the nearest chair and hurl it through like a cowboy in a saloon fight. He wanted to kick holes in the wall and tear pictures from the walls and drag the house down around his ears.

He didn't.

He stood and shook and endured his own terrible anger. Then he forced himself to walk into the kitchen. He sat at the table and clasped his hands in front of him and tried to get a grip on his own sanity.

He didn't know where all this anger had come from, but he knew it wasn't about Mackenzie. This was all for Edie and himself. This was about his failed marriage, not the woman he'd fallen so precipitously and recklessly in love with. Trouble was, at this moment in time, he couldn't for the life of him separate the two things.

He dropped his head into his hands, fingers pressing against his skull. A single, hot tear ran down his cheek and dropped onto the table.

For the first time he admitted to himself that the past five months had been damned hard. The hardest of his life. Dealing with Edie, keeping up appearances for all his friends and his business partner and his brother. Assuring everyone that he was a bit messed up but that essentially he was okay.

On one level, it was true. But on another, it was a thin, fragile lie.

He'd believed in his marriage. Even though he could see now that it had been flawed, he'd believed in it and invested in him and Edie. And she had smashed it all to pieces, destroying parts of him in the process.

In the midst of that chaos he'd met Mackenzie, and the world had seemed good again. He'd fallen, hard, eating up the happiness and certainty that she seemed to bring.

But nothing in life was certain. Certainly, people weren't.

He had no idea how long he sat at the kitchen table. A long time. He grew colder and colder. At some point, Strudel joined him, curling up at his feet. Finally the need for heat forced him to his feet and into the living room. He stoked the fire and threw on another log and stood staring into the flames, feeling depleted and exhausted and oddly numb.

When the fire was blazing again he grabbed a blanket and stretched out on the couch. Strudel jumped up to lie across his legs and he drifted into almost-sleep, his thoughts chasing themselves in circles, indistinct images flashing across his mind's eye.

He must have eventually drifted off properly, because when he woke it was very dark, the only light the glow of the embers in the fire grate. His neck was sore from being crooked at an awkward angle on the arm of the couch. He sat up slowly and circled his shoulders, then his neck. Then he stood and placed the screen in front of the fire.

"Come on Strudel, bedtime."

He wasn't sure what made him check out the front window before he headed for bed. Some innate, primitive instinct, perhaps.

He pulled the curtain aside enough to see into the street, expecting to see nothing but empty road where the Ferrari had been.

The big red sports car was still there, its paintwork shining dully in the moonlight.

Oliver stared at it for a long moment as an echo of his earlier rage and jealousy rippled through him. He closed his eyes.

He believed in Mackenzie. He really did.

But he couldn't do this.

His brother had been right. It was way, way too soon for him to be throwing himself headfirst into a serious relationship. Even if he was crazy, madly in love with Mackenzie. Even if he felt as though life was full of possibilities when he was with her.

There was too much pent-up emotion pushed down inside him. Too much ugliness. He was nowhere near ready to trust again. Nowhere near ready to place his heart and happiness in the hands of another human being. Even if that person was Mackenzie, whom he admired and loved and desired.

Maybe especially if it was her, because if she failed him, if she was even now lying sated in her ex-husband's arms… Oliver couldn't guarantee his own sanity. He really couldn't.

He didn't have it in him to risk that kind of betrayal and unhappiness again. Not at the moment. Maybe that made him a coward of the highest order, but so be it.

He turned away from the window and walked to the kitchen. Even though he'd put the fire screen in place, he wanted to be sure the fire was out so he poured a jug of water onto the ashes. Smoke and steam billowed up the chimney. Once he was satisfied that the fire was extinguished, he went to the bedroom and packed his bag. It didn't take long, no more than ten minutes. It took a little longer to collect his tools from around the house, but within half an hour he'd checked the shed, locked the back door and the windows and loaded the car. His mind carefully, thankfully blank, he ushered Strudel into the backseat, then went to secure the front door.

The car engine sounded loud in the stillness of the early hours. He reversed into the street and drove away, not once looking back.

CHAPTER SIXTEEN

MACKENZIE WASN'T SURE what woke her. A sound out in the street, maybe Mr. Smith moving around out in the hallway. She sat up in bed, blinking in the darkness. Only then did she register the dark outline of a figure in her bedroom doorway.

"It's just me," Patrick said. "It's bloody cold out on the couch."

"Then grab another blanket from the hall cupboard. You know where they are."

"I was thinking I could maybe get in with you. Share some body heat."

She didn't need to see his face to know that he was wearing his winsome, cheeky little-boy-lost expression. She wasn't exactly surprised by his approach. She'd been expecting it from the moment he'd pointed out that he'd drunk too much wine with dinner to be safe driving home.

"As if, Patrick." She didn't bother hiding her exasperation.

"We'll just spoon, I swear. I know you've got something going on with what's-his-name next door."

"Go spoon with Smitty on the couch. He's good at the kind of spooning you're talking about, by all accounts."

She waited for him to go, but instead he entered the room. The bed sank as he sat on the corner.

She sighed heavily and reached out to flick on the bedside light.

He was wearing nothing but his jeans, the fly wide-open, his hair mussed and endearingly ruffled. His body was camera ready, with clearly defined abdominal muscles and hairless pectoral muscles.

She guessed she was supposed to be overcome by desire at the sight of his gym-honed physique. Or something like that.

She pulled the covers higher so that her shoulders were warm. "I'm not going to sleep with you, Patrick."

"Okay. I respect that." He studied her, his expression pensive. "I miss you, Mac. That's really why I came down today. I wanted your advice, but I miss you."

Not so long ago, she might have been moved by his confession, even though she understood that it came from a place of self-interest and was bound to end in nothing but unhappiness for both of them. Tonight, she felt nothing beyond a tinge of sadness that Patrick still clung to something that had never worked.

"Did you miss me when I was in hospital? When I was in rehab for all those months?" she asked.

"I know I was a shit, not coming to see you. But you have to understand, seeing you like that…it was bloody hard, Mac. I didn't feel as though I had anything to offer you. So I stayed away, because I figured you didn't need to take on my grief and whatever as well as your own."

"Big of you."

His gaze dropped to the floor. "You're angry with me."

She thought about it for a moment. "Yes, I am. But mostly disappointed. At the very least, I thought we cared about each other as friends."

"We do. Jesus, there's no one else in my life like you, Mac. You're up there on a pedestal, all on your own."

"And yet you couldn't put aside your own stuff to be there for me when I needed you."

It wasn't a question.

He flicked a look at her and she saw that his gaze was anguished.

"I'm sorry, Mac. I know you think I'm a selfish, pointless bastard, but I do love you. More than anyone or anything."

She believed him, but his love was not the same as her love. Her love was all-encompassing and forgiving and resilient. Her love would have demanded that she sleep night and day by her lover's side if he'd been in a life-threatening accident. If Oliver had been torn apart and crushed by flying metal, she would have moved heaven and earth to let him know that he wasn't alone, that he was loved, that they would get through whatever lay ahead together. Then she would have followed through on her promises, because his happiness meant more to her than her own.

She stilled as she registered the thought, a little stunned by the insight she'd suddenly gained into her own feelings.

She was in love with Oliver. Profoundly so.

"What?" Patrick asked.

She shook her head. She wasn't about to tell him she was in love with Oliver—Oliver should be the first person to hear those words, not her ex-husband. It was nothing to do with Patrick. At all. He was the past, and Oliver was the future.

An almost unbearable happiness swept through her as she absorbed the truth of the realization. It didn't matter that Oliver lived in a different city in a different state. She could move, or he could. It was irrelevant. The important thing was that they'd found each other in this tiny sea-swept town on the edge of nowhere. Amazingly. Impossibly.

She glanced at the clock, wondering if it was too early to go next door and slip into Oliver's bed.

"Another private joke, I take it?" Patrick said.

"Just private."

Patrick's gaze was searching. "You're serious about this Oliver guy, then?"

"Yes."

Patrick dropped his gaze to the floor. "I always knew it would happen sometime. That you'd meet someone else."

He looked lonely and sad, sitting there in his seducer's clothes. A beautiful, confused man who didn't know what he wanted.

"It'll happen for you, too, Patrick. If you want it to."

His head came up. "You think I didn't want it with you?"

She chose her words carefully. This wasn't about them, after all. They'd been finished for a long time. "I think that we never really understood each other."

His mouth thinned, his expression becoming bitter. "You really believe that, don't you?"

"You don't?"

"I think that if you'd put half the energy into our relationship that you put into your career, we'd still be married."

She managed to stop herself from rolling her eyes. Barely. Patrick had always considered her career the enemy, but it was an old battle and a pointless one and she wasn't prepared to go there yet again.

"You don't believe me, do you?" he said. "You can't see it."

"Patrick, I don't want to get into this stuff. It's late, I'm tired…"

Patrick stood.

"You're a great producer, Mac. You know why? Because you're fearless. You know what you want and you don't stop until you get it. You don't let anyone or anything get in your way. But you never believed in us like that. You always held back. Always."

He left the room. Mackenzie stared at the empty doorway, feeling more than a little sideswiped. She'd put off Oliver tonight to help Patrick out—and this was her thanks? An unsolicited, sulky critique of her commitment as a wife.

She turned out the light and turned onto her side and told herself not to let him get to her. He'd wanted something from her and he hadn't got it and he'd simply been striking out. She was not going to lie here and stew over what he'd said. She refused to play into his hands so readily.

Except…

On a very basic level, he was right. She *had* always held back with him. Even at the very height of their relationship, in the heady days when they'd decided to get married and were making plans for the future, she'd always made sure there were options available if she needed them. She'd loved Patrick, but she'd never felt safe with him. She'd never felt as though he would be there, no matter what. And so she'd always kept a small part of herself in reserve. And when push had come to shove, when she'd finally acknowledged to herself that they were fundamentally incompatible, she hadn't gone to the mat to save her marriage.

Patrick was definitely right about that.

She stared at the wall and wondered what would have happened if she had fought for her marriage the way Patrick said he wished she had. If she'd insisted on them having counseling, if she'd pushed him to talk to her more, to share with her more, and to be prepared to listen to her and really engage. Would they have survived? Would they still be together now?

Her gut said no. Mackenzie didn't believe that people were doomed to repeat the same mistakes over and over, that personalities were intractable and behaviors immovable. But she did believe that the fundamentals of most people remained the same throughout their lifetimes. People who were generous usually remained generous, unless life taught them not to be. And people who saw the world through the prism of their own needs first and foremost would always be that way.

Patrick was one of those people. It was simply the way he'd been conditioned. And maybe that would shift for him if he met someone who took him outside of himself…or maybe not. But certainly that person had not been her, and she had not been prepared to fight for both of them. Because that was what it had come down to. Patrick said he'd wanted her to fight for them, but he hadn't been in the trenches, either.

She closed her eyes. This was all ancient history, and while she was mildly pissy with Patrick for dumping on her like that, she wasn't going to lose sleep over it. It simply wasn't worth it.

WHEN MACKENZIE WOKE again it was daylight and she could hear someone moving around the house. For a moment she let herself hope that it was Oliver, that he'd let himself in and was doing something sweet and lovely like making her breakfast.

She knew better, though. She pulled on her robe and walked out to find Patrick making himself breakfast in her kitchen. She eyed the crumb-covered counter and the many coffee cups and reminded herself he'd be gone soon.

"Good morning," he said. He shot her an assessing look.

"If you're wondering whether or not I'm going to rip your head off, relax. Game, set and match to you."

"Ah. You don't even want to play anymore."

"No, I don't."

She wanted to play with Oliver. And she wanted to play for keeps.

She walked to the French doors, pushing the curtains wide so she could see Oliver's place. There was no movement next door, however. She wondered if he was still in bed.

She glanced at the time and saw it was nearly eight. A perfectly civilized time to call.

She grabbed her phone and discovered the battery was dead. Typical. She padded into the study and plugged it in, waiting for it to come to life. After a minute or so it did and she saw she'd missed a call from Oliver last night.

He was such a sweetie. He'd probably been calling to say good-night. She smiled to herself as she hit the button to return his call. She hoped he was still in bed. She would make him toast and come join him, Patrick be damned.

The phone switched to voice mail almost straightaway. She pulled a face, disappointed, and waited for the beep so she could leave a message.

"Hi, it's me. I was kind of hoping I could come over and make you breakfast. Call me, okay?" She ended the call to find Patrick watching her.

"Sorry if I'm in the way," he said.

She shrugged her good shoulder. "It's fine."

"Sorry if I was out of line last night, too."

"Yeah, well. Did you decide what you're going to do about the movie?"

"I'm going to take it. If I can buy the time from my contract."

"Tell them you'll walk when it's time to renew if they don't come to the party. That'll make them sweat."

"Would it make you sweat?"

She gave him her shark's smile. "That would be telling."

He swallowed the last of his toast and brushed his hands together. "On that note…"

She watched as he made a halfhearted effort to tidy up before grabbing his jacket and paperwork. Mr. Smith followed them both as she walked him to the door.

"Drive safely," she said as Patrick stepped onto the porch.

He looked at her for a beat, then leaned down and kissed her cheek. "Look after yourself, Mac."

She watched him walk down the driveway, then glanced next door. She wasn't sure what she was hoping for—Oliver standing on the porch with a big red bow around his neck?—but she frowned when she realized his wagon was missing.

Huh. He must have been up super early this morning.

She went inside and finished cleaning up after her ex-husband. Once she'd put the blankets in the hall cupboard, she had a shower and made her own breakfast and went to check to see if Oliver's car was in the driveway.

It wasn't. She tried his phone again, and again got shunted to voice mail.

"This is getting ridiculous, Smitty. Where is he?"

By midday she was starting to feel a little twitchy. She didn't understand where he could have gone that would take so long, or why he wasn't returning her calls. She was considering calling the local hospital to double-check there hadn't been any accidents when her phone rang.

"Oliver," she said as she took the call. "Hello. I've been wondering where you'd got to."

"Sorry. I was driving and my phone was in the back."

"That's all right. I was just wondering what you were up to today and what time you want me to make our booking for dinner tonight."

She could hear traffic in the background, lots of it.

"I was actually calling to let you know I'm on my way to Sydney."

"What? Has something happened?" The worst possible scenarios started playing in her head—deceased relatives, house fires and other catastrophes.

"No. I mean, not in the way you mean. No one's dead or anything."

"Well, that's a good start, I always think," she joked, even though her heart was racing. There was something about the way he sounded, so flat and emotionless....

"Are you okay?" she asked.

"This isn't going to work, Mackenzie. I thought it would, but I'm not up for it. I'm sorry."

It took her a moment to understand he was talking about them. About their relationship. She reached out a hand to steady herself on the kitchen counter.

"Okay. Um...sorry. You've caught me on the hop here a little," she said. "Can I ask what's changed? Because yesterday I thought things were going pretty well."

He'd been lovely, making her breakfast and holding her hand on the beach and making her laugh. She'd felt precious and cherished and, yes, loved, and she'd finally acknowledged to herself that she was in love with him.

And now he was on the way to Sydney.

There was a long silence on the other end of the phone.

"It's hard to explain. Last night...wasn't good. *I* wasn't good. I'm not ready for this. I'm not ready for you."

She attempted to push aside the fear crowding her thoughts and listen to him, to understand. "Because of Edie? Because of the divorce?"

"Because of everything. I'm not ready to take anything on faith right now, you know? Last night made that pretty clear. You have no idea how close I came to jungle crawling beneath your window so I could find out what was going on between you and your ex."

There was bitter humor lacing his words.

"You thought something was going on with me and Patrick? Because nothing happened. There was nothing going on."

He'd seemed so cool when he'd bowed out and left them to talk. Utterly at peace with the fact that her ex-husband had shown up out of the blue.

That was before Patrick had inveigled his way into staying first for dinner and then the night, of course. She closed her eyes as it occurred to her how it must have looked when Patrick's Ferrari remained parked in front of her house all night.

"I wasn't exactly rational," Oliver said. "Which is pretty much my point. You don't need me in your life right now, Mackenzie. And I can't handle you."

She was holding the phone so tightly her fingers ached.

"Nothing happened with Patrick, Oliver." It was worth repeating. In fact, she'd repeat it ad nauseam until Oliver finally heard what she said. "He had too much wine with dinner and I put him to bed on the couch. End of story."

"You don't have to explain yourself to me, Mackenzie."

"Of course I do. I care about you. You care about me. You absolutely have a right to know that even though my ex-husband stayed the night, he didn't do it in my bed."

"Okay."

He sounded so…distant. A million miles away. How could they have gone from him holding her against his heart while he slept to being a universe apart in twenty-four hours? How could she have been planning her life around him at four in the morning and now he was on the road to Sydney? It didn't feel possible.

"I'm sorry. I didn't mean to hurt you, Mackenzie."

Tears burned her throat. She tried to find something to say that wasn't a plea.

"Can we at least talk about this?"

"I'm still on the road. But I'll call you when I get home."

"Okay."

"Stay well, Mackenzie."

She couldn't get anything past the lump in her throat. The next thing she knew, she was listening to the dial tone.

She stood frozen for a long moment, utterly stunned by how quickly things had turned. Then reality caught up with her as key parts of their conversation hit home.

I'm not ready for you... I can't handle you, Mackenzie... I'm not ready to take anything on faith right now.

Oliver was walking away. He'd stormed into her life like a freight train, riding to her rescue, enduring her antisocial rudeness, reminding her that there was more to life than rehab and producing a TV show. He'd made her feel sexy and desirable and alive again. He'd reignited her long-buried passion and dreams. He'd made her feel full of possibilities.

And now he was pulling the pin. Because he wasn't ready for her and because he thought she didn't need him in her life.

"Bullshit," she said, the word rising from her belly on a wave of disbelief. She slapped her hand on the counter.

Bullshit he wasn't ready for her. And bullshit she didn't need him. She needed him like she needed air. She needed him like she needed heat and light and laughter. She needed him so much it hurt.

When he called again, she would tell him. She would apologize for what had happened with Patrick, and she would let Oliver know in no uncertain terms how she felt about him.

Until then, she was—somehow—going to have to hang on to her patience and her sanity and not panic. Because this was not over. Not by a long shot.

Because she needed something to do to keep the anxiety at bay, she pulled everything out of the hall cupboard. She worked methodically, refolding linen, pairing pillowcases with sheet sets, culling ragged towels and putting them aside for the ragbag. She couldn't stop thinking about last night as she worked, about what it must have been like for Oliver. She'd been so *stupid,* so unthinking. If she'd only stopped to consider the situation for a moment, she would have understood that Patrick barging in and attempting to take over would have sent up all sorts of flares for Oliver.

After all, not six months ago, he'd discovered his wife had been having an affair for almost as long as they'd been married. With a man she'd been involved with beforehand.

Mackenzie couldn't even begin to comprehend what the discovery of his wife's betrayal had done to Oliver's sense of trust. Edie's breach of faith had been so profound, so all-encompassing….

And last night, Mackenzie had blown off her plans with Oliver because Patrick had conned his way into her house. Worse, she'd foolishly, blindly, agreed to let Patrick sleep on the couch, and she'd missed Oliver's phone call….

God.

She felt sick, thinking about what must have been going through Oliver's mind as he sat next door while she pandered to Patrick's ego. What he must have been imagining, or trying not to imagine.

Somehow she managed to make it through the afternoon. As the light started to fade from the sky, she began pacing by her phone, willing it to ring. She should have asked where Oliver was so she'd have some idea when he might arrive in Sydney. As it was, the best she could do was pace and fret and chew her nails to the quick.

When he hadn't called by seven she called him and got voice mail. She left a message for him, but when he hadn't called back by nine o'clock, she knew he wasn't going to.

So, what, that's it? He drives off into the sunset and you're supposed to nod and chalk up the best few weeks of your life to experience and move on?

It was much easier to be angry than to give in to the horrible despair lapping at her ankles.

He'd made promises to her. Not verbal ones, perhaps, but his body had made promises to her every time they slept with each other. He'd made love to her with a single-minded intensity and cradled her afterward as though she was important to him. He'd told her she drove him crazy and that this wasn't only sex and that he wanted them to keep seeing each other when he went home.

He'd made her believe that they'd found something special together despite the geographical challenges and the flux in both their lives.

And now he was retreating at a million miles an hour and not returning her phone calls.

If only Patrick hadn't turned up on her doorstep yesterday. If only she'd told him to leave the script and she'd call him when she'd read it. If only she'd insisted that Oliver come over for dinner, or that she'd gone to him when she'd finished with Patrick.

If only.

Sick at heart, angry, confused and hurt, she went to bed. She lay awake for a long time, having imaginary conversations with Oliver where she said all the right things and he responded in all the right ways and the horrible, hollow feeling in her stomach went away.

I don't want this to be the end. How can this be the end?

It was her last thought before she fell asleep. The first thing she did on waking was check her phone to see if there was anything from Oliver. There wasn't. Short of bombarding him with phone calls until he picked up or getting on a plane and confronting him in person, she was out of options.

She was on the verge of giving in and making another call when she heard the sound of the mailman's motorcycle out in the street. Mail was a rarity for her, since she handled most of her bills online, but sure enough, the mailman stopped at her letter box.

The back of her neck prickled with prescience and she shoved her feet into the nearest pair of shoes and made her way up the driveway in her pajamas. There was a lone envelope in the box and she knew before she picked it up that it was from Oliver.

He was too good a man, too nice a man to simply cut her off at the knees. So he'd written her a letter and caught last night's mail and now she was supposed to read it and accept his decision and move on.

She stared at his sloping, elegant handwriting for a long moment, then she walked slowly to the house. She set the letter on the counter and crossed her arms over her chest and stared at the envelope some more.

She felt as though she was standing at a crossroads, two unknown paths stretching before her. The path where she curled up in the corner and accepted that what had happened between her and Oliver had been nothing but a beautiful bubble that had been destroyed by the intrusion of reality on one side. And the path where she clung to the reality of her feelings for Oliver and his for her and chose to believe that even though there were so many odds working against them, they were meant to be together.

For some reason, Patrick's words from yesterday echoed in her mind.

You never believed in us like that. You always held back. Always.

It hit her then that she'd never held back with Oliver. Right from the start she'd given him nothing but honesty. She'd been brave with him and she'd been bold and she'd chosen to believe in them.

She still chose to believe in them.

Which meant that, really, there was only one path before

her. She would have be brave and bold again to take it. She would have to pursue love with the same kind of fearless zeal she employed in her working life. She would have to put herself out there in every possible way.

She took a moment to appreciate the depth and breadth of her decision. Then she picked up the envelope, opened it and read Oliver's letter, because she wanted to know what ground she'd be fighting on when she went to find him.

His letter made her cry, because, as always, he'd been honest to a fault. He apologized for his hasty departure and explained that at the time, it had felt as though he didn't have a choice. He told her in painful, exposing detail how paranoid and anxious he'd been, sitting on his side of the fence knowing that she was alone with her very charming, very handsome ex-husband.

He told her that in the short, in the perfect weeks he'd known her she'd made him feel as though the sun had come out from behind the clouds in his life. He told her that she was beautiful and sexy and clever and courageous and that he wanted her to be happy and to find the next thing in her life that would make her smile. And he told her that that thing could not be him right now because he was too messed up, too angry, too scared to be any good to anyone.

Finally, he told her that he did not expect her to wait for him, because he knew that he had hurt her by leaving the way he had and that he understood that a man only had one chance in life to get it right with a woman like her.

"Oliver...you foolish, beautiful man," she whispered when she'd finished.

Then she wiped the tears from her face and went to pack.

CHAPTER SEVENTEEN

IN OLIVER'S DREAM, he and Mackenzie were walking along the beach, joined together by Mackenzie's crazy scarf.

It was cold but they were warm and she was laughing. Then his dream self reached for the scarf and started tearing at it. Mackenzie watched him, her eyes huge pools of sadness, but she didn't say anything. When he'd finished, the scarf was severed and she drifted away from him, her eyes accusing now. Asking him why he'd destroyed something that was good, something that made them both happy.

He woke in a sweat, blinking rapidly to try to dispel the image of her standing alone on the beach.

He made his way to the bathroom and used a towel to dry himself off. Then he went into the kitchen and poured himself a glass of water. Strudel padded into the room, her look questioning.

"Just a bad dream, sweetheart. You go back to bed," he told her.

She stared at him fixedly for a moment, then crossed to the sink and settled at his feet with a heavy sigh. She'd been out of sorts, too, since they'd come home four days ago. Mooching around, off her food.

Did dogs miss each other the way people did? Did Strudel dream about Mr. Smith?

For her sake, he hoped not, because he missed Mackenzie so much his bones ached with it. It shouldn't have been possible that someone he'd known for so short a time could have such a huge impact on his life. The fact remained, however, that he thought about her, he dreamed about her, he missed her, he craved her....

He'd had her, too, for the briefest of times, before he'd screwed it up.

He couldn't think about that night without feeling anxious and panicky and ashamed all over again. He never wanted to be in that place again, so desperate and angry and out of control. He definitely didn't want to inflict that kind of crazy on Mackenzie. Didn't want her to see him flailing around in his own bullshit. Didn't want her to know how nuts and scary it was inside his head sometimes.

He wanted only good for her, and he was not good. He was messed up and scared. He'd told her so, too, in the hardest, most revealing letter of his life. He figured it would be more than enough to convince her that she'd had a lucky escape.

And if it wasn't, if she was feeling even close to as shitty and sad and lonely as he was...well, then he was an asshole of the highest order. He'd had no business getting involved with her when he was so screwed up. He should have resisted the pull of attraction and turned his back on the sense of connection he'd felt with her. He should have barricaded himself inside his aunt's place and worked through his crap on his own instead of inflicting it on her.

He tried to reimagine the past several weeks if he'd done just that. If he'd kept his distance. If he hadn't kissed her after she listened to him spout off about Edie. If he had turned her away when she showed up at his door, determined to seduce him within an inch of his life. If they hadn't shared all those dinners and open fires and nights in her bed.

He couldn't. It was impossible to imagine himself not responding to her. Not being attracted to her. Not wanting her.

So maybe all roads led to him standing at his kitchen sink in the middle of the night, sweaty and anxious and full of regret. Maybe he'd always been destined to break her heart—and his own—because he'd met her at the wrong time, because he couldn't handle the way she made him feel and the corresponding fear that came with all the good stuff. Fear that she would betray and hurt him the way Edie had. Fear that he would never be able to trust her or anyone. Fear that his divorce had broken something inside him and he'd never repair it.

He clicked his tongue and nudged Strudel gently. "Come on. Let's go back to bed."

Strudel heaved herself to her feet and followed him to the bedroom. She did her usual circle routine on the mattress before settling with her head resting over his feet, her big brown eyes watching him solemnly.

He closed his eyes, unable to bear her steady, loving regard. He didn't feel very lovable right now.

His thoughts roamed as he lay in the darkness. To Flinders and back, but always circling around Mackenzie. Wondering what she was doing. How she was feeling. If Patrick had stepped in to console her.

Oliver hadn't heard from her since he'd sent the letter. Which was the way it should be. He'd spelled out in no uncertain terms why he'd left and why it was best that he'd gone. There was no way she could fail to understand that she was better off without him.

Heartily sick of himself, he reached for his iPod and called up a playlist. He listened to the heartfelt lyrics of Crowded House and Paul Kelly and Peter Gabriel and consoled himself with the notion that maybe he'd get a decent song out of all this.

Pretty thin gruel.

The street outside grew noisy as the day started—car

doors slamming, engines firing, the roar of the garbage truck. He contemplated getting out of bed, but there was no great rush. Rex didn't want him back at the studio for another few days, since there was still time left on the free-lancer's contract.

Oliver had nowhere to go, no one expecting him, nothing to do. If he wanted to, he could stay in bed all day thinking about how he'd missed out on something amazing because he'd met Mackenzie at the wrong time and place in his life.

A car door slammed, followed by a single, low-pitched bark. Strudel stirred, lifting her head. She blinked, cocked her head, then leaped from the bed in a show of athleticism worthy of her pre-knocked-up days. Tail wagging furiously, she scrambled out of the bedroom and toward the front door.

He was still staring after her in bemusement when the doorbell rang.

Well, that explained Strudel's antics, at least. Although she wasn't normally so attuned to visitors.

He got up and grabbed the pair of jeans he'd flung over the end of the bed last night. He had a fair idea he was a far cry from his usual groomed self—unshaved jaw, bed head, stained T-shirt—but anyone who called this early could take him as they found him.

Strudel was whimpering and scratching at the door when he joined her, so excited she was trembling.

"Calm down. It's probably someone selling raffle tick-ets."

Then he opened the door and found himself looking into Mackenzie's intense blue eyes. She scanned him head to toe a couple times, then a slow, tremulous smile curved her mouth.

"You're alive, then. That's a good start," she said.

Mr. Smith was at her feet, enjoying an intense sniff fest

with Strudel. Oliver tried to find something to say but his mind was a blank.

Mackenzie solved the problem by stepping forward and slipping her arms around him. She lay her head on his chest and held him tightly, her eyes closed. She felt so right, so good against him that he couldn't stop himself from returning the embrace. She turned her head and pressed a kiss to his chest, her arms tightening around him even more.

After a long moment they both loosened their grip and Mackenzie took a small step backward and laid her palm along his jaw.

"How are you? Are you okay?" she asked.

There was so much tenderness and compassion in her touch and her voice that he was embarrassed to feel the prick of tears.

"I'm fine."

Her gaze searched his intently. "Are you? Really? Because I'm not. I miss you like crazy. I think about you all the time. I want to know what you're doing, how you're feeling. I want to be with you."

His heart did something weird in his chest, banging against his rib cage as though it wanted out.

"Mackenzie..."

"Don't tell me that you don't feel the same, because I know you do. I know you feel as connected to me as I do to you. I know you've been dreaming about me. I know you love me, Oliver, because I love you so much it hurts." She blinked away tears.

"Don't cry," he said.

He couldn't stand to see her unhappy. Especially when he knew it was his fault.

"Right now, that is not an option."

"Nothing has changed, Mackenzie. Nothing I put in that letter has gone away."

"I don't care."

He laughed, the sound hollow and hard. "That's because you don't know how screwed up I am."

"I don't care."

She was so brave, appearing on his doorstep, her heart in her hands. Offering to take him on, no matter what.

"Maybe I'm not as strong as you," he said quietly.

"Because it's scary trusting someone again?"

He swallowed the last of his pride. She deserved the truth.

"Yes."

She caught one of his hands in both of hers. Her eyes were brimming as she looked at him. "I understand. I understand that you need time. I understand that what happened between us wasn't on your agenda. I understand that there might be some rocky times ahead, for both of us. But I'm still standing here." She held his gaze, her chin tilted in challenge. "And I still love you. And I'm not going to stop loving you. It's taken me nearly forty freaking years to find a man who makes me feel the way you do and I am not going to let that slip away because you want to spare me what you think are the worst parts of yourself.

"So be afraid. Be angry. Be jealous. Be possessive. Be whatever you need to be. But please, let me come along for the ride. I promise I will hang in there with you. I promise you that there is far, far more good between us than there will ever be bad. I promise you that your heart will always be safe with me. Always."

Her hands were trembling as she pressed a kiss to the back of his hand.

"All I ask is that you don't shut me out. Let me walk beside you. Let me be there for you. Let me love you."

He'd never cried in front of a woman in his life, but apparently there was a first time for everything. He blinked and turned his head to wipe his face on his shoulder. Then he hauled her into his arms and held her so tightly his shoulders cracked.

"I love you. I don't want to hurt you," he said fiercely.

"I know. I don't want to hurt you, either. I figure if we're both trying, if we're both careful, we're in with a pretty good chance. Don't you think?"

She pulled back to gauge his response and he saw that she was crying in earnest, too.

"It kills me when you cry," he said.

"I can't even begin to tell you what it does to me when you do." She captured his face in both her hands, brushing his tears away with her thumbs. "Don't be afraid of me, of us, Oliver. Give us a chance."

He wrapped his hands around the fine bones of her wrists. "Do you honestly think I have anywhere near the strength to walk away from you twice?"

She smiled. "Thank God."

She kissed him then, her body straining toward his. He let go of her wrists and wrapped his arms around her and lifted her off her feet as they kissed. She laughed against his mouth, her arms circling his neck.

"I love you, Mackenzie," he said.

The words felt so good in his mouth.

"At the risk of repeating myself, thank God." She kissed him, hard, then glanced over his shoulder. "What are the odds that there's a bed in this house somewhere?"

"Very high."

"What are the odds I might get to inspect it anytime in the next sixty seconds?"

"Even higher."

She gave a whoop as he bent and picked her up in a firefighter's hold.

"Oh, yeah. This was worth a trip to Sydney," she said as he strode down the hall to his bedroom.

The dogs skittered after them, excited by all the noise, dancing back and forth. He turned into his bedroom and let Mackenzie fall onto the bed as gently as he could. Then he went to the door and whistled the dogs away from the bed.

"Outside, now," he said.

Strudel gave him a wounded look before slinking into the hallway, Mr. Smith trailing after her. Oliver kicked the door shut and reached for the hem of his T-shirt, pulling it over his head.

Mackenzie propped herself on her elbows and watched him undress, her cheeks flushed, her hair spiky on one side.

"Worried about having an audience, huh?"

"Worried your dog will pick up some new tricks. He's already got enough moves."

He shucked his jeans and moved toward the bed, impatient to be skin to skin with her again. Needing the rightness of it.

"You missed me," she said, her gaze dropping to his thighs.

"Like crazy. Take your clothes off."

They undressed her together, his hands caressing each inch of skin as it was exposed. Finally they were lying chest to chest, hip to hip. The warmth of her supple body against his was like a benediction. He rubbed his cheek against hers and closed his eyes and simply lived in the moment, savoring her.

There were a lot of things that could go wrong between them. They still had to sort out who lived where. He needed to negotiate his divorce. She needed to rekindle her career.

A warm certainty came over him as he felt the rise and fall of her chest against his. It might get complicated. There might be days when there was more shade than light. But all of that was manageable. All that truly mattered was Mackenzie loved him, and he loved her.

He figured it was a pretty solid starting point. And then some.

"Those new tricks you mentioned..." Mackenzie murmured near his ear.

He smiled. "Didn't anyone ever tell you patience is a virtue?"

"Virtue is highly overrated."

She wrapped her arms and legs around him and proceeded to prove her point in the best possible way.

EPILOGUE

Two years later

THE SCREEN DOOR SLAMMED behind Mackenzie as she let herself into the house. She could hear music playing in the kitchen and she hastened her step, buzzing with anticipation. She couldn't wait to show Oliver what she had in her purse.

The dogs must have heard the door because she was barely halfway down the long hall when they came running to greet her, Tinkerbell leading the charge. To be fair, neither Mr. Smith nor Strudel had much of a chance to beat her, Tinkerbell's long legs giving her a distinct advantage. That was what came of having a Doberman for a father.

As always, Mackenzie found herself grinning like a loon as Tinkerbell butted her big, black head into Mackenzie's belly, demanding an ear scratch. For as long as she lived, Mackenzie would never forget the day Strudel had given birth to Tinkerbell and her three siblings, all of whom had long since found good homes. She could still recall in vivid detail how stunned both she and Oliver had been when they inspected Strudel's offspring and discovered that instead of long, thin dachshund bodies, courtesy of Mr. Smith, they had huge feet and pure black fur.

Oliver had been very quiet for a few minutes before admitting that before he packed up his wagon and drove south to Flinders, Strudel had been hanging out with Brutus, the

Doberman who lived two streets over. Mackenzie had waited until the vet had confirmed their observation that Strudel had, indeed, produced four good-size Doberman-Schnauzer cross puppies before suggesting that Oliver might owe Mr. Smith an apology. A really big one.

To his credit, Oliver hadn't hesitated, but every now and then Mackenzie liked to remind him of the many lectures he'd visited upon poor Mr. Smith leading up to Strudel whelping. In part because Oliver always came up with new and novel and hilarious ways to express his regret.

Dogs hard on her heels, Mackenzie entered the vast living area at the rear of their new home to find Oliver busy making dinner. Even though she was eager to share her news, she paused for a moment to appreciate the scene—her big, bad man, elbow-deep in spices and herbs, poring over a recipe book as though it held the key to life itself. He wore his hair a little shorter these days, but he hadn't lost one iota of the appeal of the man who had knocked on her door two years ago. In fact, he'd only grown more appealing.

Once the divorce had been finalized eighteen months ago, he'd lost the tight look around his mouth, and the crease between his eyebrows had eased. The laugh lines in his face had taken over, and the inherent warmth and goodness and humor in him was now evident in every smile, every glance, every gesture.

God, she was lucky.

Never in a million years did she think she would say that about herself. Not after the accident. She'd counted herself supremely *unlucky* to have suffered that terrible year of pain and uncertainty. But without the crash and recovery, she wouldn't have met Oliver, she wouldn't have been ready for him, and she certainly wouldn't have appreciated him. She wouldn't have rediscovered Mary and her own passion for documentaries, either, or developed a growing appreciation for simply stopping and enjoying her life instead of sprinting toward the next finishing line.

Oliver glanced up, one finger remaining in the book to mark his place in the recipe. “Hey.” A slow, sexy smile curved his mouth.

A delicious warmth unfurled in her belly and chest at the sight of that smile.

Yeah, she was lucky. The luckiest woman alive.

“How was your day?” he asked as she moved to his side and lifted her face for his kiss.

His arms came around her, pulling her against his chest. She inhaled his familiar smell and made a “more, please” sound when he started to lift his head. After a moment she pulled away. He was in the middle of cooking dinner, after all, and they were no longer in the honeymoon stage of their relationship. She would give him another five minutes, ten tops, before she dragged him off to the bedroom to have her wicked way with him.

“My day was good. It’s better now, of course.”

“Naturally.”

She gave him a gentle nudge with her elbow in response to his teasing. “What are you cooking?”

“I’m attempting to make a marinade for the chicken I bought for dinner.”

“Yum.”

He cocked his head a little. “Why are you looking so bright-eyed and bushy-tailed?”

She pushed her hair behind her ear. It wasn’t quite back to its former swishy glory, but it was nearly to her shoulders now. Oddly, it had grown back with a pronounced wave in it since the accident. She was still trying to decide if this was a good thing or a bad thing.

Before she could say anything, Oliver’s smile became knowing. “You finished the edit, didn’t you?”

"We finished the edit," she confirmed.

He reached for the tea towel hanging on the oven handle and dried his hands. "Let's go, baby. Show me what you got."

She loved that he was as excited about this film as she was. Loved that he understood without her asking that she wanted to share this moment with him. The disc in her handbag was the culmination of years of work. It was the first thing she'd created that was entirely hers, born of her vision. And she couldn't have done any of it without him by her side.

"I love you," she said.

As always, the expression in his eyes grew soft as he looked at her. "I love you, too, sweetheart."

It hadn't been easy for them to get to this place. There had been times over the past two years when things had been tense and unhappy. She'd uprooted her life in Melbourne to come to Sydney, and they'd weathered what had turned out to be a messy divorce, thanks to Edie's ever-changing demands and priorities.

But Mackenzie and Oliver had made it. They'd purged the last of his past when they sold the house he'd shared with Edie, and three months ago they'd moved into this bigger, brighter house by the water in Rose Bay.

In short, life was good. And it was only going to get better with this man by her side.

Taking her hand, he led her into the living room. She slid the disc into the DVD player and they sat side by side on the couch as the screen filled with the credits for her Mary De Garis documentary. Clever, intricate guitar music accompanied the images flashing across the screen, underpinning the moody, slightly edgy vibe the production designer had created.

Oliver's music, of course. It had taken her four whole

months to convince him that she wasn't "throwing him a bone," as he called it, commissioning him to create original music for the documentary. It was only when she played him some of the alternative compositions she was considering and he understood how very wrong they all were for the project that he'd given in.

The result, everyone agreed, was wonderful. Subtle, unassuming music that worked with the themes the documentary explored rather than declaring itself and demanding the spotlight. He'd helped give her project heart, plucking at emotion when the narrative needed it, drumming with bravado when Mary was on the warpath, filling the blanks in the story with wordless emotion.

Mackenzie slid her hand into his as the narrator's voice rose above the music, accompanied by a series of images of turn-of-the-century Melbourne. A thrill raced down her spine as she watched the way it all effortlessly flowed together.

After a few minutes, Oliver lifted her hand to his lips and pressed a kiss to her knuckles. She glanced at him.

"It's really good," he said.

"God, I hope so. I hope I'm not completely deluded after months of staring at this footage in the edit suite."

"You're not deluded. You're clever and talented and passionate and committed. And you did it, sweetheart. You did it."

Tears filled her eyes. "Because of you. Everything is because of you, Oliver."

Because he believed in her. Because he loved her. Because he rubbed her shoulder and hips when they were sore and made sure she ate properly and forced her to sleep when she needed it. Because he was a true life partner, someone who was in the trenches with her, fighting at her side.

Because he was Oliver.

He didn't say anything, simply pulled her into his arms. They rested their cheeks together, arms tight around each other. For a moment, her love for him was an ache in her chest, a tangible thing.

"Once upon a time, I used to think I was happy," Oliver said after a moment of perfect silence.

She drew back a little so she could look into his eyes. "And now?"

"Now I *know.* Beyond the shadow of a doubt."

She took a slow, deep breath, savoring the moment. There would be many others like this, she knew. But this one was still precious, and she was going to treasure it. She was in the right place at the right time with the right man, and it was *good.*

Best of all, they'd done enough miles and weathered enough storms to know it. It didn't get much better than that.

* * * * *

COMING NEXT MONTH FROM

HARLEQUIN® SUPERROMANCE®

Available February 5, 2013

#1830 WILD FOR THE SHERIFF

The Sisters of Bell River Ranch • by Kathleen O'Brien

Rowena Wright has finally come home to the Bell River Ranch. Most townspeople thought this wild child would never be back, but Sheriff Dallas Garwood always knew it. She *belongs* to this land. He's doing his best to steer clear of her. The last time they tangled, he almost didn't walk away. And now there's too much at stake for him to risk a second round with her.

#1831 IN FROM THE COLD

by Mary Sullivan

Callie MacKintosh is good at her job. That's why she's been sent to this Colorado town—to persuade her boss's brother Gabe Jordan to relinquish his share of the family land. But she soon learns there's more to this situation than she knows. And her skills are no match for a family feud that runs deep...or for her growing attraction to Gabe!

#1832 BENDING THE RULES

by Margaret Watson

Nathan Devereux has big dreams—and they don't include family. After years of raising his siblings, he's ready for some time to himself. But what is he supposed to do when faced with an orphaned thirteen-year-old daughter he didn't know about? He can't turn his back on her—or ignore her very appealing guardian, Emma Sloane. But when Emma announces that she wants to adopt the girl herself, all Nathan's personal rules about family suddenly seem to change.

#1833 THE CLOSER YOU GET
by Kristi Gold

As a country music superstar, Brett Taylor seems to have it all. But appearances are deceiving. He's learned the hard way that relationships and family don't mix with a life on the road. Then Cammie Carson joins his tour group, and the pull between them is intense. Suddenly he sees an entirely new perspective...with her by his side.

#1834 RESERVATIONS FOR TWO
by Jennifer Lohmann

Opening her own restaurant has been Tilly Milek's lifelong dream—and she's finally done it. And all it takes is one bad review to derail everything. Of course The Eater, the anonymous blogger all of Chicago reads, was there on the worst possible night! But when Tilly meets Dan Meier and discovers that he's the reviewer, she's determined to make him change his mind—no matter what it takes.

#1835 FINDING JUSTICE
by Rachel Brimble

For Sergeant Cat Forrester, there is only right and wrong. But when former lover Jay Garrett calls to say their friend has been murdered, those boundaries blur. Especially when he admits he's a suspect in the case. She needs to think like a detective and find the truth. But can she balance these instincts with her feelings for Jay?

Wild for the Sheriff

by Kathleen O'Brien

On sale February 5

Dallas Garwood has always been the good guy, the one who does the right thing...except whenever he crosses paths with Rowena Wright. Now that she's back, things could get interesting for this small-town sheriff! Read on for an exciting excerpt from *Wild for the Sheriff* by Kathleen O'Brien.

Dallas Garwood had always known that sooner or later he'd open a door, turn a corner or look up from his desk and see Rowena Wright standing there.

It wasn't logical. It was simply an unshakable certainty that she wasn't gone for good, that one day she would return.

Not to see him, of course. He didn't kid himself that their brief interlude had been important to her. But she'd be back for Bell River—the ranch that was part of her.

Still, he hadn't thought today would be the day he'd face her across the threshold of her former home.

Or that she would look so gaunt. Her beauty was still there, but buried beneath some kind of haggard exhaustion. Her wild green eyes were circled with shadows, and her white shirt and jeans hung on her.

HSREXP0113

Something twisted in his chest, stealing his words. He'd never expected to feel pity for Rowena Wright.

She still knew how to look sardonic. She took him in, and he saw himself as she did, from the white-lightning scar dividing his right eyebrow to the shiny gold star pinned at his breast.

Three-tenths of a second. That was all it took to make him feel boring and overdressed, as if his uniform were as much a costume as his son Alec's cowboy hat.

"*Sheriff* Dallas Garwood." The crooked smile on her red lips was cryptic. "I should have known. Truly, I should have known."

"I didn't realize you'd come home," he said, wishing he didn't sound so stiff.

"Come *back,*" she corrected him. "After all these years, it might be a bit of a stretch to call Bell River *home.*"

"I see." He didn't really, but so what? He'd been her lover once, but never her friend.

The funny thing was, right now he'd give almost anything to change that and resurrect that long-ago connection.

HSREXP0113